"They Say That Music Calms the Heart, Gwenyth . . ."

Robert drew his fingers across the strings, and the ripple of music that filled the small rock chamber echoed clear and sweet.

"You've made me feel as if I could touch the hills," she murmured. "You have enchantment in your singing, Robert Gavin."

"Aye, enchantment . . ." but he was not thinking of his song. The girl was magic, her beauty dangerous sorcery. He heard a roaring in his ears, and his hand shook slightly as he put down the harp. She reached out as if to entreat him to play again, and their hands brushed. She heard him catch his breath, and she was filled with a yearning that was almost pain.

Then, his arms were about her, the hard muscle like iron.

She felt herself melt into that hardness . . .

Dear Reader,

We, the editors of Tapestry Romances, are committed to bringing you two outstanding original romantic historical novels each and every month.

From Kentucky in the 1850s to the court of Louis XIII, from the deck of a pirate ship within sight of Gibraltar to a mining camp high in the Sierra Nevadas, our heroines experience life and love, romance and adventure.

Our aim is to give you the kind of historical romances that you want to read. We would enjoy hearing your thoughts about this book and all future Tapestry Romances. Please write to us at the address below.

The Editors
Tapestry Romances
POCKET BOOKS
1230 Avenue of the Americas
Box TAP
New York, N.Y. 10020

A Loving Enchantment

Cynthia Sinclair

A TAPESTRY BOOK
PUBLISHED BY POCKET BOOKS NEW YORK

Books by Cynthia Sinclair

Beloved Enemy
Journey to Love
A Loving Enchantment
Promise of Paradise
Winter Blossom

Published by TAPESTRY BOOKS

An *Original* publication of TAPESTRY BOOKS

A Tapestry Book published by
POCKET BOOKS, a division of Simon & Schuster, Inc.
1230 Avenue of the Americas, New York, N.Y. 10020

ISBN: 0-671-60356-6

First Tapestry Books printing December, 1985

10 9 8 7 6 5 4 3 2 1

Chapter One

"THE SUN—OH, THE WONDERFUL SUN." GWENYTH tipped back her head to the welcome light that spilled into her green eyes and turned her hair to golden brilliance. "I thought we'd never see it again." She smiled at the elderly man who rode beside her. "Perhaps it's a gift of the Old Ones and Merlyn himself."

"Why not? You're Owen Glendower's daughter, and many call him heir to the great magician, Merlyn." Dafyd ap Tybach, the grizzled captain of Glendower's fighting men shrugged out of his sopping mantle, adding, "First those two rainy weeks spent at Cadwen Castle waiting for your sister to be brought to childbed and then the rain that followed us along the coast. By St. Cynog, my lady, that's

1

A LOVING ENCHANTMENT

enough rain to wash the English back to their own accursed borders."

"We're not the only ones to celebrate the end of the rain, Dafyd. Listen."

They were nearing a small village by the banks of a swift-flowing river, and the wind carried sounds of distant music and laughter. One of the young men riding behind them said hopefully, "It's a place called Rowyn, Captain. Can we stop, do you think? Sounds like a wedding."

"Tam, you dunce, we're here to escort Lady Gwenyth back to her father," Dafyd growled, then relented. "Well, we can stop for a moment and water the horses, but that's all. We're only a few miles from the seacoast and there's many miles between us and Eyri."

Gwenyth followed his eyes inland. To the north lay the uplands with their remote heights and steep, forested valleys, and beyond this the half-circle of the Snowdonia Mountains where Snowdon hid its peak among the clouds. "At least two days' journey," she murmured.

The young soldier behind her protested eagerly, "We'll soon be there, my lady, and you'll be bringing news to the prince, your father. Owen Glendower'll be glad to hear of Lady Mairi's firstborn son."

Dafyd added, "It's not too many sisters who'd travel five days to help at a birthing."

Memory of that tiny, healthy mite brought more warmth than the sun. "He's a beautiful baby, isn't he?" Gwenyth was beginning eagerly when a shrill voice interrupted her.

"It's the lady from Eyri. No wonder the rain stopped!"

A shepherd's lad was peeping down on them from a grassy slope. His eyes were round as buttons, and when Gwenyth smiled and called up to him, he flung down his staff and pelted toward the village. Dafyd frowned as he watched the lad run. "They should set out sentries to guard against English raids. We could have swept down on that village and killed every man before they knew what hit them."

"It's just a small place," Gwenyth soothed, thinking that it was a pretty one as well. In the early May sunshine Rowyn's wide green fields and stone houses made a peaceful picture. Sheep and goats grazed on hillsides covered with marigolds and cuckoo flowers, and the warm scent of grass and flowers and wet earth brought back unasked-for memory. "Look, there are the people. Don't roar at them, Dafyd, please. You'll frighten them."

"Old Henry IV of England'd frighten them a lot more," the captain grunted, but he held his peace as they approached the village and the knot of people who waited there. They appeared to be dressed in their Sunday best, and many of the younger women wore circlets of flowers in their hair. At the center of the throng stood a young man and a young girl.

The girl's eyes went wide. "It's the prince's natural daughter. She's magicked out the sun for our wedding."

Gwenyth was conscious of a ripple of unease among the people of Rowyn at mention of her so-called magical powers, and she ignored the reference to the fact that she was Owen Glendower's bastard daughter.

"*Diawl,* that's foolishness," Dafyd snapped. "The sun came out because it was tired of drowning, that's all." He waved a big hand, adding, "We don't want to inconvenience any of you, but some water for the horses and a glass of wine for the lady would be welcome."

An old woman now stepped forward and curtsied deeply. "We are glad to do anything for followers of Prince Owen Glendower. You'll have water and oats for your horses, and we beg you to stay and join us for the marriage feast." She added shyly to Gwenyth, "My grandson Taliesin and his bride, Ceinwen, have just been wed. It would mean a great deal if Glendower's daughter put a magic blessing on them, my lady."

"Oh, please, my lady," the girl in white begged. Gwenyth was tempted to tell them that she had no magic to offer, no power with which to bless, but it would have been useless and unkind. She turned to Dafyd. "We've all been riding a long time, and it would be good to rest for a few moments. Besides, my father would want me to give blessings in his name."

"Then let me help you from your horse."

The new voice was deep, holding both sun and shadow, and she looked down at a man who stood at her stirrup. Sunlight turned his gray eyes to silver, softened the strong planes of a proud-nosed, firm-jawed face. She had a moment's impression of height and of broad-shouldered, lean-muscled strength, and then he smiled. "Will you let me help you dismount?"

Warmed by the smile, she put her gloved hand in his lean, tanned one, then caught her breath as she slid from the horse and found herself for an instant enclosed in his arms and pressed against the length of a whipcord-tough body. Perhaps because of her many hours in the saddle, she felt slightly unbalanced.

"Are you all right?"

Some quality in that deep voice set him apart from the others in the village, and he was not dressed like them, either. He was garbed for travel in a short tunic belted at the waist with a leather girdle, and from this belt hung a serviceable dagger. She glanced up, half expecting to see a bow slung across his shoulder, and found instead a five-stringed harp.

"I'm Robert Gavin, at your service. It's not often that a poor bard has the chance to assist a princess of Wales." When he bowed the sun found auburn highlights in the rich darkness of his hair. She drew a bracing breath and found the air tinged with a clean, vibrant male scent that was distinctively Robert Gavin.

"What is a bard doing in the village of Rowyn?" she wondered aloud.

"Minstrels get their music by traveling the lengths of the land." He touched long, tanned fingers to the harp on his back. "Today I'm here to sing at a wedding."

Reminded of her promised blessing, she turned to the villagers, who had respectfully clustered around.

"Will you come with us to our house, lady?" the new bridegroom asked humbly, and she followed them to a carefully washed and swept house made of stone and wood. In front of it was spread a table covered with simple food for the wedding guests.

Knowing how hard everyone had worked, she praised the hearty fare of vegetables from the fields, flat, thick-crusted bread, and rich farm cheese. Then she joined the young couple's hands. "Live in peace and happiness, raise healthy children, and always love each other," she said. "My father, Owen Glendower ap Gryffth Vychon, prince of the Welsh, joins me in blessing you and yours."

As she finished the blessing, Robert Gavin's harp rippled behind her and he started to sing. It was an old, familiar country love song, but sung in the deep, resonant voice it seemed somehow different—somehow personal. "No longer will you be alone, my heart, not when I hold you safe in my arms . . ." The old words seemed to reach out to her, and involuntarily she turned toward him. Sea-gray eyes held hers for a moment. The brief, shared look had the impact of a caress.

Dafyd's hand on her shoulder startled her. "If we don't get away now, Tam and the other susceptible young fools will start making sheep's eyes at the girls. You gave the blessing and the horses have been watered and fed. Time to leave, my lady."

She wasn't sure whether she was grateful or unhappy, and she avoided looking back at Robert Gavin as she nodded. "Call the men and we'll ride," she told the captain.

Laughter and singing followed her as she walked toward her horse, but the harp had gone silent. Before she could reach her mount she heard a step behind her and knew instinctively whose it was. "That was a kind thing you did," the remembered voice said at her shoulder. "It means a great deal to these folk that Glendower's daughter should have given a blessing on this day."

"I hope they have many happy years together," she replied, and then honesty made her add, "But I fear they may not. There's little joy in our country now. Taliesin might be called to fight the English within the month. Is that happiness?"

"Happiness means different things to different people. Don't you believe in your own magic?"

She glanced up at him and saw that he was smiling down at her so infectiously that she smiled also. "Do you?" she asked him.

"It's my trade to believe. In fact, I intend to write a song about a gold-haired lady who rode into Rowyn and blessed two young people. Someday I'll climb Mount Snowden and knock at the gates of Eyri and sing it to you."

"My lady, will you mount your horse now?" Dafyd stalked over to them and frowned pointedly at the tall bard as he added, "Let me give you a hand up."

He muscled his way between Robert Gavin and Gwenyth, and the bard raised a hand in salute. "Godspeed, then," he said. "Remember to believe in your magic."

Dafyd glowered after him as he returned to the

wedding. *"Diawl,* that minstrel has an over-quick tongue. But then, that's the trick of their trade, eh? Who'd give coins to a slow-witted bard?"

It was true. Also true, no doubt, that their meeting had meant no more to Robert Gavin than a chance encounter that could be made into a song. Gwenyth held the memory of smoke-gray eyes and strong arms for a moment and then let the image go. There were many more important things to think about on the way homeward—such as a safe place to spend the night.

"Where do we rest tonight, Dafyd?" she asked.

"We'll make camp when we reach the Valley of the Old Ones, and tomorrow will see us home. I'll be glad to see the gates of Eyri again. Eh, lads?"

A chorus of eager agreement rose from the escort behind them, and Gwenyth wondered why she did not feel more joy at going home. Try as she would, she could not feel the heart-tugging anticipation of returning to a beloved place. Perhaps it was because she would always think of another place as "home" even though that place had ceased to exist for her.

Her horse whickered suddenly, and jolted from her thoughts, she saw that they were riding down a narrow path bordered by tall grass and scrubby underbrush. Everything was quiet, too quiet. There was no song of summer insects, and even the birds were quiet. "Dafyd," she exclaimed, "something's wrong!"

As she spoke, the underbrush just ahead of her parted, and a man leaped out onto the path. His nose and mouth were covered with a mask, his bow held at the ready. "Stand where you are," he barked.

"*Diawl!*" Late afternoon sun stained Dafyd's sword red as he drew it. "It's an ambush! Tam, Jonas, protect the lady and ride back toward Rowyn. The rest of you lads, let's teach these buggers a lesson. . . ."

As he shouted and spurred his horse forward, other masked attackers poured out of the scrub or leaped from the concealment of grass. "Back, my lady, back!" young Tam screamed. Out of the tail of her eye she saw Jonas fall, and she turned her horse and began to gallop back the way they had come. "My lady—look out!" Tam yelled again as four men leaped at them. Gwenyth slashed one across the face with her quirt. As he yelled and fell back, she heard Tam's cry of agony, and looking back, she saw the young man toppling from his horse.

She started back to help him but Dafyd shouted, "Ride back to Rowyn! Too many for us to hold off. Ride now. . . ."

It was an order that couldn't be ignored. She could do little against an ambush, but she could get help from the village. Bending low over her horse's back, she set spurs to his side, but before she had ridden more than a few hundred yards a burly man on horseback blocked her passage.

"You're going nowhere, Mistress Gwenyth," he told her.

His voice was muffled by the mask he wore across

the lower half of his face, but somehow it was familiar and so were his distinctive rust-colored eyes. Defiantly she faced him. "Since you know who I am, you must also know what'll happen to you if you lay a hand on me."

He hooted with laughter. "You've got spirit—that's good. I like a woman with some fire in her."

Now she knew who this was. With disgust and outrage she recognized a castle lord who lived on the northwest Welsh coast. She had seen him at Eyri, once, when he attended a meeting of her father's allies. "Get out of my way, Huw ap Reese!" she cried. "Did you think I couldn't see you hiding behind your mask?"

He cursed, and she saw him hesitate. Taking advantage of this, she bent close to her horse's back and spurred it hard so that it galloped past Reese and down the road. If she could only get back to Rowyn—but she knew almost at once that it was hopeless. She could hear the hooves of his powerful stallion pounding almost at her shoulder, and looking back, she saw him riding like a man possessed.

"You won't get away, witch," he snarled.

Her long, loosened hair streamed back over her shoulders as she bent even closer to her horse's neck. Behind her in the distance she heard a shout of despair and prayed that it wasn't Dafyd's death-cry. As the thought filled her mind, the big man drew alongside her and seized her horse's reins.

Years of learning to control her emotions kept her still until he began to dismount. Then she slid from

10

the saddle and, picking up her skirts, began to run down the road. She was fleet of foot and for a moment she thought she might get away, but after a few moments he caught up to her and yanked her back against him with cruel force.

"I have you," he panted.

Even though she knew it useless, she struggled. "What you have is trouble. I swear to you that if you kill my men, if you harm me, you'll rue it."

Russet eyes rolled angrily. "Have done, hellcat. You've brought this on yourself. I intended for my men to ambush you and take you prisoner so that I could 'rescue' you and earn your father's gratitude and a higher place in his Welsh alliance. Now . . ."

His words trailed off, and she repressed a shiver. *Now* what did he intend to do with her? "Let us go, now, and I will say nothing," she told him.

He jerked down the cloth that masked his lower features, and she saw that he was smiling. "Let you go? Hardly likely, Gwenyth. But don't worry, I don't intend to kill you. As for your men, their lives are in your hands. Your people are outnumbered ten to one. They'll be cut down, every one, unless you're prepared to do as I say."

She knew he meant it, and her heart twisted in sick panic. "What do you want from us?" she whispered.

"It's you I want." His grin broadened. "Well, mistress? Do I give the order to stop the slaughter, or do you think you're worth so many men's death?"

She thought of young Tam on ground red with his

11

own blood. She thought of grumpy, kind old Dafyd.
A wave of nausea swept through her as she whispered, "Stop it. Stop it now. I'll do whatever you want."

He drew a horn from his girdle and lifted it to his lips. At the first raucous note, there seemed to be a sudden halt in the noise of battle, and he blew it again. This time a distant voice called— "Hold!"

"What will you do with Dafyd and the men?" she asked. "Many are hurt, some grievously. May I not tend their wounds?"

But he was shaking his head. "No time for that."

Her eyes flashed. "I agreed to do as you said only if you spared their lives. If you hurt any of my men . . ."

Again he seemed to hesitate. "Those still alive will be bound hand and foot and left by the side of the road. Eventually they'll work themselves free or passersby will free them, and they'll make their way to Eyri." He nodded as he read her thought. "By the time Glendower learns of this incident, it'll be too late for him to do anything about it. You and I will be safe in Castle Reese—and we'll be wed."

She repeated the last word with sick horror and then with ringing scorn. "You think that I would marry you, Reese? I'd rather mate with a pig. Or perhaps that's the custom in your castle?"

His eyes narrowed and he snarled, "Keep a civil tongue in your head. I spared the lives of your escort on the condition that you'd do my will. I can easily order their throats cut." As the horror of that thought took hold, he began to lead her back toward the horses. "There's nothing you can do, Gwenyth, except come with me and do exactly as I say."

Chapter Two

THE WIND WAS DAMP AND CARRIED THE SMELL OF SALT and wet sand. Gwenyth shivered and then winced as the sea-wet thongs that tied her wrists together cut into her flesh. Now that the sun had gone, it had turned cold along the long line of coast. They had been riding for several hours, and yet the desolate sea road stretched ahead of them between sandy beaches and dull, tan hillocks of bracken and gorse. To one side lay barren bogs, to the other the gray and wrinkled sea.

Her thoughts kept returning to Dafyd and the other men in her train. She did not even know who lived, who was dead, and she prayed that somehow they had all survived and had managed to work loose from their bonds. That is, if Reese had kept his promise and let them live.

"Tired, sweetheart?"

Though exhausted, she stiffened her spine at the sound of the hated voice and heard the burly man chuckle. "We'll make camp soon, I promise you, and you can rest then. There's a place ahead where the rocks and cliffs make a natural fortress. We need a place where I can defend. I know your father too well to underestimate him."

She could not help crying, "You're a member of his Welsh alliance! How can you betray him like this?"

"Glendower was too powerful for me to challenge, but I was irked that men like Merdyn Pryse and Madog ap Kerr held higher positions than I did in the alliance. Even though Glendower knows that he needs me to hold the northwest coast against Henry's navy, he's treated me as only a minor ally."

"Do you think that these foul tricks will make my father love you more?" she cried.

"As I told you, you upset my plans to pretend to rescue you from your abductors. It doesn't matter. Once we're married, he'll agree to everything I want." He lowered his voice. "When we make camp tonight I'll show you what else I want."

Disgust and fear sent bile into her throat, and she swallowed convulsively. "If you touch me," she spat, "you'll do so at your peril. If you so much as come near me, you'll rue it."

She had meant that she would fight him with every ounce of her strength. To her surprise he drew his breath in sharply. Twilight did not disguise the look in his eyes, and she realized suddenly that Reese was afraid. He feared her supposed magic! She struck quickly before he could control that fear.

"You called me 'witch' before," she said. "You're right about that. I know magic. My mother is not Lady Margaret, the lord Glendower's wife, but a hillwoman long dead. She was wise in the ways of the Old Ones. She taught me things that would shrivel you up with fear. You'd better be careful, Reese, before you think of harming me."

She heard him swear under his breath as he moved his horse a little away from her. "I'm not afraid of your cursed magic," he muttered. "The priest gave me a charm against your spells."

"Do you think that any charm a priest gave you will hold up against the power of the Old Ones?" She laughed. "Aren't you afraid to be riding along the sea road with me?"

For a moment he hesitated, then shook his head. "If you could have done anything, you'd have done it when I captured you," he said. "No, my charm against you is working." His voice grew harsher as he said, "Once you're my wife, your magic will help my men ride against their enemies and come back victorious, with loot and ransom in their saddle-bags!"

He spurred his horse and rode away from her, leaving her close to tears. She knew now what he was really after. It wasn't the Welsh alliance that mattered to him, but the profit he'd make as one of Owen Glendower's most trusted lieutenants. More, he wanted the wealth and power he felt sure her "powers" could help him acquire. She wished with all her heart that she had one hundredth of that power so that she could escape, but when she looked around her she saw that she was ringed by Reese's followers. And even if she managed to break away, where would she go? Neither the marshland nor the sea would hide her. She felt the onset of panic but forced herself to hope. Perhaps when they made camp, she could get away and hide in those rocks.

The coastline became more rockbound as they rode along, and as twilight slipped into dusk and dusk to night, the sea road began to climb up a cliff of natural stone. As they went higher the path became narrow and then narrower still, until it could barely accommodate one rider at a time. Gwenyth's horse grew nervous, and at Reese's command one of his men dismounted and led it along by the reins. "What is this place?" she asked the man.

"Cleddau Rock—Sword Rock," he replied. He was a big young fellow with a flat, rather stupid face, and she noticed that he took care not to meet her eyes. "From the top of the cliff you can see for miles. That's where our master is going to make camp."

The rock was well named. It rose high above the sea like a drawn sword, and as they rode up the narrow road, Gwenyth looked down at the sea far below and despaired. What chance did she have of escaping now? On so clear a night, a lookout from the top of the rock could see anything that moved for miles around. But even while she registered defeat, she sensed something new in the air. She took a deep, questing breath and now she smelled it clearly. Over the harsh odor of brine and kelp, her hill-trained nose scented rain in the wind.

Rain! Instantly she was clear-minded, thinking rapidly as she scanned the sky. It was clear still, but in an hour there would be rain. If it stormed hard enough, there was one chance in a thousand that she could race down the narrow path and hide in the rocks along the way they'd come. It would be difficult for horses to follow her into the rocks, and perhaps she could find a cave in which to shelter. Glendower had often spoken of secret caves dug by the Old Ones in Roman times.

"Time to rest now, pretty one."

Her thoughts of escape shattered as she looked down into Reese's heavy features. They had reached the craggy crest of the rock, and his men were already dismounting and hurrying to start a fire, secure the horses, and erect shelters. "Come," he said to her, and loathing his touch, she had to endure him helping her to dismount. Helpless, her hands still bound, she felt the burly strength of his arms and drew in the rancid odor of his sweat and sour wine. "Now, that's more friendly," he approved.

His face was inches from hers, and she felt sickened. She tried to pull away from his grip, but he only laughed and kissed her soundly on the mouth before letting her go. "We'll get acquainted later," he promised.

Some of his men guffawed and others grinned in appreciation. Resisting the impulse to spit her mouth clean, she spoke with supreme contempt.

"I'm thirsty, and I would like my hands free to eat. That is, if you intend to feed me?"

Reese hesitated, then pulled his knife from his belt and slit her bonds. "Mog," he shouted. "You're in charge of this woman. Give her a drink from your waterskin, but don't take your eyes off her until I come and give her something else to think about."

That raised another laugh, but Gwenyth noted that the big young man who had guided her horse up the path wasn't laughing. Instead, he approached hesitantly, his waterskin in his hand. Her heart gave a small surge of hope as she saw the scared way in which he looked at her. If she could just play on his fear. If the weather did change. If!

"So your name's Mog," she murmured.

He had a stricken look in his eyes, and she saw him make the sign against the evil eye. "Aye," he mumbled.

Averting his eyes as much as possible, he brought her some dried beef and hard, flat bread, and though the unsavory food stuck in her throat, she forced herself to eat as well as drink. She needed all her strength. She could hear Mog settling himself on a rough blanket nearby, and she knew that he was watching her. Finally she murmured, "It's a shame. You're much too young for such a cruel death."

Out of the tail of her eye she saw him start, his flat, foolish face full of superstitious dread. His hand closed on the spear at his feet. "What mean you?" he mumbled.

"Do you know what risk you run, Mog? I'm sure Huw ap Reese knows, but I doubt if he told any of

19

you. Why should he? No man would be foolish enough to go to his own death . . ." In the darkness she saw the man swallow, his Adam's apple moving up and down convulsively. She glanced up at the sky and saw to her great joy that it was clouding over. "You know, don't you, that Glendower is going to rescue me?"

"Aah, you speak foolishness." Mog spoke loudly, blustering. "We'll be safe in Castle Reese by tomorrow."

"There's not going to be a tomorrow, Mog. Not for you or for your leader or any of your friends. Glendower will come." She pointed to the sky. "Do you see how the clouds thicken? My father and I can talk together through the clouds. Through the winds. He knows what has happened to me and where I am."

A low, soughing wind came up from the sea and brushed their faces like a clammy hand. "Stop it," Mog snarled.

"Don't you know that my father can control the elements? I taught him much of his magic and it was I who helped him win his battles with the English king." She lowered her voice. "He rides the thunderclouds, you know. Like a great eagle."

Some distance away from them, Reese sat with his men around the fire. They were talking and laughing and passing a wineskin around, and she knew that the castle lord was drinking to raise his courage. She had to hurry, terrify Mog into obeying her before Reese got up from that circle by the fire and came to her. She looked up at the sky again, noting that it was now full of scudding clouds. Aloud she said, "He's come to save me once before. I tell you this because you've given me water and food and because I feel sorry for you."

Mog cleared his throat. "Look, my lady, I do only as I'm told." There was a whine to his voice as he added, "Huw ap Reese is my master, and what he says to do, I do."

The laughter around the fire was louder now, and Reese's voice rose higher than the laughter, telling some obscene story about a woman and what he'd done to her. God, Gwenyth prayed, please. Send the storm now, while there's still time.

As if in answer, there was a flash of lightning and a low rumble of thunder. The men around the fire hardly noticed it, but Mog's entire body went rigid. "You see?" Gwenyth whispered. "He's coming to take me away from here."

The man's eyes were rolling in his sockets. "By the bones of St. Dygrig," he moaned, "I never meant to harm you, my lady. I never did, did I? It was Reese who took you prisoner. . . ."

"You helped him. I've seen Glendower blast men for less." Another flash of lightning, and now she could almost feel the rain on the wind. The young man began to plead, and she said, "There's only one way to help you, and that's to get you away from the top of this rock. Glendower will destroy everyone here with his lightning."

"Lady, save me!" Mog's wail was so loud she was sure that Reese would overhear. "I'll do anything you say."

"We're going to take a walk, you and I. You will escort me past the sentries. If they question us, you're to say that your lord gave me permission to attend to my private needs." Another rumble of thunder, nearer and louder, echoed over the sea, and she glanced at Reese's back. "Now," she whispered. "Carefully. If your master sees us, if he tries to stop us, I can't help you."

Licking his lips, Mog got to his feet. He motioned for her to follow him and noiselessly they backed into the darkness. As they came to the edge of Sword Rock, Gwenyth saw her captor get to his feet and stretch. "Hurry," she whispered.

She felt sweat, clammy and cold, trickle between her shoulder blades as they began to descend the narrow rock path. In a few moments Reese's sentry challenged them. Gwenyth held her breath but Mog said, "She's got to be alone for a few minutes to attend to her needs. The master gave his permission."

As he spoke, a slash of lightning jagged across the sky, and a boom of thunder followed. At the same time she felt the first drops of rain on her face and heard the men around the fire scatter to take cover. "Quickly," she whispered. "My father's coming for me!"

Slipping and sliding in their haste, they hurried down the path. As they did so she heard Reese's bellow behind her. "The woman—where in hell has she gone?"

Mog turned a frightened face to her as she ordered, "Stand here and stop any who come after me.

I'm going to meet Glendower farther down the path. If you move, no one can save you."

Without waiting to see what Mog would do, she began to run down the path. The rocks were sharp underfoot, and as the rain beat down, the narrow trail became slippery and treacherous. Behind her she could hear shouts and the sounds of a struggle, and Reese bellowing that Mog had gone insane. They were close behind her—so close! Clutching her skirts hard against her, she whispered a prayer for safety and ran.

As she ran the rain came down. It didn't fall but beat down on her in a solid wall of water. She couldn't see where she was going, but she knew that one false step would mean falling into the sea. Slowing her pace, she began to fumble her way along the rock-face, and above the roar of thunder and the blasting rain she could hear bits and snatches of men's voices shouting the news that the sorceress had escaped.

A flash of lightning showed that she had reached the base of Sword Rock, and that she was standing almost on the edge of the sea. Looking backward, she could see the black shapes of men hurrying down the path, and she thought she recognized Reese in the forefront. He was shouting, "There she is. After her quickly, damn you."

It wasn't possible to run on sand. She found that out quickly and made instead for the tumble of rocks that formed a natural breakwater against the sea. For some time her hillwoman's training helped her, but as she sprang from rock to rock, she slipped on a clump of wet kelp and stumbled to her knees. Agony seared through her as her knee smashed against jagged rock, and for a moment she was doubled over by the pain of it. Then the sound of shouting behind her had her up on her feet again, limping across the rocks until she could go no farther. "Mother of God," she prayed, "help me find someplace to hide."

Lightning flashed again, and it was then she saw it—a small crawl space between two rocks. The space was so tiny that she had almost missed it. She started toward it and then stopped, caught by the fearful truth: even if she managed to squeeze into that space, lightning would give her away.

And then she remembered a lesson that her mother had taught her long ago. "When in a field of clover, become the clover . . ." She could almost hear Merryn's voice repeating words from lost, happy times. When in a field, become a blade of grass. And among rocks, become a rock.

She crawled to the rocks and drew a long, calming breath. Then, wrapping her mantle tight about her, she curled up into a tight ball and went motionless. All around her and mingling with the sounds of the storm, she heard her pursuers hot on her trail. Some of them were on horseback, for she could hear the thud of hooves tearing up raw sand. Others ran over the rocks, looking for her and shouting to each other. Their voices came closer. Closer still . . .

She forced fear away and remained motionless. Deep within her heart she retreated to the beloved time on the hill where nothing could harm her. She let the warm content of perfect belonging, perfect peace, and all-encompassing love fill her. She was with her mother, and nothing could hurt her. "Feel the stillness of the rocks," she almost heard her mother saying, "think the stillness, *be* the stillness."

"Curse me, but she isn't anywhere. Do you think she vanished into air?" Memories went still and her feeling of peace drained away as she felt the thud of a man leaning against the stone where she lay concealed. "God's feet, we've searched all over. How can a mortal woman run faster than horses and just—disappear? She can't have changed herself into a fish—or a rock."

There was uneasy laughter, and she held her breath. Then another voice said, "She'll not get away. Our master has ringed the sea and the marsh with watchers, and when the dawn comes we'll get her. Witch or not, I pity the girl when he gets his hands on her."

They moved off, leaving her in bitter despair. She might hide in the darkness, but with daylight her hiding places would be gone. Hurt as she was, she couldn't go far before the dawn. For a moment she felt despair at the futility of it all, and then she recalled Reese's coarse cruelty. "No," she whispered out loud. "He'll not find me alive."

She left her hiding place and began to limp along again through the rocks. She had hoped to escape into the bogland on the other side of the rocks, but if Reese's men were patrolling the marshes, that would be impossible. She made her way along the beach until she could no longer walk, and then she began to crawl.

The rain had lessened now, and the thunder had drawn farther away, but she was not aware of it. She had lost track of time as she crawled. All her faculties were trained on staying alive, all her attention focused on listening for Reese's men. She had no idea where she was going, and she concentrated on one hope. If Dafyd had recognized Reese's men, if Dafyd were alive and had managed to get loose— then he would be riding down the coast road, searching for her. If she could stay alive until Dafyd found her, she'd have a chance. "Please," she prayed under her breath. "Let Dafyd be alive. Let him find me. . . ."

Suddenly, up ahead of her, she heard the slithering sound of a footstep. Desperately she listened, but all she could hear was the lessening roar of the storm and the sound of the tides coming in. Perhaps, she thought, she hadn't heard the footstep after all. But as the hope formed in her mind, she heard the triumphant male laughter.

"There she is!"

Lightning flickered overhead and in that feeble light she saw two men some distance from her. She tried to get to her feet to run, but such pain flared from knee to thigh that she collapsed back onto the wet sand. The men ran toward her, their daggers in their hands, and one of them snarled, "This time you're not going to get away."

Rough hands seized her, dragging her up, and she cried out in agony. "My knee—I can't walk!"

"You'll walk, all right. No more of your witch's tricks," the other man told her. She caught her lip in her teeth as he grabbed her arm and twisted it cruelly behind her. "Move," he commanded.

"Is that any way to treat a lady?"

The unexpected voice seemed to come from the sea itself. Gwenyth's captors whirled, their weapons catching the glint of lightning which momentarily limned a man's figure standing by the water. Then he sprang forward and one of Reese's men pitched over to lie motionless on the sand. The other hefted his dagger and went down into a fighting crouch. "Curse you, whoever you are," he snarled. "This is no business of yours."

The newcomer did not answer. Instead, he moved. There was a blur of speed, a gurgling death-cry, and the second of Gwenyth's captors went down. Her rescuer rolled the limp body over with his foot. "Quickly," he commanded, "before the others come."

The voice was familiar even in the darkness, but before she could place it another streak of lightning lit the sky and glittered momentarily on steady gray eyes and a stern, strong-boned face. She choked back a cry of surprise. It was the minstrel, Robert Gavin.

Chapter Three

HE WAS THE LAST PERSON SHE HAD EXPECTED TO SEE, and for a moment all she could do was stare at him. "What are you doing here?" she gasped.

Impatience tinged his answer. "All in good time, my lady. Were these brutes the only ones after you?"

She shook her head. "All of Reese's men." It crossed her weary mind that he might not know who Reese was, but he only nodded.

"Put your arms around my neck." She did as she was told and was lifted effortlessly into strong arms. "Am I hurting you?"

Her knee throbbed fire, but strangely she was not conscious of pain but of his nearness and of the hard-muscled warmth that cradled her chilled flesh as he strode toward the water. "I'll soon have you safe," she heard him say.

Safety, here? But before she could ask him where they were going, he explained. "I was on my way to Bryn Celyn on the coast when the storm broke. By blind luck I found shelter in a cave."

"But Reese's men might also find it—"

"Not now. At high tide the sea comes right up to the cave opening. Hold on tightly," he added. "I'm taking you into the water."

As he spoke he plunged thigh-deep into the waves, then waist-deep. Though she felt the push and pull of the tide against them both, she felt no fear. The hard arms that held her were strong and sure, and even in the cold water she retained the warmth of his body. "The cave opening is ahead of us in those rocks," he told her. "Bend your head."

It had been dark outside, but here was total blackness. Within this blackness, the roaring of the sea became a menacing bellow. Still waist-deep in water, Robert Gavin strode forward. "Not far now," he told her. "It becomes drier as we climb higher."

Then he was silent, and she knew he was concentrating on his footing as they began to climb a slope that led away from the pound of waves. She tried to gauge the distance they had come. A hundred yards above the sea? Two? She did not know, but suddenly and incredibly the darkness was no longer profound. Light flickered orange up ahead, and the raw smells of kelp and wet salt became mixed with woodsmoke.

"A fire—here?" she exclaimed.

"I'm a man who likes my comforts." As he spoke they turned a corner and entered what almost looked to be a small room carved in the rock. In the middle of this room burned a fire complete with meat roasting on a wooden spit. Before the fire a cloak had been spread out to dry, and in one corner of the stone chamber, propped against the wall, were a stout staff, a knapsack such as travelers carry, and the Welsh harp.

He lowered her gently onto the cloak, and starved for heat, she leaned forward almost into the heart of the fire. As she did so she felt a stir of air against her cheek, and looked upward.

He nodded toward the left. "The cave is really a tunnel. I followed that path over there, and it leads up into the marshland. Someone long ago must have used this way to get to the sea."

"The caves of the Old Ones," she murmured. He looked surprised and she explained, "The Druids built these secret caves years ago to hide from their enemies."

"As you are hiding from yours." He wrapped the folds of his cloak about her shoulders. "What happened to you on your way back to the mountains?"

"Huw ap Reese ambushed us." Speaking of that ambush brought back the terror of that moment, made her remember Tam and Jonas and the cries of agony that she had heard behind her as she rode toward Rowyn. "There were too many of them and I—I tried to get help, but Reese caught me. He said he'd spare my men if I came away with him peacefully." A tight hand seemed to be squeezing her throat as she added, "He was taking me to his castle on the coast, but I managed to get away."

He reached out and took her hands. The palms were cut and lacerated. "Blood of Christ, girl," he swore, "did he do this to you?"

She shook her head. "I hurt my knee trying to get away, and I had to crawl."

The cold had numbed her, but now with returning warmth her hands were beginning to hurt. Robert Gavin saw the flicker of pain cross her face and felt his anger mount. "I've heard of this man. He lives in a castle on the northwest coast. He's much feared by the English because he raids their holdings across the border and takes many prisoners. I'd not heard he needed to be taught a lesson in manners."

He spoke quietly, almost gently, but in the firelight his eyes were as hard as gray ice, and the strong bones of his face seemed carved from rock. She recalled his swiftness, his deadly fighting skill. "You are a strange minstrel, Robert Gavin," she murmured.

He laughed, and some of the hardness left his eyes. "But a good one. After you've had your supper, I might even sing you my new song." He reached for his knapsack as he spoke and drew out linen bandages and a small wooden box. "But first those hands must be cleaned and bandaged."

She was too weary to protest as he poured water from his waterskin over clean linen and began to cleanse her wounded hands, but soon tiredness changed to surprise. He was not only gentle but skilled and knowledgeable. Glendower's personal physician, dead this past harsh winter, had worked on wounded warriors with just this concentrated, sensitive skill. When Robert Gavin opened a small box, she saw that it contained a rare salve she recognized, and she could not help an exclamation.

"How did you come by this? It's made with rare herbs. My mother taught me to gather them when we lived in the hill country near the great mountain Cader Idris."

"Bards have been known to be swept along in wars. I've been in a few places where a man had to survive by keeping his wounds clean." He began to bandage her hands, adding, "Your mother was a healer, then?"

"She knew the knowledge of the hills—the wisdom of the Old Ones. I lived with her until I was eight, which was the year she died." She added, slowly, "I thought of Cader Idris today when we rode into Rowyn. It was so lovely and peaceful in the hills. When she was young, she met my father there . . ."

She caught herself, astounded that she was speaking of Merryn and her love for Owen Glendower. It was a love she thought of often, but could not talk about to anyone in Glendower's household. Still, something in Robert's silent attention made her go on. "My mother didn't tell me how she met my father; she didn't even tell me who he was. That I found out from the kind priest who took me to Glendower after her death."

"Then she never spoke of him?"

"Only once. She told me that she had been given a choice of never loving or of feeling both great love and great sorrow. She said that she had never been sorry for choosing as she did."

Her voice stilled, and Robert watched her green eyes become soft with the memory. The expression of her lovely face had changed and become very young and vulnerable. In the warmth of the cave chamber her clothing and hair had begun to dry, and her face was now framed in soft, curling gold. He found himself thinking that if her mother had looked as Gwenyth did now, Glendower was a fool to have ever left Cader Idris.

He cleared his throat and asked, "And so you went to Glendower's household when you were a child. Were they good to you at Eyri?"

Her nod was swift. "Certainly they were. My father didn't know I existed, for Merryn had never tried to communicate with him. He did not have to acknowledge me as his love child and neither did his wife, Lady Margaret. But when he saw me and learned that my mother was dead, he wept and told me I'd always have a home with him."

He'd heard good things about Owen Glendower, and his opinion of the man rose higher. And yet, even while she spoke, he saw the wistful curve of her mouth, the darkening of her clear eyes, and knew instinctively that though she had been cared for, she had never again been the joyous child who had played on the hills near Cader Idris. How many times had she cried herself to sleep, he wondered, and he had to fight an incomprehensible urge to take her into his arms and comfort her.

His voice was purposefully brisk as he added, "Your hands will do well enough. Now your knee." She frowned a little and he said, "It might be broken, and you can't hope to escape Reese on a broken leg."

"I can care for my knee myself," she protested, but he deftly lifted the skirt of her riding habit to her knee and peeled down the torn stocking to probe the aching joint. "There's not much swelling. Does this hurt?"

It was not pain that made her tense. Her nerve ends had come alive, suddenly awake and alert to the touch of sure, sensitive fingers. That touch burned like cool fire, and as he bent closer, she drew in his remembered scent—clean, male, vital. She realized that if she moved forward, her cheek would brush the wet darkness of his hair. She could almost feel its crisp silkiness against her skin.

"Your kneecap's not broken," he was saying in a relieved tone. "There's a bad bruise, but it will mend given time. Even so, I doubt that it will be able to bear your weight tomorrow. It's lucky that you have a safe place to hide."

Safety—she repeated the word to herself as he began to rub the salve into her knee, and sudden knowledge made her gasp. He looked up quickly, misreading the reason for her stifled cry. "I'm sorry if I hurt you, but the salve must be rubbed into the muscle or it won't do any good." She shook her head and he asked, "What is it, Gwenyth?"

In her anxiety she did not realize that he had used her name without title. "My lord father!" she exclaimed. "I must get word to him before Dafyd does. Reese's men were masked, but I saw through the disguise. If I could do so, Dafyd must also know who attacked us. My father mustn't fight Reese because of me."

He frowned down at her. "I'd think you'd want the bastard's head on a stake!" he exclaimed.

"Not if civil war is the result." He did not look convinced and she realized that being a bard he might not know about the Welsh alliance. She began to explain. "My father has managed to get most of the great Welsh lords to unite."

"I have heard of the Welsh alliance, but not of its members. Does Reese belong, also?"

He spoke offhandedly, but she sensed that he was keenly interested. "My lord father has kept the names of his allies a secret," she explained. "He knows that if the English king learned of its strength, he'd move at once to try and crush the alliance."

He nodded thoughtfully, and she watched him pack away his salve and thought again that this man was like no minstrel she'd ever known. There had been plenty of songmakers wherever Glendower went, for he loved to hear the old heroic ballads and rewarded bards richly for their services. She'd met old harpists who could coax their instruments to sing and had known poets dedicated to their art as well as adventurers who played for their supper and had an eye for drink and women. Robert Gavin fit no mold.

She looked up at him and saw that he was watching her, one dark eyebrow raised quizzically as if waiting for an answer. So deep had she been in her thoughts that she hadn't heard the question. "I'm sorry," she told him. "I didn't hear you. I must have been half asleep."

"No wonder." His face gentled. "Are you too exhausted to eat before you sleep? The meat is done." He sliced off a piece for her with his knife, adding, "It's better to sleep on a full stomach."

She thanked him and took the meat for politeness' sake, but once she had tasted it, she found that she was ravenously hungry. The meat was cooked crisp, well salted, and flavored with wild thyme. So he could cook, too, this strange fighting bard. She ate slowly, savoring the food and watching him from the shadow of her long eyelashes.

Long ago her mother had taught her to notice the small details that told so much about a person, and yet all that she learned about Robert Gavin puzzled her. He ate with relish but with manners that might have graced a lord's table. His movements were swift and economical and everything about them suggested a man of action, not a musician or poet. He had the voice of a minstrel but the reflexes of a fighter. And as he moved and the firelight caught his dagger hilt, she thought that the weapon suited him more easily than his harp. Suddenly she wondered where he had been going that night and why he had been there to hear her cry for help.

She realized he was asking a question. "How did you escape from Reese? From what little I saw of the man, he isn't an easy man to outwit." She told him of Mog and the storm, then, and his eyes kindled. "Well done, my lady Gwenyth." He added thoughtfully, "You say you have no magic, but your knowledge of people and of nature is worth more than a hundred spells." Warmth and pleasure flooded through her at his approval, but his next words brought back reality. "Fearing your 'magic' as he does, I'm surprised Reese dared to abduct you."

She explained his original plan and how that had been thwarted. "He told me he wanted to marry me." At the blunt words the warmth of the fire, the comfort of Robert's cloak, and the taste of good food ebbed away and left her afraid again. "He made it plain that it's not me he wants but my 'magic' on his side. He feels that a little sorcery can help him become a rich and powerful man. He still thinks that he can catch me and force me to do his will."

She spoke bravely, but he saw horror quiver beneath the surface of her calm words, and though her face was grave and controlled, he saw her shiver. The anger he had felt against Reese before was nothing compared to the cold fury that swept him now. "The bastard," he said, and then he gentled his voice with effort. "You need not fear, Gwenyth. Here you are safe."

Instinctively, she knew he spoke the truth. There was a promise in his words that matched the strength she had found in his arms. In the sudden quiet between them her eyes rose involuntarily to seek his, and the firelight reflected their flame in their gray depths. Yes, she thought. With him, she was safe.

She did not know that her mouth had relaxed into softness, that her eyes were the color of spring leaves, that firelight spun gold through her long hair. She only knew that something changed, moved in his strong face. Then he turned away and reached for his harp.

"I promised you a song after your supper," he was saying, "and I'm a man of my word. They say that music calms the heart and brings rest, and you need both after this hard day."

He drew his fingers across the strings, and the ripple of music that filled the small rock chamber echoed clear and sweet. She closed her eyes and listened as the strong, deep voice began a song about the wedding at Rowyn. The words were poetic, filled with images of sunlight and laughter, and listening to the rich, deep voice, she relaxed.

Then the music changed and he began to sing about the Welsh mountains. As his deep voice told of valleys and high passes of perilous beauty, the cave and the sea faded away and she felt almost as if she were back on a sun-warmed hilltop. The meadow, the round blue lakes fringed with flowers—they were all still there, waiting for her. And there was more, a feeling of completion, a sense of belonging and peace. When he stopped singing, that feeling stayed with her still.

"You've made me feel as if I could touch the

hills," she murmured. "You have enchantment in your singing, Robert Gavin."

"Aye, enchantment . . ." but he was not thinking of his song. Instead he watched how her face had brightened as if turned to the sunrise, how against the still-wet fabric of her riding dress her high breasts heaved with emotion. The girl was magic, her beauty dangerous sorcery. He heard a roaring in his ears, and his hand shook slightly as he put down the harp. "But that's enough of enchantment for one night. You should rest."

She reached out as if to entreat him to play again, and their hands brushed. She heard him catch his breath, saw that his eyes were the color of storm-clouds on the hills, and she was filled with a yearning that was almost pain. Then his arms were about her, the hard muscle of them so tense that when they gathered her against him, they were like iron. She felt herself melt into that hardness as his mouth came down on hers.

His lips were cool and sure. The taste of those lips, the texture of his mouth, and the rough, male rasp of his cheek against hers—his hand stroking her cheek as they kissed, his arm cradling her possessively— she had not known how sweet a man's touch could be. With trembling fingers she traced the corner of his mouth, the lean, hard line of his jaw.

He took his lips away from her mouth just long enough to kiss her fingers. That light caress was more of his magic, she thought. It seared her with a heat that seemed to reach into her bones. When he touched her tonguetip with his own, tasting the periphery of her lips, her mouth yielded to the bold invasion of his tongue.

"My heart—" She did not know whether he had said the word or whether she had thought it, or whether it was part of the music that was still filling her senses. It didn't matter, it was all a part of the magic. His lips and his hands awoke sensations she had never known. Deep within her at the core of her being some unknown part of her was opening, turning toward him as a flower turns to sunlight. There was an aching in her to become closer, to kiss more deeply, to touch even more. She could feel her heart hammering against the hard wall of his chest as he held her pressed against him.

"Sweetheart." This time he did say it, and the deep voice was another caress. And yet even while her mouth responded to his kiss, she heard the echo of another voice that had spoken that same word, spoken it derisively, cruelly.

She didn't want to think of Huw ap Reese, and she tried to beat back all thoughts of him. It was no use. She remembered his coarse laughter, his foul kiss on her mouth. God in heaven, he, too, had kissed her this night. The warmth and the magic died, and she felt frightened, cold, a little dizzy.

Robert felt her go rigid in his arms and realized that the slender, lovely body that had pressed against him so eagerly was now as tense as a wild creature in a trap. Instantly alert for danger, he loosed his arms around her and reached for his dagger, but there was no sound except for the lap of the fire and the sound of their own ragged breathing. "There's nothing to fear, sweeting," he said, and reached for her again.

But she would not have it. She put her small hands against his chest and held him away from her. "No," she whispered. "No, please—do not. I beg you. No."

Her voice was low, scarce above a whisper, but he read the fear in it. Though she was making a valiant attempt at controlling herself, she was shivering. "We must not," she was saying. "I am tired, and the song was full of magic. That was why we—that was why this happened."

Looking down at her bent head, he realized she was making sense. He had saved her from her peril and the memory of that danger had sent her into his arms. That was all—the answer to the madness that had swept them both. He was a fool not to have recognized her emotion for what it was.

"You're right," he told her somberly. "This is no time for singing songs when Reese may have men on patrol outside." He loosed her completely and got to his feet. "Wrap yourself in my cloak and lie down by the fire. I'll stand watch while you sleep."

Before she could speak again, he had caught up his dagger and was walking away from her. As he disappeared into the darkness, the cave went quiet. And yet it was not entirely empty, for she could sense the memory of his presence, feel the whip-lean hardness of his body and the sweetness of his kiss.

To put an end to such thoughts, she lay down on his cloak and gathered it close to her for warmth, but this was a mistake. The mantle carried his scent, and its warm folds enfolded her like a lover's arms. She felt her pulse quicken, and instead of quietening, her fear grew. Who or what was Robert Gavin that he could make her feel like this?

Chapter Four

SHE AWAKENED IN DARKNESS. FOR A MOMENT SHE WAS disoriented, confused, and then she remembered. The wedding at Rowyn, the ambush, her escape from Reese, and Robert Gavin's rescue—the jumbled images coalesced on that thought, and she whispered his name into the still darkness.

Only the faint echo of her own whisper answered her, and Gwenyth sat up and began to feel about her on the stone floor. She needed light, and though the fire had burned out, a few red embers glowed at its heart. She found the wood that Robert had piled in a corner and started the blaze again. As she watched the flames turn the darkness ruddy, she saw with relief the minstrel's knapsack and harp. He still stood watch—unless Reese's men had found him and outnumbered him.

The thought brought back memories of last night's desperate flight, and she could no longer bear to crouch helpless here in the cave. She got to her feet and gingerly tested her foot, found that the pain was bearable now. Pulling a burning branch from the fire, she used it as a torch and began to walk away from the chamber—not the way she had come, but through the passageway that led, Robert had said, to the marshes.

The passageway was narrow and snaked through rock and earth. She could smell the cold sourness of clay and feel hairy tree roots brush against her as she crept down the tunnel. After a while it became so narrow and low that she had to bend nearly double to pass, and then suddenly she could see light. A gust of cool, fresh air extinguished her makeshift torch. She pressed on, climbing again, her eyes riveted on the circle of brightness up ahead, and then the passageway widened and she found herself standing in bright morning sunlight.

For a moment the dazzle of the sun blinded her, and she could only hear the song of larks and thrushes and draw in the fragrance of grass and flowers. Then she saw that the tunnel had ended in a small copse of trees at the edge of the marshes. She scanned the area around her anxiously, but the green marshlands stretched away from her in perfect peace until they reached the sea. There was no sign of Reese's men anywhere. Nor was there sign of Robert Gavin.

Cautiously she left the tunnel's mouth and slipped

out among the trees. Mostly ash and birch and oak, they were too sparse to offer a hiding place, but after the sea and the cave, she welcomed their living presence. Also, she could hear the sound of water tumbling and running nearby, and she was thirsty. Very carefully she followed the water sound until she found a creek running swiftly through a tangle of grass and brier. There she knelt down and, removing the bandages from her hands, drank and bathed her face and hands in the clear, cold water.

A man's shadow fell across the water and a hand dropped to her shoulder. She twisted free, her entire body poised for flight, then realized who was behind her. "What need to frighten me to death, Robert Gavin?" she cried.

"Why did you leave the cave?" he retorted. "The marsh is crawling with Reese's men, and so is the sea coast. It's God's mercy they didn't find you before I did."

Sunlight threw his strong-boned face into relief, and she saw the worry in his eyes. "You are right," she said contritely. "I wasn't thinking. When I awoke in the darkness—" She broke off and repeated, "I'm sorry to have put you in danger, too."

"And I am sorry you were alone in the dark, but it couldn't be helped." She shook her head slightly, and it occurred to him that this was not the first time she had been left lightless and alone. "If we are to get away to Eyri, we needed horses. There is no other way that you can cover the distance."

"You've found horses?" He nodded, and she

exclaimed, "How did you—and did you say 'we' were going to Eyri?"

"I told you that I wanted to climb Mount Snowden and visit the Glendower stronghold." He was smiling now. "Mind you, 'horses' might be too good a name for those sorry nags. Reese should be grateful I took the poor beasts off his hands."

Her eyes widened. "You stole Reese's horses? But weren't his men on guard?"

"Too busy searching for you and jumping at shadows. Your 'powers' are much feared, apparently." His grin was suddenly merry, and for an instant he was as she had first seen him at Rowyn—the smiling, dark-haired man with laughing eyes. Then he grew serious again. "I've hidden the horses some distance from the cave opening and seen to their needs. We'll ride after sunset."

"But if Reese has men everywhere—"

"If I'm not mistaken, he'll ride homeward tonight. Now that you've gotten away, he has to fortify his castle against a possible attack from your father. He'll leave some of his men behind, and it's my guess that they'll be searching for you along the road to Eyri. But then, I imagine that there are mountain roads that they don't dream about."

It was the way any fighting man would reason, she knew. He continued, "Of course, I'm only guessing. You have more knowledge of Reese and Eyri than I. Do you have another plan?" She shook her head and he said, "We're agreed, then. If you'll return to the cave, you'll find some bread and dried meat in my knapsack. I want to see that the horses remain well concealed.''

Her knee had gone stiff, but it was not discomfort that made her frown as she retraced her steps down the narrow tunnel. Robert Gavin had spoken of Reese's movements with calm authority, and despite his jest, she knew it had taken both skill and daring to "acquire" those horses. The man was swift and shrewd—and well versed in woodcraft, too, for even her keen ears had not heard his approach this morning. Suddenly she stopped in the close, earth-scented passageway. Was it only to sing his songs that this man wanted to go to Eyri?

The question nagged at her even when she had returned to the rock chamber and had replenished the fire and brought out bread and the meat as he had directed. "Why?" she asked herself out loud.

"Why, what?"

Again she hadn't heard him coming. She said with some sharpness, "You walk softly, Master Gavin."

"That has saved my hide many times over." There was no amusement in his voice, and he faced her squarely across the fire. "You asked a question, I think. Why, what?"

"Why do you want to come to Eyri?" she asked him bluntly.

"Even a poor minstrel would be less than a man if he left a woman alone among so many enemies." The smoke-silver eyes were steady. "Besides, as I told you, I want to meet Owen Glendower. I hear he has a good ear for music and is an excellent patron."

It made sense, she told herself, but something made her persist. "And this is your only reason?"

There was an edge to his reply. "What else, my lady? Perhaps you believe that I've fallen hopelessly in love with you."

She turned away from him, and he saw the color flow and then ebb along the lovely line of her cheek. He was angry with her for questioning him, and even more irritated at himself for feeling that anger. Beautiful she was without question, but then he was no stranger to beautiful women. Many had loved him, and he them, but he had always kept his head. This woman upset his inner balance, and this annoyed him. He told her shortly, "If you would like to go on to Eyri alone, I'll not stand in your way."

Suddenly she smiled. "Your pardon, Robert Gavin." Whatever he had expected, it wasn't an apology, and the warmth of her smile caught him by surprise. She went on, "I forgot that I owe my life to you—and I fear I have questioned your honor." She held out her hand, adding, "Will you forget what I said?"

Without speaking, he took the small hand. When he turned it over, yesterday's cuts were still sorely apparent and reminded him of what she had suffered. "If you'll forget my bad humor," he said, and without waiting for her answer lifted the hand to his lips.

The touch of his mouth brought memories. It seemed as if her skin, her flesh, her entire body was suddenly alive with radiant energy. "You must not fear Reese. I'll see you home, and safely. Did I not pledge you my service when we met at Rowyn?"

"Yes—yes, you did." Her lips had gone dry, and she could only speak with effort. "Everything, even the ambush seems long ago. And Dafyd—and poor Tam, poor Jonas. God grant some of them are alive."

"Amen to that." He let go of her hand at last, and she hurried to divide the food she had set out. They ate in silence, but to her the quiet was alive with his nearness, and she was conscious of even his smallest movement. Well, she reasoned, she was nervous—and little wonder. Huw ap Reese outside waiting for her, and the long journey in the mountains ahead of them.

"Tell me about Eyri." He broke the silence as if he had read her thoughts all along and was continuing an unspoken conversation. "I know that when Henry of England first brought his armies against your father, he left his other mansions and retreated into the Snowdonia Mountains to build a mighty fortress. It's said that his magic is strong there and that no matter who tries to get to Eyri, they can't find it unless Glendower wishes."

"Do you believe such tales?"

He shrugged. "Owen Glendower is a master strategist. I'd hoped his daughter knew of some little-known way to get to Eyri."

Taking a piece of charred wood from the fire, she scratched a map on the stone floor. "Here we are on the northwest coast. We must ride through the forests of the uplands in a southeasterly direction, skirt the great Llanberis Pass, and reach the valley near the Cliff of the Old Ones, where we'll find a secret road to Eyri. The only trouble is that members of the Welsh alliance also know this route."

"And Reese belongs to the alliance." She nodded. "Well, that can't be helped." He then asked her several questions about their route, and she could sense that he was gauging time and distance. At last he got to his feet. "If we travel all night, we'll reach the Cliff of the Old Ones by morning. But now you must rest for the journey."

"And you?" she asked.

"Minstrels are used to going without sleep. Besides, I want to see what our friend Reese is up to."

Mindful of his advice, she must have dozed, for when she woke, Robert was bending over her. "It's an hour after sunset, and Reese and half of his men have left for their castle. The rest of his henchmen have spread out toward Llanfair. Time we were going, too."

He had readied the horses and they stood saddled and waiting in the little copse outside the tunnel. As Robert had said, they were sorry-looking beasts, but they also looked strong and biddable. She paused to stroke their rough noses, and they whickered, softly. "Be surefooted and take us safe to Eyri," she murmured.

"I hope they listen to you." He was close behind her, and even at such a moment she had the giddy sensation that if she leaned back, she would be in his arms. She drew a bracing gulp of cool twilit air as he helped her mount. "It will be a long journey," he was saying.

It was also dark in spite of a half moon which rose over the ragged trees as they made their way toward the hilly interior. Picking their way through unmarked woods, they were soon riding into the uplands through stretches of thick forest and up hills pitted with shale and limestone. The ground here was often treacherous and several times they had to dismount and lead their horses, but Robert seemed confident of his way, and Gwenyth saw him looking skyward.

"Do you know how to read the stars?" she asked, surprised.

He nodded. "An old sailor taught me how to follow the North Star."

"Is there nothing you do not know, Master Harpist?"

"Many things," he replied promptly. "For instance, I know little about you. Tell me more about Cader Idris. You were happy there in the southern hills, weren't you?"

"Happy—" the word was spoken almost like a prayer, and he saw her tip her head back as if to draw in the light of the moon. For a moment she did not speak, and then the words came swiftly, as if held back for too long. "Sometimes, on fine moonlit nights, my mother, Merryn, and I walked in the hills gathering herbs. She taught me to be a part of nature, to hide by blending in the shadows, to become so still that a doe and her young would come and graze nearby. Once a wee fawn took food from

my hand and pressed its soft nose into my palm—"
She laughed softly at the memory.

He could barely see her face, but he knew her eyes
would be wide and soft with memory. Like green
velvet kissed by silver moonlight.

"I think I understand," he told her. "When I was
a lad, my parents died of fever. I was brought up by
my uncle—a decent man who tried to do as much for
me as he did for his son. He and my aunt did their
duty to me, and I to them, but understanding and
love did not come into it."

Instinctively she knew that the matter-of-fact tone
hid some ancient sorrow. His words made her remember nights when she had cried herself to sleep
for loneliness, ways in which Glendower's handsome
wife and trueborn children had made her realize that
she would always be an outsider. He was saying,
"People like you and me learn early to rely on
ourselves, to turn inward to find strength. Perhaps
we are lucky. We know we can count on no one
except ourselves."

She protested. "That sounds so selfish, and in my
case it's untrue. I truly love my father. I am grateful
that he loves me, also. I honor his wife and family.
Besides, I'm needed in Eyri. We have no doctor, and
my herb lore is much prized."

"But still you feel yourself an outsider," he murmured.

He was too quick, she thought, too shrewd.
Somehow this strange minstrel seemed to understand not only how she felt but why she felt as she
did. How could a man she had known for a handful

of hours see into her heart more clearly than did even the wise Owen Glendower?

The question nagged at her as they rode through the night, and it was still with her when dawn came to light the craggy hills through which they traveled and the cloud-covered peaks of the Snowdonia Mountains beyond. Gwenyth pointed out a deep valley between two hills. "If we follow that valley, it will lead us to the Cliff of the Old Ones."

"Reese's men might be watching for us, so we must go carefully." He paused to add, "I'm sorry. I know you need rest, but there's no safety here."

He looked concerned, and she hastened to reassure him. "I've ridden farther than this without rest."

She was tougher than she looked, this hill-princess. Even so, he could see the lines of fatigue in her face and the shadows that lay like bruises under her clear eyes. Again he silently cursed Reese for forcing this ordeal on her. "I'll go first. If there's fighting, you're to ride back along this way. No trying to help—you'd only be in the way. Understood?"

Without waiting for her reaction he spurred his horse and rode down the rock- and brier-strewn hillside that sloped into the valley below them. She was frowning as she followed. Once again he had spoken with the unconscious authority that suited a soldier far more than it did a minstrel. . . .

Suddenly her thoughts went still. They had almost reached the valley floor, and thickly growing banks of beech, rowan, and oak rose up to meet them.

Those woods seemed quiet and peaceful, but—
"Everything's wrong!" she exclaimed. "I can't explain it, but I feel it."

Instead of asking questions, he snatched up her reins and spurred his horse, making for the cover of the nearest trees. As he did so, there was a hissing noise, and spears flashed silver in the early sunlight. A moment later four men on horseback broke from the woods, and even at this distance, Gwenyth recognized them by the color and cut of their clothing as Reese's followers.

"Ride for those woods." His voice was very calm, almost cold, and she caught a glimpse of his face as he turned to meet their attackers. She also whirled her mount to look back at Reese's men and saw sunlight flash on their upraised swords.

"You're not armed—" Her dismayed cry was cut short as he rode out to meet them. For a moment he stopped to let them sight him, and then he turned his horse and galloped down into the valley.

He was leading them away from her, giving her a chance to escape. She must not waste the opportunity. And yet, how could she ride away and leave him to be cut down? In agonized indecision she watched as she saw him whirl his horse again, this time to face his pursuers. Sword blades arced up, and one of the four yelled triumphantly as he closed in.

There was a scream, and she shut her eyes. But they wouldn't stay shut. As they flew open she saw Robert Gavin bending sideways in his saddle, gripping one of his three attackers by the arm. Next moment he had dragged one man from his saddle.

As Reese's henchman fell, the minstrel tore his sword from his grasp.

But before he could even straighten, the other three were upon him, hacking viciously with their weapons. She cried out as he parried a brutal sword slash, raised his own sword for a blow. Another of Reese's men went down, and her heart leaped in thanksgiving, but thanks were premature. As he fell, the man caught Robert around the arm, dragging him halfway down from his horse.

He was up on his feet at once, but the remaining two men on horseback circled him, stabbing with their swords. Now she hesitated no more. Digging her heels in her horse's flanks and shouting an old Welsh battle cry Dafyd had taught her, she spurred not away from but toward the battle. She saw Reese's men turn toward her involuntarily, and that moment was what Robert Gavin needed. One of his attackers fell, sword-pierced. By the time Gwenyth had reached the scene of battle, Robert had dragged the other from his saddle.

"Yield or die." She heard the hard ring of his deep voice but could not hear the other man's reply. Apparently, he decided to yield, for Robert stepped back. As he did so Gwenyth saw that one of the fallen men had gotten to his knees, a dagger clutched in his hand. At the same moment the one who had yielded sprang for Robert's throat.

Shouting a warning, she spurred her horse between Robert's unguarded back and the man with the dagger. He snarled a curse and tried to catch her reins, but her horse reared, knocking him down.

Next moment Robert had dispatched one attacker and had swung his sword on the other. The man fell without another sound.

It was over. They stood facing each other across the bloodied valley floor. For a moment there was no sound but their ragged breathing and the squawking of frightened magpies and jays in the trees about them, and then he said, "Didn't I tell you to ride away at the first sound of trouble?"

"You also told me that I'd be useless in a fight," she retorted. "It seems to me that I just saved you from being stabbed in the back."

Steely gray eyes met stormy green ones. Then he threw back his head and laughed aloud. It was a warm laugh, joyous and infectious, and though she didn't want to, she began to smile. "Only a fool would laugh after nearly being killed," she scolded.

"Peace, my lady princess." Still shaking with laughter, he caught her by the hands. His action took her by surprise, and before she could protest, she was being drawn from the saddle. He held her for a moment against him and then lowered her to stand within the circle of his arms. "You have saved my life this day," he told her softly. "Now I'm even more at your service."

His eyes danced with flecks of silver, and his face was alight with laughter. Against her breasts she felt the rise and fall of his breathing. She tried to give light answer, but she could not find the words, and as — she struggled with her thoughts, she saw his face change. The amusement died but the light in his eyes did not. Unable to meet this new brightness, her long lashes fluttered down to shield her eyes.

"Gwenyth." At the deep vibrance of his voice something deep at the core of her shivered into life. Her body felt heavy as if filled with languorous honey, and her lips parted. Almost as if the weight of her hair was too much to bear, her face tipped up to his.

"Release the woman!"

As the harsh cry filled the air, she felt Robert's arms stiffen about her. Horrified, she watched as a troop of mounted, armed men rode down into the valley. Next moment she was being caught around the waist and almost hurled into the saddle. "Ride," Robert commanded her harshly. "Ride and don't look back, do you hear me? I can't hold them for long."

Shaking her head, she scrambled down from the horse. "You don't understand. It's Dafyd and his men. They've come to take us to Eyri."

Chapter Five

"HE'S TAKEN HIS TIME GETTING HERE." AS THE TROOP of grim-faced men rode up, Robert lowered his sword and addressed their leader. "Well, Captain. A shame you missed the fun."

The veteran captain's eyes narrowed. "Whoever you are," he barked, "stand away from the lady and drop that sword. You're all right, my lady?" he continued anxiously. "This fellow . . ."

". . . has twice saved my life," Gwenyth interposed hastily. "He helped me get away from Reese, Dafyd."

For a moment the veteran hesitated, and then he nodded. "In that case I'll be craving your pardon. I took you for another of these bastards—saving your presence, Lady Gwenyth—who follow that cur." His eyes turned frankly murderous as he added, "But there'll soon be a reckoning. Some of these lads will escort you back to Eyri, my lady, while the rest of us go on to Castle Reese."

It was what she had been afraid of. "My father ordered you to attack Castle Reese?"

"What did you expect?" the captain growled. "Aye, those churls that attacked us were masked, but I've not fought at my lord Glendower's side for thirty years without knowing a thing or two. I knew who was behind the ambush, all right. Of course we were going to get you back."

Her eyes had been busy, searching the ranks of the men, and now she interrupted. "How many were hurt by or—how many, Dafyd?"

"Jonas is dead, poor fellow, and Harries and Cradog ap Evans. Tam is hurt so bad it's feared he'll die—took a spear near the heart. Almost everyone was hurt bad, my lady, that's why I had to go back to Eyri to get reinforcements before following Reese. It needs avenging."

A low, angry mutter of agreement rose from the waiting men. Feeling the same cry for vengeance welling up within her own heart, she still shook her head. "It won't do our men any good to start a civil war." Dafyd began to object but she persisted. "You know what will happen if you attack Castle Reese. His friends will come to help him fight you. Then the Pryses and Kerrs and Vychans will come to our aid. Soon all the Welsh lords will be at each other's throats."

"And easy picking for the English," Robert interposed. "The lady is right."

The grizzled captain frowned down at him. "Now it comes to me. I've seen you before, at that wedding in Rowyn."

"I'm deeply flattered that you remember."

Dafyd frowned at the amusement in Robert's voice. "No wonder you counsel peace. What do harpists know about war or fighting?"

Hastily Gwenyth interrupted. "At least return with us to Eyri and see what our lord Glendower has to say now that I'm safe. You know that he's worked hard to unite Wales, and as Robert Gavin says, civil war will please the English king only too well."

Dafyd chewed the inner wall of his cheek for a moment. "Very well, my lady, we'll all return to Eyri and see what our lord has to say." He looked doubtfully at her horse and added, "Is that sorry beast yours?"

Tension broke as she laughed. "Aye, he is. Along with saving my life, Robert relieved Reese of these two mounts. They're good enough to take us to Eyri."

Several of the men at arms guffawed at the thought of a minstrel stealing horses from Reese, but Dafyd didn't join in the laughter. "Did you say, take 'us' to Eyri, my lady? That's impossible. No one goes to Eyri without an invitation from your father. The minstrel can't come with us."

"Don't you think he would wish to thank the man who saved my life?" Gwenyth reached up and rested a small white hand on the captain's arm. "Remember how much my lord father enjoys good music. We have had so little of it lately, with only sour old Gwyllym to sing to us at night. I've heard you complain that his voice could curdle milk."

"That's true, it can," one of Dafyd's men ventured. "Gwyllym is cousin to a crow. Many's the time I've wanted to drown him in the lake, but minstrels are sacred—or so the lord Glendower insists."

Scowling, Dafyd stared down into Gwenyth's uplifted face. "Don't try to get around me, my lady. It won't do any good," he scolded, but watching them, Robert could hardly hold his laughter. The hardbitten veteran was no match for the coaxing in Gwenyth's eyes.

"He only wants to sing to Glendower. It's little enough reward for saving my life. Reese's men chased me in the storm, and two of them had actually caught me when Robert Gavin rescued me."

Dafyd threw up a hand in surrender. "Have your way, my lady. Like enough you're right, and your father will want to reward the man." He paused and swung around to face Robert, his voice turning harsh again. "But if you are not wanted in Eyri, minstrel, remember I'll be there to throw you out. Bodily, if need be."

Robert said nothing, but Gwenyth saw the tightening of his fine lips and the momentary narrowing that turned his eyes cold. As Dafyd turned to shout an order to his men, she put a hand on his arm. "Please, do not mind what he says. He is a good man, and he and his wife and granddaughter have been friends."

Her low voice was packed with feeling, and looking down into the lovely, upturned face, Robert felt his momentary anger dissolve in a wave of totally inappropriate tenderness. "I cannot hold a grudge against anyone who has been your friend," he told her, and held his breath to see the radiance of her smile.

They rode throughout the morning and reached the Cliff of the Old Ones by noon. After the well-wooded valley, the place came as something of a surprise: a stark hill of limestone brooding over a narrow, glacial lake. Robert leaned back in his saddle to look up at the cliff wall, and Gwenyth said, "The lake is said to have been here since the beginning of time. According to many legends, Merlyn came here. He's supposed to have put the cliff and the caves here, also."

"I see no caves," he protested.

"You will."

Dafyd had called a halt and sent back a patrol to make certain that no one was following them. This done, he led the way around the lake to the base of the cliff. "Watch closely," Gwenyth instructed, and as she spoke, Dafyd seemed to disappear into the ground. Robert swore softly. The cave was not in the limestone wall but below it. His horse whickered in fear as he urged it down through a concealing line of bushes and into the earth.

Gwenyth said, "In a few moments we will be at the other side of the cliff."

She was right. Even as they entered the darkness of the cave, Robert could see light streaming in from the other side. "The legends must be right about Merlyn's magic. It would have taken mortal men years to tunnel under this mountain of solid rock."

"Perhaps. But my mother told me that there was a time long, long ago when huge mountains of ice moved across Wales and fell into the sea. The mountains gouged out valleys and lakes and dug huge holes into the sides of mountains, she said. I've often wondered whether this cave be one of those holes."

Awed, he looked about him at the huge opening gouged in the rock. "That story is even stranger than magic, but perhaps it is true. It would explain the cave, anyway."

She could not explain the warmth of pleasure she felt at his words. She had never told Merryn's strange story to anyone before, not even to her father, and yet she had instinctively confided in Robert Gavin. As they emerged into sunlight at the other side of the mountain, she heard him add as if to himself, "At Oxford we were taught to seek the reason behind all things and not simply accept what was told to us. I know several learned men who would be interested in Merryn's tale of the moving mountains."

"You were at Oxford—in England?"

She knew him well enough to note the slight

tension of his shoulders, the tightening of his hand on the reins, but he hesitated only a moment. "I went there as a boy to be educated. So did Owen Glendower himself, many years ago."

That was true enough. Many noble Welsh families, in the days of peace before Henry IV came to the English throne, had sent their sons to England for their education. But she had never heard of a minstrel with Oxford training.

He explained, "My uncle was a rich man, and he sent his own son to Oxford, so I was sent also. I lived in Queen's College, the coldest and poorest of the lodgings. It was so cold in the winter that we had to suck our fingers to warm them enough to write."

Shocked, she said, "Your uncle was rich and yet he sent you and his own son to such a miserable place?"

"My cousin was older, so he lived elsewhere. I shivered at Queen's College with a lad who had lost his mother and whose father cared nothing for him." Then he seemed to catch himself. "But that story is too dull to interest you. I'd rather hear more about the moving ice mountains."

She sensed that he was hiding something. Some inner sense warned her that she should seek Dafyd's counsel, and yet she remained silent as they rode along. She owed this man too much to cast suspicion on him, especially when she had no real reason to suspect he was anything but what he claimed to be.

Even so, she found herself watching him some time later as they climbed the steep mountain road.

It was no easy passage, so narrow at times that the horses had to be led through perilous passes or coaxed over rope bridges that swayed over rocky chasms, but Robert Gavin was as surefooted and as adept as any of Dafyd's veterans. They rode throughout the long afternoon, and toward sunset Gwenyth felt each separate bone in her body ache with exhaustion. Only sheer force of will kept her in the saddle, but the gray-eyed minstrel who rode behind her seemed tireless and alert, and as they went along she heard him murmur something under his breath.

When she turned to look at him, he was staring intently along the road. "See there." He nodded as two bright flashes of light ahead reflected the dying sunlight. "I have been watching the signal lights flashing back and forth and have been trying to learn the code. There must be a different meaning to each lightflash, and of course Glendower can communicate across great distances using reflected sunlight. No wonder he has poor English Henry on the run."

There was genuine admiration in his voice, but again she was troubled. "You have sharp eyes," she murmured.

For answer he urged his horse forward, drawing up beside her on the narrow road. Frowning, he said, "Sharp enough to see you're exhausted," he said. "Dafyd must call a halt. You can't ride like this."

"We won't have to ride much farther." He looked doubtfully at the forest around them and she explained, "Eyri is nearby but you will not see it until we are almost upon it. My lord father has built it to blend in with the surroundings."

As she spoke they followed a curve in the mountain road. Expecting the path to continue, Robert was astonished to find that they had come to a broad natural plateau on the side of the mountain. The area had been cleared of trees and he could clearly see the glint of a mountain lake, but it took a full minute to realize that he was looking straight at Glendower's mountain fortress itself. He had to resist an impulse to rub his eyes. In the gathering twilight the fortress literally seemed to blend into the side of the mountain.

"This is better than magic!" he exclaimed.

"When I was accepted into his household, my lord father asked me to teach him Merryn's art of concealment," she explained. "He used hillcraft to build Eyri."

He had indeed, but there were military features to the place as well, Robert noted. Eyri was easy to defend, and as they rode closer he could see that Glendower had diverted the water from the nearby lake to fill the moat that circled the mountain fortress. A wooden bridge was now lowered over this moat and heavy gates swung open to let them in.

Surprisingly, it was homelike within the walls. As Robert followed Dafyd and Gwenyth into Eyri, he was struck first by a sense of bustle, a comfortable and welcoming mixture of noise and smells and activity as the people of Eyri surged around the homecoming party. Suddenly a small girl came running out from among the crowd, shouting, "Granda—Granda Dafyd, you are back!"

"That's my Bronwen." Dafyd's hard face creased in a fond smile, and he reached down from the saddle to take the child up before him. The little girl then turned to Gwenyth.

"Oh, Gwenyth, I am so glad to see you. Grandmama Olwen and me, we were worried about you. I cried when they said you'd been stolen away. I prayed that you would come back to us."

Gwenyth's weary face brightened, but before she could speak, another voice drowned her out.

"Please, my lady, Tam's in a bad way. I have hoped that you would return before he died. They say no one can heal him, but I know you can."

"Only let me greet my father and the Lady Margaret, and I'll come." She turned to Robert, adding, "What think you of Eyri?"

"It's a fair place." It was also large and well appointed. In the half-light he could make out a large square building built in the center of the compound. This was no doubt Owen Glendower's home. Surrounding it were other smaller dwellings, a large warehouse, larder houses hung with newly pressed cheeses. There was even a pigeon loft standing beside a small but vigorous orchard of fruit trees.

"We lack for very little," Dafyd interjected proudly. "My lord Glendower has made this as comfortable a home as any of the others he owns all over Wales—such as remain." He hugged his grandchild closer to him as he added, "May God damn those Englishmen to hell, for they have stolen many of my lord's manors and lands. And that's not all. It was one of the earl of Stoake's men who killed my Bronwen's father. Her mother, my only daughter, died of a broken heart."

As he spoke the doors of the large house were drawn open, and a tall man was silhouetted for a moment against the light. Robert did not need Dafyd's sudden attention to realize that this was Owen Glendower, leader of the Welsh people.

As the lord of Eyri came forward, Robert bowed with the others, noting that Owen Glendower bore no resemblance to his fair daughter. Dark, intelligent eyes glinted under thick black hair and his face was narrow and bearded. A smile of relief and welcome softened the strong face as he exclaimed, "Gwenyth, thank God and His saints that you are safe!"

He helped Gwenyth from her saddle and held her for a long moment. She was grateful for his support. Now that she had reached Eyri, she had begun to tremble with weariness and reaction. "My lord father, I'm unharmed," she told him. "I escaped from Reese with help from this gentleman—Robert Gavin."

"Master Gavin." Dark eyes swung over Gwenyth's shoulder toward the still-mounted Robert. "The sentries told us you were coming. Come down from your horse now, and be welcome in our hall, both for bringing home our daughter and for helping to avert civil war." Gravely he kissed Gwenyth's forehead and then let her go. "I had not relished the thought of attacking Castle Reese, no matter how well its master deserved it. Now that you are back, the alliance can be preserved."

So she had been right. Gwenyth felt close to tears of relief. "I thought so, my lord father. Bold though he is, Reese himself does not wish war with you. He only wanted what he thought was my 'magic' on his side." Glendower nodded, and she would have said more had not a handsome woman appeared at the door flanked by a tall youth and a pert, dark-haired young girl. At sight of them Gwenyth curtsied deeply. "Lady Margaret," she murmured.

"Welcome, Gwenyth—we were very worried, Joan and Ivor and I," the woman was saying, but her smile was forced and Robert's ear heard no affection in her voice. He watched as the young people came forward to greet Gwenyth, but again he could feel little warmth.

He then realized that Glendower's wife was addressing him. "Master Gavin, I add my welcome to my lord husband's for saving Glendower's honor. Will you not come into our hall?"

"I'd be honored, lady." Dismounting, he bowed again to Glendower and then to his wife. Removing his dagger as custom demanded, he handed it formally to the master of Eyri and then followed him into a well-lit hall that was large enough to accommodate the many people who crowded in after their lord and lady. At one end of the hall stood a dais set with two chairs. Near this dais a long corridor connected the hall itself to other rooms and steps led upward to another level of Glendower's house.

There was a silence while Glendower and his lady took their seats and while Gwenyth and her half sister and brother came to stand beside the dais. Then the knights of the household and their ladies took their places, and Dafyd stepped forward somewhat apologetically. "My lord Glendower, you must forgive me for bringing a stranger here without your consent. Lady Gwenyth said you would wish it so since he had saved her life and was a minstrel to boot . . ."

"A bard!" There was surprise and real excitement in Glendower's voice. "Now you are doubly welcome, Robert Gavin. When the servants have washed the dust of the road from your feet and you've rested, perhaps you'll play for us."

From her place near the dais, the dark girl tugged his sleeve. "Father, ask him to sing now. We have not heard a good song in so long."

Glendower shook his head at the girl, but his lady said fondly, "My daughter Joan is a bold minx, but she is honest. You see that all of us crave music here in Eyri."

Robert glanced worriedly at Gwenyth. He had hoped that this gathering in the hall would be formal and brief and that then she would be allowed to go to her chamber and rest, but no one seemed to be paying her any heed, and now there was no polite way of declining to sing.

He lowered his harp from his shoulder and turned over songs in his mind. Should he sing a stirring battle song of the hero Rhys ap Gruffyd or of Rhodri Mawr who drove away the Norsemen? As he began to strum his harp, his eyes returned to Gwenyth. In the shadows of the hall her golden beauty shone like a star. Suddenly he knew what song to sing.

"Tonight I will sing to you of Gwidion, the man of ancient sorcery, who fashioned a maiden out of flowers," he announced.

As his strong voice filled the hall, everyone leaned forward so as not to miss a note of the music or a word of the song. Gwenyth didn't blame them, for the song was among the finest she had heard. Yet, instinct told her that this was no ancient poetry but a song of Robert Gavin's own making.

"Golden roses for her hair," Robert's voice chanted, "green velvet leaves for her eyes. She is as beautiful as the sun, my lady of flowers." She caught her breath as he met her eyes across the length of the hall, and she felt the caress of his voice in her innermost heart.

As the last harp note rippled away, there was an almost universal sigh of appreciation, and Dafyd unabashedly wiped his eyes with the back of his hand. "Master Gavin," he exclaimed, "I take back the words I said against you! If you hadn't come to Eyri, I would never have heard that fine song. Ah, but it was as if Gwidion himself were here in the hall, telling of his love for his golden lady."

"Perhaps he was here, seeking his lady of flow-

ers." Robert's words seemed to come almost in spite
of him. In the momentary hush that followed his
words, Gwenyth felt dizzied, unbalanced. Without
her volition she felt herself take a step forward as if
to go to him.

Glendower's voice broke the spell. "By St. Cynog,
I haven't heard such fine music for years. A talent
like yours should not go unrewarded, Master Minstrel."

It was a moment before Robert answered. "I have
been rewarded already, my lord, in being permitted
to come to Eyri."

"Still, there must be something we can offer you
so that you'll remain with us." The master of Eyri
suddenly began to smile as he added, "You spoke of
magic tonight, Master Gavin. Knowledge is the
greatest gift of all, and so I offer it to you. Stay at
Eyri and sing for us, and in return you'll be taught
the 'Welsh magic' of Owen Glendower."

A murmur ran through the great hall and Robert
looked surprised. "It's a great gift, my lord."

"Then you accept. Glendower turned to Gwenyth. "Daughter, you have every reason to be grateful to Master Gavin. If you're willing, you will be his
teacher."

Before Gwenyth could reply, Margaret Glendower spoke sharply. "Why should she not be willing?
He saved her life, didn't he? Besides, but for him,
the Welsh alliance would be crumbling."

It was true. Without Robert's help, Gwenyth
would be a prisoner, trapped and dishonored. In-

stead she was safe here in Eyri and free to teach Robert, be with him, and hear his voice—a sudden wave of dizzying joy filled her, and as she straightened her shoulders to meet his questioning gray gaze, all her heart trembled in her smile.

"I will gladly teach you, Robert Gavin," she said.

Chapter Six

"THE WOUNDS LOOK WELL TODAY. NO SWELLING, NO sign of infection. You're healing well, Tam."

As Gwenyth smiled down at him, the young man's pale face brightened, and beside him his elderly mother wiped her streaming eyes. "I've not stopped thanking God that you returned in time to help him, my lady. If not for your power, Tam and those others hurt by Reese would be dead by now."

"The only power I have is in the herbs and ointments I use." But it was no use, Gwenyth knew. Whatever she said, Tam's mother was convinced that her son was being cured by magic.

She gave Tam's shoulder a gentle pat. "I will be back tomorrow." Then, to old Ethelwyn she added, "Today when I go into the mountain, I'll gather red

clover and brew it into an infusion that will strength-
en his blood."

"Then the lessons with Master Gavin continue?"
Gwenyth nodded. "He is a kind man," said Ethelwyn. "Each day he comes to sing and play his harp
for us common folk. And him so busy, too."

Gwenyth felt inexplicably happy at the affection in
the old woman's voice. All of Eyri was impressed
with Robert Gavin, and all of Eyri had taken him to
its heart. This wasn't strange in view of the fact that
in the few weeks he had been at the mountain
fortress, he had willingly turned his hand to whatever task that needed doing: hunting, fishing in the
fish-stocked lake, even helping old Medwas the
armorer. Even Glendower, who had learned of
Robert's Oxford days, sought him out for discus-
sions about Welsh history and politics. And yet even
with all that, there had been time for lessons in what
he called "Welsh magic."

She thought of these lessons now as she left
Ethelwyn's house and walked toward the great
house where Robert was waiting. Together they had
ridden up the steep slope of Snowdon, and here she
had showed him healing herbs and their uses: how
raspberry bark could cure dysentery while spikenard
roots helped to knit bones. They had also ridden
down to the Cliff of the Old Ones, and here, while
telling him the legends of the place, she had taught
him Merryn's tricks of seeming to blend into natural
surroundings.

She was pleased and astonished at his attention

and the swiftness with which he learned, and the fact that he was so good a pupil made her want to teach him more. That was the only reason, she told herself, that she hurried her footsteps as she entered the great hall and climbed the stairs in search of him. From past experience she knew that he would either be in the little herb room she had installed on the topmost floor of the house, or in Glendower's private study.

Today he was in the study. She could hear his deep tones as she passed the solar on the second floor where Lady Margaret was overseeing some women who were spinning. Margaret Glendower took no notice of Gwenyth, but Dafyd's rosy-cheeked wife Olwen winked at her. "It's high time you came to fetch Robert, my little one," she told Gwenyth. "The men have been talking politics so loud that they have bored us silly."

As she spoke Gwenyth heard her father say, "Henry of England is no fool. He tried to bring us to our knees the only way he can, by turning us against each other. Even now, the English earl of Stoake bribes lawless Welsh renegades to attack their own countrymen. But so far he hasn't succeeded in breaking the Welsh alliance."

An angry voice which she recognized as that of her youthful half brother, Ivor, cut in. "I can't understand even the worst Welshman siding with the English. I spit on them. They have taken everything from us, even our country's name."

"This I know," Robert said. "Our country was

called Cambria, and it was the Saxons who called us *Vealh,* or 'foreigners.'"

His voice was peaceable, but Ivor's rose angrily. "And that's not all. Henry has made it a crime for English and Welsh to intermarry, as if we were somehow less than human. I say death to all Englishmen."

In the silence that followed his words, Gwenyth could hear Dafyd's voice outside the great house. He was shouting to his men and urging them on with their training. Suddenly she longed to be away from Eyri and in the quiet hills, and she crossed the solar and knocked on the open door of Glendower's private room. Her father and brother were standing by a large table covered with maps, but Robert was facing the door, and his eyes lit up at sight of her.

"Good morning, my lady Gwenyth," he said, and his voice was as glad as his eyes.

"Time for another lesson, I see." Glendower also smiled, but his eyes remained troubled. Somewhat wistfully he said, "It's a fine day to be out on the mountain. I almost wish I could join you."

Young Ivor spoke savagely. "None of us will ever be able to enjoy a walk on the mountain until we rid ourselves of Henry, father. Until then, it's only songsters and women who can pretend that there's any such thing as peace or safety."

He strode past Gwenyth and out of the small room, and Glendower sighed. "He's young and hot-blooded, but in a way he's right. There will be no peace and safety unless the alliance holds."

"Surely it will," Gwenyth said, troubled.

"I hope so." Glendower ran a long finger from marked points on the map on the table. "Here is Castle Pryse on the Conwy River, guarding the northern border between England and Wales. Here the Hanmers keep central Wales safe. Here are the Kerrs to the south. But unless Reese repents and returns to the alliance, our northwest coast and the Lleyn Peninsula is unguarded."

"Reese." Robert did not raise his voice, but there was steel under its softness. "Would you still count him an ally, Lord Glendower?"

Dark brows pulled together in a frown. "For Wales I would ally myself with the devil himself. None of us matters, Robert Gavin, only Wales matters." Quietly, as if repeating a prayer, he added, "Wales is my blood, my bones, my heart. I will do all I need to do, whatever I need to do, to keep it free from English rule."

There was a silence in the little room. Outside, mingling with Dafyd's shouts, rose the high, clear call of a lark. Listening to it, Gwenyth spoke impulsively. "Come with us into the mountain, my lord father. You are worn with care and should rest."

The frown melted away and Glendower smiled. There was a remarkable sweetness as well as power in the smile, and Robert understood why all of Wales had flocked to this man's colors. "You alone know how I have missed the peace of the hills," he told his daughter. "The hills and Merryn—the love of my youth. But I cannot come today. I must send

messages to Merdyn Pryse and to the other lords of
the alliance to gather at Eyri so that we can consider
what is to be done about Reese's actions." Gently
but firmly he waved Robert and Gwenyth to the
door. "Go and learn more 'Welsh magic,' the two of
you."

Gwenyth felt a heaviness clouding the bright day.
Robert seemed to feel it, too, for he was silent as
they left the great house and walked to the stables
near the great wooden gate. Only when they had
ridden out of Eyri and taken a narrow path that led
away up the mountain did he shake off his mood.
"Well, my lady of flowers, where are we going
today?"

"Up into the mountains. I am going to show you
the enchanted lake. You'll be pleased, I think."

"There is always pleasure in being with you."

The day seemed to brighten at his words, and her
heart lifted. "Ethelwyn tells me that you have been
coming to sing to Tam. That is kind."

"Singing is something I enjoy, though I can't say
as much for everything else I have been doing
lately." He grimaced. "You should have talked to
the man in charge of your father's fishponds. Hob
was disgusted with me for scaring the fish away. And
Dafyd is certain I'll never be a soldier. He feels I
know nothing about military strategy."

"Why should you?" She turned to look at him in
surprise. "What would you want to know about
military strategy?"

"Your brother is right in saying that there's little

79

peace these days." Abruptly laughter left his face. "Even a minstrel has to face the facts that songs won't turn aside a sword."

"What made you want to be a bard?" she asked him curiously. "You never told me."

"I always enjoyed the old tales, and I can sing and play the harp. I have no fortune of my own, and I craved adventure." He smiled down at her. "Now it is my turn. Do you agree with Ivor in his hatred against the English?"

She was surprised. "What kind of question is that?"

"I merely ask if you hate all Englishmen— enough, say, to kill them all."

She hesitated. "My mother believed that life was sacred. She taught me that the life of a flower, a tree, an animal, a man—all are sacred." She shook her head in exasperation. "I don't like your question, Robert Gavin."

"But I must ask questions. How else can I learn from you?" He was smiling, but she had the feeling that he was turning some thought over in his mind. As they rode up the mountain she was thoughtful, too. She had always thought of the English as the enemy, as the evil ones who had killed little Bronwen's mother and so many others. Yet surely God would not create an entire race of evil men, and so there must be good Englishmen, too.

She was glad to lay aside these thoughts as they came around a bend in the mountain and Robert exclaimed with pleasure. Before them the mountainside fell away into a valley, and at the heart of that valley, bordered with fir and beech, was a large turquoise lake.

"This is the enchanted lake of the moving island," she told him. "The king of England thinks that my lord father is so strong in magic that he can make islands move. Today you will have to guess how the 'island' in the middle of the lake can move."

Spurring her horse, she rode down into the valley ahead of him and he followed, watching how the sunlight turned her braided hair to deep, rich gold and brought color to the lovely line of her cheek. When he spoke it was with effort. "What you say sounds impossible—but there must be an explanation."

For answer she turned and smiled at him, and the irresistible mischief in that smile took his breath away. He had to restrain an impulse to lean across and kiss her soft mouth as she said, "Wait and see. I wager that you cannot discover the secret of my father's moving island."

"A wager paid with what?" he called after her as she rode away from him.

"You will never guess the secret. See? There is the island."

He helped her dismount and then walked to the water's edge. Narrowing his eyes, he looked across the bright blue water. The island she spoke of was some quarter mile from the shore, a small, sturdy bit of land covered with green rushes and waterweeds and surrounded by lavender water hyacinth. He studied it for some time and then said, "This movable island must be used in times of war, so it would be used for the movement of arms. But how it moves I cannot guess. Unless the island is not an island at all."

Wonder filled her voice as she gasped, "How did you know?"

"That's it, of course. A boat—or a raft." He was astonished at the sheer simplicity of it. A huge raft covered with silt, planted with living reeds and anchored by heavy rocks so that it remained immovable. And the military significance of such an invention was considerable. The lake lay in the midst of this mountain valley. By using the 'moving' island Glendower could move men and arms quickly, all the time confounding his enemies with his 'magic.'

"In the hills where my mother and I lived, there was a much smaller lake. To get from one side to another, we used a raft of logs lashed together. And so that the raft would remain concealed, we covered it with branches of trees. I told this to my lord father, and he—" She broke off, troubled, her earlier laughter stilled.

She had wanted to astonish him when she brought him here, had been sure that he would not even come close to the truth, and yet he had gone unerringly to the heart of the puzzle. How? she wondered, but before she could pursue the thought, he was saying, "Don't fear, Gwenyth, your secret is safe."

Instinct told her that this man's word would never be broken, and yet how could he have guessed, this bard who had been at Oxford, this minstrel who was interested in military strategy. Questions without answers eddied in her mind, and to give herself time to think she walked away from the lake to a grassy knoll some distance away. Here she sank down on the warm grass. He followed her, saying, "Henry's soldiers will be confounded when your father plays the trick of the floating island on them during battle."

Involuntarily she cried protest. "You must not bring the thought of killing here," she begged him. "No matter what Ivor says, in the mountains there is still peace. When I am here, I feel as if I belong as I do not—"

She broke off, but he ended the sentence for her. "As you do not belong in Eyri. Is that what you meant to say?"

It seemed ungrateful, but here by the sun-splashed lake and in the flower-scented air, she could only nod sadly. He did not move toward her or touch her, but she felt his nearness and his understanding as she said, "Sometimes I feel I do not belong anywhere except in the hills. Here, I am home."

"What was that you said?"

His puzzled eyes told her what she had done. "I ask your pardon," she stammered. "I was thinking of the hills and I—I forgot for a minute that you couldn't understand me. Merryn and I had a language that we invented, and we used it to talk to each other. I don't use it anymore, but sometimes when I'm thinking of my mother it slips out."

Even so, some from Eyri might have heard her whisper in her secret tongue, and this had no doubt made the superstitious even more convinced that she was a sorceress. Robert frowned as he seated himself on a tree stump by the water and watched her downcast face. He could sense the ache of her loneliness, and he wished he could think of something to ease it.

"I think I know what you mean," he said at last. "At Oxford I felt cut off from the rest of the world. My cousin had his own circle of rich friends and did not come near me, and I knew no one well besides the lad I met at Queen's College. In our mutual misery we made up a few words of a secret tongue. When we were feeling wretched, we used to use it to pretend the world was a better place."

"What was your word for 'friend'?" she asked eagerly.

They compared words. She had known he had a quick ear and a gift for sounds, but even so she was astonished when he began to string Merryn's words together into recognizable sentences. She laughed merrily when he told her that he was hungry, but then the laughter stilled. Until now, teaching him hill lore and using the secret language had seemed to bring the hills closer. Now, suddenly, reality filled her like a dark wave, and the hills seemed far away. She would never return to them again, she thought sadly.

As the thought filled her mind, she felt a shadow between her and the sun, and looking up, she realized that he had come to kneel beside her. He took her hands in his, and the motion that linked them seemed as natural as breathing. "Gwenyth," he said. "Do not go away from me. Don't shut me out of your thoughts."

Something in his voice compelled honesty. "I cannot keep my thoughts from you," she whispered. "I don't know why. Who are you really, Robert Gavin? You are unlike anyone I've ever known."

He hesitated, and again she sensed that he was considering some thought. Then he shook his head. "That won't do. No more questions until you have paid your wager. You did say I'd never find the secret of the enchanted lake, didn't you?"

"And how do I pay you?" she asked, and saw the answer in his eyes as he drew her into his arms. Locked against him, breasts, hip, and thigh, she had no moment to think, much less protest, before his mouth found hers.

And then she knew she did not wish to protest. She well knew the touch and taste of his lips. Knew and remembered the slow-building heat that was forged at their joined mouths and filtered like sunfire through her skin and blood and pulse. Against her softness she felt the strong, sure beat of his heart, and his mouth on hers was sure, too, as he rubbed her lips with his and then stroked the inner recesses of her mouth with his tongue.

She was so sweet to kiss—the thought formed deep in his mind as his lips traced her softness. Her mouth, her tender chin, the hollows of her temples, her throat—and back again to her seeking lips. He felt her arms go about his neck and the firm press of her breasts against him, and he raised his hands to loosen her braids. Her long hair fell in a waterfall of golden silk, and he stroked it and her shoulders and back and the rounded curve of her hips. Then his hands moved up to caress the high slopes of her breasts, and against her mouth he formed the words, "My sweet lady of flowers. My lovely one."

His words she registered within her heart, within the tumult of senses brought by his kisses. Ripples of fiery pleasure filled her as his hands touched and stroked her, and she murmured with pleasure as his fingers smoothed the taut and yearning nipples under her bodice before bending to seek the still-clothed buds with his lips.

Wordless, he drew her down with him on the warm, fragrant grass, and she caught her breath that was filled with crushed flowers and the distinctive scent of him. For an instant she saw herself reflected in the depths of his eyes, and then her lashes swooped shut as he kissed her again, and yet again while he drew the bodice from her shoulders and breasts to kiss the white, cool satin of her skin. She felt the rasp of his cheek against her inner breast, his open-mouthed kisses caressing the pale areolas, his tongue nudging the taut peak.

Her murmur of want was sweet in his ears as he covered her eager nipple with his mouth, sucking it lightly and then more boldly as she moved against him. He was on fire with wanting her, and the desire mounted with every pulse of his blood. Her breasts, her waiting mouth that met his with answering desire—every flower-scented, eager young curve cried out for his loving. "My Welsh princess," he whispered, "before God, I worship you."

The sound came suddenly, out of nowhere, shattering the golden stillness around them. Magpies screamed and crows cawed, taking angry wing. Robert's arms tightened around Gwenyth, pulling her with him to a sitting position. "What in the name of God?" he exclaimed.

"It's the horn—the sentries are sounding an alarm." Gwenyth heard herself speak as if from a faraway place. Her heart was hammering so loudly that she could feel it leaping against her ribs. "Oh, God, the English are here to destroy us."

His arms loosened about her, and for a moment it seemed as if she were looking into the eyes of a stranger. "The English!" he exclaimed, and the spoken words awakened her to full reality. As she pulled away from him, she could feel the rasp of his shirt against her bare, kissed-tender nipples, and a sense more of confusion than of shame swept through her.

With trembling fingers she pulled her clothing to rights. "We must get back to the fortress before they shut the gates."

Swiftly he got to his feet and, catching her hands in his, drew her up also. The grim look in his eyes softened. "Don't worry, I'll see that you're safe."

He had said those words before, and her pulse quickened at the memory of those dangerous times. Then as now his touch and his nearness had brought its own madness, and its own danger. Was it the lake that had enchanted her into forgetting the questions she had about this man? Or had he taken her into his arms to make her forget those questions? It was almost as if some sorcery had waited for them beside the enchanted lake.

She glanced up at him and saw that he looked grim. "Are you all right?" he asked. "We must ride swiftly to reach the gates. There's no telling what we may find there."

But when they reached the gates, there was no sign of knights or men-at-arms racing to repel an invading force. Instead, the wide-eyed gateman gave them the news. "There's trouble on the border. A message just came that Castle Kerr has been attacked by Welsh renegades and that Madog ap Kerr needs our help. All the knights and guardsmen who can walk or crawl have assembled in the great hall."

That much was true. There was scarcely room to move in Glendower's hall, and Gwenyth and Robert had to squeeze their way through the throng of men waiting for their lord's command. As they pushed their way toward the raised dais, Gwenyth heard her father say, "Madog ap Kerr is a staunch supporter of my alliance, and he's been put under seige by renegade Welshmen paid by the English to harry the border castles. He managed to get word to me asking for help." He paused. "Dafyd, choose a third of the men to stay here and defend Eyri. The rest will ride with me."

Young Ivor was flushed with excitement. He jumped onto the dais and lifted a naked sword, brandishing it high. "This time we'll hammer those English-paid traitors into the ground." He looked around the loudly applauding assembly, and his eyes lit on Gwenyth and her companion. "Master Minstrel!" he shouted as Robert approached the dais. "Will you ride with us or stay here safe at Eyri with the women and old men and babes?"

Owen Glendower frowned, but Robert replied peaceably, "I am a bard, young sir, not a knight or a soldier."

Ivor laughed. "Listen to him!" he exclaimed, and before any could stop him, he had lifted his sword point to touch Robert's throat. "I always maintained that a singer of songs was no true man. . . ."

There was a blur of sound and of shadow, and then Ivor's sword clattered to the floor. Next moment Ivor himself was pulled off the dais, with Robert's arm locked tight around his neck. The bard spoke gently. "You are young, Ivor Glendower, but not too young to learn a lesson in courtesy."

A babble of voices rose and then fell into a stunned silence. Into it Robert released the youth and bowed to the master of Eyri. "I regret the incident in your hall, my lord, but I don't enjoy a sword point at my throat."

For the space of a heartbeat the silence continued, and then Glendower began to laugh. Dafyd followed, and then laughter echoed through the hall. Only the flushed young Ivor was not smiling as his father said, "You're full of surprises, Master Gavin." He leaned closer. "You refused Ivor's ungentle offer, but tell me now—will you ride with me if I ask it? We would have use of both your sword and your music."

This time there was no possibility of refusal. Robert bowed low. "As my lord commands."

Ivor blustered, "You took me by surprise, Master Gavin. Don't think that you can do the same to the Welsh renegades. They are fierce fighters and know every filthy trick there is. It may be that you will not ride back with us to Eyri."

Over the buzz of noise, over the heads of hurrying knights and men-at-arms, the minstrel's gray eyes met Gwenyth's. "I'll be back," he promised.

Chapter Seven

"GWENYTH, PLEASE TELL ME A STORY. YOU HAVEN'T told any stories in a long, long time."

The child's coaxing voice rose over the conversation in Lady Margaret's solar, and the women gathered there looked up smiling from their various tasks.

"Bronwen, Gwenyth is busy carding wool. She hasn't the time to tell you stories," Lady Margaret reproved. She added, "It's your fault, Gwenyth. You tell the old tales so well that the child keeps bothering you."

Gwenyth smiled at Dafyd's granddaughter. "It's no bother, my lady, and I can tell a story while I work. But what story will it be? About King Math who could read your thoughts, or about the magic white horse?"

Small Bronwen cuddled close against Gwenyth. "I like the one Robert told about Gwidion and the lady he made out of flowers. I miss his songs—and Granda Dafyd, and everyone else."

Gwenyth's fingers still carded wool, but she felt a tightening of the heart. The sun-bright solar seemed to grow darker, and the busy women fell silent. Olwen, Dafyd's wife, looked troubled, and Lady Margaret's eyes went involuntarily to the wide bed that stood in the center of the solar. Briskly she said, "That is why so many of us have gathered here together—to keep our spirits up and make sure the work of Eyri goes on in the men's absence. It won't be long before they come back."

"But it's been seven full days without any word," Joan Glendower said, sighing. "Perhaps there'll be news today. What do you think, Gwenyth?"

She shook her head. "I wish I knew."

"Everyone knows that hillwomen have the gift of second sight," Joan protested. Gwenyth looked up to deny this and knew from Margaret Glendower's suddenly narrowed eyes that the memory of Merryn still rankled. Joan was continuing, "You can charm the beasts out of the forests. You can make yourself disappear. Surely you can tell when our men are coming home?"

Dafyd's wife came to the defense. "If Gwenyth says that she can't predict the future, she can't." She smiled at her small granddaughter. "Bronwen's right, Gwenyth. Tell us a tale to pass the time."

Mechanically Gwenyth began, but her mind was

not on Gwidion or his maiden made of flowers. The familiar words invoked Robert's song, his kisses, and his hands playing her body as he played his harp. They had shared love beside the lake that day, and now he was gone. Bleakly she wondered whether he would ever return, and her mind rejected the thought. He'd promised to come back. . . .

"My lady Margaret!"

At the hoarse shout the women stared at each other wide-eyed. A moment later heavy footsteps clattered on the stairs and one of the guardsmen came running into the room. "Good news, my lady. The lord Glendower and his men are riding back to Eyri in triumph. The signals say he should be back by dusk."

Cries of joy erupted through the solar. "Then he's unhurt?" Gwenyth cried. The man nodded, and she realized that while he thought she meant to ask about her father, she had thought only of Robert Gavin.

There was a confused tumult as women began to demand news of their men, but the message received had been only that Owen Glendower and his son were alive and well. Dafyd's wife got to her feet, her arm around Bronwen. "We'll go home now, my dear one," she said. "We have much to do before our men return."

If they all return. Gwenyth could hear the unspoken thought and saw the women watching her again. Did they truly believe she knew who was alive and who dead? To Lady Margaret she said, "I must see to the infirmary, my lady, and to my medicines and ointments."

Bowing, Gwenyth left the solar and climbed the stairs to her herb room on the topmost floor of Glendower's house. Because patients needing her care often sought her here, she had installed a bed in one corner as well as a cabinet filled with jars of ointments and dried herbs. She was already listing in her mind the herbs she would need: briony juice to cleanse wounds, yarrow and toadflax to be beaten into poultices, cypress leaves to be made into compresses that would stop the bleeding of the wounded. But together with the list of herbs, her mind also formed a prayer. Please, she begged, let him be safe.

She spent that afternoon readying Eyri's infirmary and making sure that the supply of clean linen bandages was adequate. She was helping to spread sheets on fresh straw pallets when she heard a rumbling chant coming up the mountain. She recognized a Welsh battle song. Glendower's warriors were marching home.

She ran into the twilit courtyard, where others had already gathered, all of them listening to the deep chorus. Lady Margaret and Joan stood together on the steps of the great hall while tense and pale in the gathering twilight the other mothers, sisters, sweethearts, children waited in silence. Those men who had been ordered to stay behind and protect Eyri stood at painful attention, and even Tam, ghost-pale and bandaged, had managed to drag himself to the

door of his house. As she stood and watched with
the others, Gwenyth felt her hand being taken and
looked down into a small, upturned face. "Gwenyth,
it'll be all right, won't it?" Bronwen whispered.
"Granda will come home. . . ."

Gwenyth glanced at Dafyd's wife. Olwen's face
was stoic, but there was no hiding the fear in her
eyes. Kneeling beside Bronwen, Gwenyth hugged
her tight. "It will be all right," she promised, and
wondered if her words were meant to comfort the
child or herself.

As she spoke, the marching song swelled louder,
and Owen Glendower and his son came riding
around the bend of the mountain path. Glendower's
colors and the great dragon pennant of Wales flew
over their heads. "There's Granda!" Bronwen exclaimed. "Gwenyth, look—he's hurt."

Swiftly Gwenyth scanned Dafyd as he rode behind
his lord. The grizzled captain looked pale, and his
left arm had been bandaged to the shoulder, but he
held his seat proudly. "Don't fear, sweeting, he's not
badly wounded," she breathed, and her eyes darted
among the other riders, searching for Robert.
Where was he?

A wail of sorrow rose from among the women,
and Gwenyth's arms goose-pimpled as she saw that
now the wounded and the dead were being carried
into Eyri. Was Robert among these? she wondered,
and then gratitude filled her as she saw him. He was
on foot, leading his horse and walking beside the
litters of the wounded. He seemed unhurt except for

a bandage around his left arm, and she breathed a prayer of heartfelt thanks.

As if he had heard the unspoken words, he looked up and their eyes met across the crowded space. It was too dark to see his face, but she could feel the intensity of his gaze. She started toward him, and he left his place in the ranks and began to push toward her, but before they could reach each other a shout of welcome announced that Glendower had dismounted and was embracing his lady. Margaret was close to weeping as she said, "We prayed for your safe return, my lord. For all our gallant men."

Glendower kissed his wife and then drew back to face his people. "We return with good news. Castle Kerr is safe and many of the renegades were captured. They admitted to being paid by the English to try and break the alliance." An angry mutter rose, and he raised his hands for quiet. "In the struggle, five good men were lost and many were wounded."

As he began to name the fallen, a deathly silence fell on his people. Then a woman's broken-hearted wail pierced the quiet like a spear. "My son, my son—God could have taken me instead of you."

"He could have taken any of us," Glendower said somberly. "Both Ivor and Dafyd were close to death. If it wasn't for Robert Gavin, they might have been killed by those renegade Welsh." He paused, looking around him. "Master Gavin, come here and receive our thanks."

Robert had almost reached Gwenyth. Now he turned to Glendower. "My lord, you exaggerate. I was the closest to Ivor and Captain Dafyd, that's all there was to it."

Dafyd objected to this. *"Diawl,* boyo, you came like the wind. I was down on the ground, a spear at my throat, and Ivor was fighting off a half dozen of those bastards when you got to us."

"He killed three of them almost at once." Ivor's eyes glistened as he recalled the incident. "Then we fought, shoulder to shoulder, until we had dispatched the others. Ah, that was a brave fight." He paused and then added with some embarrassment, "Master Gavin, I want to say that I was wrong for what I said to you in the hall. Minstrel or no, you're a fine fighter, and I owe you my life."

It was a handsome apology, and the people of Eyri shouted their approval. Robert knew he must reply but for the first time in his life the right words eluded him. He had been in perfect command of himself until he saw Gwenyth kneeling in the dust with Dafyd's granddaughter in her arms. All his powers of reasoning had not been proof against the one jolting moment when their eyes met, and now he could think of no one but her.

Lady Margaret was smiling through her tears. "Your silence shows your modesty as well as courage. We're all in your debt."

Her husband nodded. "When Wales throws off the English yoke, I'll reward you with land and title for your valor. Meanwhile, enter my service, Robert Gavin. I promise you that you'll be one of my most valued knights."

There was a moment's silence and then the bard said, "I'm a minstrel, my lord Glendower, not a man of war. To enter your service as a fighting man would mean the end of my way of life. I'd gladly serve you, but with my harp."

The master of Eyri began to protest, but his lady put her hand on his arm. "Master Gavin might change his mind in time."

"I hope so. Perhaps we can convince you to settle in Eyri and marry one of our maidens." For a moment Gwenyth felt her father's eyes on her and the warmth of his knowing smile. Then he added, "But now it is time for other things. Come with us into the hall, Robert, while others see to the honored dead and take charge of the wounded."

Organized confusion followed. Now women mourned their dead or waited to help Gwenyth treat their wounded. Amid the noise Gwenyth felt her hand being taken and looked up into Robert's eyes. "I prayed you'd be safe," she whispered. "But are you wounded? Your arm . . ."

"A scratch. Your prayer kept harm away." Why was it that her heart sang when he smiled down at her? "I know you must tend the wounded, and I have been commanded to go into the hall with your father. There will be time later," he promised.

But the caring for the wounded lasted deep into the night. Assisted by Olwen and the other women, Gwenyth cleansed and stitched wounds, set limbs, soothed burns. Most of the wounds were minor, but two of Glendower's soldiers died from loss of blood.

Their deaths tormented her even though she knew she had done everything possible, and a bruising misery filled her as she walked back to her father's silent house. Her family slept now, and her footsteps echoed emptily as she climbed the stairs to her herb room to ready tomorrow's supply of medicines and ointments. In spite of the oil lamp she carried, it was very dark in the little chamber, and as she stood in the doorway she had the feeling that in all her life she had not felt so alone.

"Have I come too late to seek your skill?"

He was standing in the doorway of the stillroom. In the fragile light of the lamp he looked enormous, his shadow looming across the bare white walls, and when he stepped into the room she saw that he had changed from the clothes in which he had ridden away. Bathed, too, for she saw the wetness of his dark hair above his open-necked tunic. She knew she should be glad that he was there, but at the moment all she could think of was death.

"You should be asleep," she murmured.

"I wanted to come to you earlier, but your father insisted I stay and play to the company. And then the families of the dead asked the same. I could not refuse. . . ." He came closer to her, his face hardening as he looked down into her face. "You have worked too hard!" he exclaimed. "How could Glendower ask this of you?"

"It is my duty to try and heal—" She broke off and added bleakly, "But many died in spite of all I could do."

A strand of hair had fallen across her forehead, and it shimmered against her skin like gold. Gently he pushed it back. "Don't blame yourself, dear one." At the loving words she felt her heart open as a flower unfurls to the sun, and she leaned forward against his warmth and strength.

"While I worked on those poor dying men," she told him, "I kept thinking how I would feel if it were you lying there. How I would feel if I could not save you."

"I promised to come back. Did you have so little faith in me?" He drew her against him, holding her gently. "My poor love, you're worn out. Rest, now, and we'll talk tomorrow."

Her heart trembled between tears and laughter, between recent sorrow and present joy. She could hardly breathe from the tumult in her heart, but her lips trembled into a smile. "I don't need to rest now that you are here."

Looking down at her, Robert felt a twisting tenderness at her smile. "That's my brave lady," he told her softly, and bent to touch her lips with his own.

He had meant it to be a gentle kiss, a tender touching of lips, for she was too weary and emotionally spent for more. And besides, he had promised himself that he must go slowly with her. But when their mouths came together, the world seemed to vanish about them. Nothing mattered to Robert except the slender, warm firmness of her in his arms, her scent of sunlight and flowers. His mouth could not get enough of her sweetness, and he lifted a hand to support the golden head against him as she kissed him back with a hungry passion that answered his own.

"I have waited—" Her ragged whisper was ended by his mouth, but she continued the thought in her heart. She had waited for this moment since the men had ridden away seven days ago. No—she had waited for him all her life. With sure and mounting joy she felt the touch of his tongue as it circled the periphery of her mouth, and then its bold invasion. She lifted her hands to touch his crisp dark hair, trace the line of his hard jaw, the musculature of shoulders and back, and something within her sang with joy at his touch. When he lifted her into his arms and, still kissing her, carried her to the narrow stillroom bed, the song within her grew still more joyous. My love, she thought, my love.

"I have missed you. Missed you sorely the days I was away from you. I thought of you constantly." He spoke against her mouth, each word an urgent caress, and under the small kisses her lips parted in welcoming. Their tongues thrust and twined, tasted, sucked each other's breath. "I left to be away from you, but I carried you in my heart wherever I went."

Eagerly their hands moved and touched, remembered, caressed. She slid her hands under his tunic and over the smooth, silk-muscled strength of his back, while he unlaced the fastening of her bodice. For a moment she felt cool night air from the open window touch her bare shoulders and breast, and then his hands were warming her, stripping away her skirt, her shift, until she was naked against him.

The rough linen of his tunic teased her bare skin for a moment, and then he withdrew from her a moment to strip off his garments. Then, still cradling her against him, he bent his mouth to trace the swell of her breasts, skirting the pale areolas before drawing the nipples between his lips. She murmured with a pleasure that was almost pain as his warm mouth covered the taut buds, as his tongue tip caressed them. Then his mouth was seeking hers again, and he was lowering her to the cool linen sheets.

Coolness against her back, Robert's hard warmth against her breasts—she was lost, drugged, spinning in a vortex of desire. Some part of her mind wondered at her want of him, at her need to touch the muscles of his chest and the crisp chest-fur and run her palms over the powerful tension of his buttocks and thighs.

Her delicate touch burned like fire, reached into the marrow of his bones. He could scarce believe her sweetness as he kissed her with slow, open-mouthed kisses and then moved his mouth to her breasts again. His sensitive fingers caressed her legs, her knees, and the tender skin of her thighs. Then he bent lower, and his mouth tormented her with new sensation as it adored each smooth rib, the flat perfection of her stomach, her inner thighs. She felt her body imploding with pleasure that spread through her like a whirlpool, a firestorm, and her body moved against him, instinctively seeking more.

"My beautiful love. You make me forget everything but you. You'd make any man forget."

He smoothed his hand between her thighs, and she shattered at his touch. She could no longer remember anything but this sweeping fire, this tormenting need of him. She wanted him. She could no longer endure being separated from him, from his tenderness and his strength.

As though in echo of her thought she heard him whisper, "I want to love you, Gwenyth."

Wordlessly she lifted her arms to circle his neck and draw him down to her. Silently she offered all that she was to him and gloried in the weight of his body covering hers. Hard chest, tense thighs, and strong male passion—it was enough, it was everything. "Love me, Robert Gavin," she whispered.

As the words left her mouth she felt his body change. No longer was his tension one of controlled passion and desire. Instead, unbelievably, he loosened his arms about her and drew slightly away. "You are weary tonight," he told her. "There will be other nights for love."

There was tenderness in his voice and something else that she could not analyze. Even his voice had changed, she thought, and now along with the melting desire that had swept through her she felt a trace of fear. "What is it, Robert?" she whispered.

"What could it be?" he parried, but she knew him well enough to know that there was something evasive in that reply.

Her thoughts were interrupted by a sudden noise below. Someone was hammering on the doors of the great hall. As the thudding blows echoed through the sleeping house, a voice began to shout. "That's Dafyd making all that noise!" Robert exclaimed.

"My lord Glendower," Dafyd was bellowing, "my lord, wake up and arm yourself. That bastard Reese is coming here with his men!"

Chapter Eight

ROBERT'S VOICE WAS HARD WITH SURPRISE. "SO THE swine is actually coming here."

She felt cold as if a sudden gust of wind had filled the herb room. "Why would he come?"

"I don't know, but I swear that he'll not hurt you again." He had begun to pull on his clothing, dressing with swift, economic movements, and now he said, "Even in all this confusion it's not wise if we were both seen coming from the stillroom at this hour. Follow me after a few minutes." She nodded, and his face softened. "Don't worry, love. Whatever he's come for, Reese will find more than he's bargained for this time."

The chamber seemed empty when he left it. As she dressed and smoothed her thick hair into golden braids, she could hear the household responding to

Dafyd's shouts. Above Glendower's and Lady Margaret's voices, Ivor's rose. "That bastard tried to dishonor us once before," he was arguing as she hurried down the stairs to the great hall. "Let's put an end to him once and for all."

She hurried down the stairs and entered a scene of confusion. While servants ran about lighting lamps, the knights of the household raced in. Some of them had buckled swords over their nightclothes, others were struggling into their tunics as they ran. Outside, horns summoned men-at-arms to their posts.

Looking about the room she saw her family standing beside the raised dais surrounded by several of their knights. Dafyd was with them, and Robert, also, and as she made her way toward them, Glendower spoke over the tumult. "Even after what he did on the road from Rowyn, we must greet Reese peaceably until we learn his intent."

Dafyd growled that the intent of such a bastard could only be evil, and Ivor agreed. "Father, let me take a dozen men down the mountain, and I'll bring you his head."

Glendower shook his head. "The sentries signaled that there were only twenty men in Reese's train. He's not here to fight, Ivor."

Unhappily, Dafyd agreed. "That's true enough, but it could be a trick, my lord. He could be pretending to come in peace while the rest of his men hide near the Cliff of the Old Ones." Dafyd paused and added, "He'll be here by first dawn by my reckoning, and with your leave I'll have my men-at-arms waiting for him at the gates. They'll be armed, but I'll make sure they don't fight unless you personally give the order."

"Do it." Glendower turned to his knights. "Unfortunately, Reese is still a part of the alliance, so we must allow him into Eyri. But, gentlemen, we'll be prepared for trouble. Your wives and children must wait in a place of safety until we're sure why Reese is coming here. If he means treachery, we'll be ready for it."

There was a growl of approval, and then the noise intensified as knights shouted for their esquirers and their armor or hurried off to prepare their families for possible trouble. Gwenyth could hear one of the knights entreating his wife to get the children to safety, and his words chilled her. It didn't take second sight to know that if Reese managed to ruin the alliance, there would be no safety in all of Wales.

She felt an arm about her waist and Robert asked, "Where will the women and children go?"

"The warehouse. It's the strongest building in Eyri," she was beginning mechanically when Glendower spoke again.

"Once the women and children are safe, the men-at-arms are to guard the gate and the doorway of the great hall. My knights and my family will await Reese here."

Robert felt Gwenyth become tense beside him and he spoke without thought. "It would be folly for Lady Gwenyth to be here when Reese shows his face."

"Why folly?" Glendower frowned impatiently. "You speak too boldly, Robert."

Angrily, the minstrel faced the master of Eyri. "You did not see how she looked that night she escaped from him. Surely you would spare your daughter pain."

"Master Gavin, I must think of Wales." In spite of his quiet voice Glendower's eyes flashed dark fire, and for a moment his narrow, bearded face grew as hard as stone. "I can preserve the alliance only by strength, and hiding my family would show fear and weakness on my part. My wife and children must remain here in the hall."

About to argue further, Robert felt Gwenyth's hand on his arm. He looked down into green eyes that pleaded with him to be silent, and with an effort he held his peace. If he opposed Glendower and was sent from the hall, Gwenyth would truly be alone.

Glendower now turned to Gwenyth. "I need you to observe Reese as Merryn taught you to do. Watch his expressions, his reactions. I want to know whether he lies or not."

Robert remained silent as she bowed her agreement, but when Glendower had moved away to issue other commands, he protested. "At least take time to rest."

To his surprise she smiled a radiant smile that was like sunrise over the mountains. "It was not sleep that I craved but you," she told him.

Then she was gone, making her way through the throng to Lady Margaret's side. Her golden head was held high, her slender back straight. He followed her with his eyes until he felt a hand fall on his shoulder, and turning, he looked down into Dafyd's sympathetic eyes.

"I know, boyo," the grizzled captain rasped, "but she will always do her duty to the lord Glendower first. A good one, that. Now, come to the armory. In case that swine wants trouble, I think you'd want the pleasure of getting a slice of him."

"You're reading my mind." Grimly the men smiled at each other and left the great hall. As they did so, a horn blew some distance away and another answered. Not far off now, Robert thought. With care he chose a sword from the armory, balancing blade after blade until he found the one he wanted. Then, ignoring the steel helmets and the armor made for arms and throat, he took a round wooden shield covered with tough hide. The grizzled captain of the guard eyed him with approval. "You look less a minstrel than you do a Welsh soldier," he growled. "Now I must inspect my men. Come with me, if you like."

It was uncanny, Robert thought, how speedily the men of Eyri readied themselves for war. Not half an hour had passed, but now the motley crowd in the great hall had been transformed into a disciplined force. Knights with swords and shields stood inside the great hall together while selected guardsmen sturdily watched the doorway. Archers with their deadly Welsh bows were at their stations on the fortress walls, while grim-eyed spearmen also held themselves ready. Another contingent of soldiers had been deployed before the warehouse where the women and children had gathered.

Well pleased, Dafyd looked around him. "The knights will do their duty to our lord and his family, and if there's trouble the rest of us will send Reese and the buggers who follow him to hell."

As he spoke, a shout came from the gate. "They're coming around the bend now. Twenty of them, like the sentries said."

Robert saw that the first gray of dawn was easing the eastern darkness. Without waiting to see what Dafyd was going to do, he strode through the ranks of waiting knights and up to the open doors of the hall. Inside, bathed in the light of oil lamps, Glendower's family waited, and his eyes went swiftly to Gwenyth, who stood with her half brother and sister at the foot of the dais. She looked tense though determined, and he felt the familiar twist of admiration blended with a desire to protect.

As if she had heard his thought, her eyes met his. His entrance was so quiet that no one else remarked it, but Gwenyth's heart leaped at the sight of him. She read reassurance in his steady gray gaze, and she tried to smile at him, but the smile died when there was a knocking at the gate and the familiar, rough voice shouted, "I, Huw ap Reese of Castle Reese and my twenty men ask entry into Eyri."

She fought back a shiver as she heard Dafyd's formal challenge. "Come you in peace?"

"In peace," Reese answered, and the heavy wooden bridge creaked down, the gates opened. She held her breath as thudding hoofbeats crossed into the fortress and neared the great hall.

Gwenyth's half sister bent to whisper, "Don't worry, Gwenyth, he won't dare insult the family a second time." But she broke off as a burly figure marched into the hall with Dafyd behind him. Outside the door, ringed by Eyri men-at-arms, his twenty followers waited.

"I come in peace, Owen Glendower." He held wide his arms to show a rich brown tunic under a dark-red, fur-tipped mantle. "See, I bear no arms."

Silence greeted this announcement, and Robert tasted bile. His fingers itched to close around the thick neck and squeeze the life out of the man, and when he saw Reese smile at Gwenyth, he had to use all his control to remain where he was. Not yet, he told himself. Wait.

Glendower was asking sternly, "Why have you come, Huw ap Reese? To ask pardon for your actions toward my daughter?"

The castle lord's eyes narrowed for a moment before he shrugged. "Perhaps."

"Meaning exactly what?" Glendower demanded angrily. "In abducting Lady Gwenyth and shedding the blood of her escort, you committed a crime against my family and against the terms of the alliance." His voice rose to a sudden roar. "What have you to say?"

"Only that I have come in peace. I stand in your hall unarmed, and I crave the hospitality that is the sacred right of any stranger." Reese's voice dropped to a purr. "I intend to pay good gold to the families of the men who were regrettably slain in that, er, misunderstanding on the road from Rowyn. And my intent in coming is honorable."

"You dare talk of honor." Robert's voice was soft, but the menace in it made the sound carry throughout the hall. "Any man who acted as you did toward a helpless woman is not fit to live."

Eyes rolling, Huw ap Reese turned to glare at the new speaker. "Say that when I have a sword in my hand," he sneered.

"Gladly." The deep voice had dropped into a feral snarl. "I will meet you anywhere and prove your guilt on your filthy carcass."

Even Glendower seemed to hold his breath as Reese took a step toward his challenger. Then the burly man hesitated, stopped. With an effort he swung away from Robert and faced the dais again. "I'd not looked for insult in your hall, prince," he snarled.

"Speak your mind." It was obvious that Glendower himself was having difficulty controlling his emotions, and beside the dais young Ivor was practically grinding his teeth. "You have invoked the laws of hospitality, and I cannot deny you that much. We will listen to what you have to say—but say it quickly."

Watching Reese smile was like seeing a wolf bare its fangs. "I come to ask for Gwenyth's hand in marriage."

In the deathly silence that followed this, Gwenyth gave a choked cry. Robert's hand flew to his sword as Glendower raised an imperious hand. "The laws of hospitality are sacred, Master Gavin. No man may draw a weapon on an unarmed man in my hall." Then he added, "It were best you leave now, Reese. While you can."

Calmly the burly man stood his ground. "It's what I should have done from the first. I acknowledge that and I crave the girl's pardon. It was the enchantment of her beauty that made me act so foolishly. Anyone can see why Gwenyth would turn a man's head." As a rumble of anger filled the hall he spoke more quickly. "Remember that Castle Reese stands on the northwest coast. Who'd watch your back against the English if I didn't, Owen Glendower? I'm a better ally than an enemy."

As his voice died away, Gwenyth spoke for the first time. "No," she said clearly, "I will not. I cannot . . ."

Lady Margaret added, "No woman would marry a man who has abused her."

Ignoring her, the burly Reese spoke again. "To refuse me would be ill courtesy, Owen Glendower, and it would doom your Welsh alliance. Here and now I say that if you refuse me, I leave the alliance. There's several that would follow me."

Gwenyth saw her father hesitate, could almost read his thoughts. But even the fate of Wales itself could not make her do as Reese wanted. As Glendower turned to look at her, she shook her head frantically. No.

"Huw ap Reese!"

At Robert's shout all heads turned to face him. He had stepped farther into the hall, and the flickering light of the lamps danced shadow across his strong-boned face as he continued, "I am not the lord Glendower's knight, nor have I sworn fealty to him. No dishonor can come to him through me when I call you liar, bully, coward, and whoreson knave."

Each clear and distinct word echoed the length of the hall, and Gwenyth saw her unwelcome suitor turn almost purple with rage. She realized that she had clasped her hands so tightly that the nails dug into her flesh as Robert challenged, "Are you man enough to meet me sword to sword, or do you only attack women?"

With a bellow, Reese threw off his mantle. It pooled down onto the stone floor like blood. "Nameless cur, I'll have the flesh from your bones."

"Not nameless, sirrah. I'm called Robert Gavin, and I am a bard." The deep voice mocked. "Doesn't that please you? Fighting a minstrel is probably only a little less difficult than tormenting a maiden."

Almost foaming at the mouth, Huw ap Reese turned to the dais. "Give me my sword and I will fight this, this—"

"Aye, you'll fight me," Robert cut in. "But first you'll openly acknowledge that our quarrel is between you and me and has nothing to do with the Welsh alliance or the Glendower household."

"The blood I shed will have nothing to do with the alliance or Glendower. Master Minstrel, I'll hack you to bits."

114

Even through her daze of horror, Gwenyth realized that Robert had shifted the responsibility of this quarrel to his own shoulders. But he didn't know his adversary or the cunning and ferocity of the castle lord. He had no idea of the danger he ran. But before she could go to him, warn him, Glendower spoke sharply.

"Hold—enough. Robert Gavin, there is no need of this. The quarrel between my daughter and Reese has nothing to do with you."

Gray eyes glittered murder, but the deep voice was steady. "Your pardon, but it does. I was the one who found her crawling over the rocks to escape this swine. I swore then not to let him get his hands on her again, and I'm bound by that vow." He paused and then asked, "You honored me earlier by asking me to join your household, my lord. Will you honor me more by allowing me to champion your daughter's cause against this villain?"

He spoke to Glendower, but his eyes went to Gwenyth. She was paper pale and her eyes were enormous, and as their glances locked, he saw her take a swaying step forward as if to come to him. "No," she was crying. "You don't know him . . ."

"Ah, but I do. Reese the coward, Reese the swine." Deliberately goading his enemy, Robert almost sang the words. "Come, my lord of the northwestern coast, have you found a sword yet?"

As if by single accord, Glendower's men moved to clear a space in the center of the hall. Dafyd stepped forward and looked questioningly at his lord, who

115

nodded. "Here's a sword and shield, Reese," he snapped, adding in a quick aside to Robert, "Be careful, boyo. He'll fight dirty if he can."

Robert smiled. "Come, sir. The gate of hell is open, and the devil doesn't like to be kept waiting."

Seizing the sword from Dafyd, Huw ap Reese began to circle the cleared space in the hall. His eyes were narrowed to slits of cunning, and the powerful muscles of his arms and back bunched under his fine doublet as he moved. "You're making a mistake, minstrel," he crooned. "A very big mistake. I'll cut off your hands so you can't play a harp again—or please a woman."

Suddenly he lunged forward, and Gwenyth screamed. But the deadly sword thrust cleaved down on air. Next instant Robert's sword had slashed down only to glance off Reese's shield. Another sword thrust, another, and then both men broke loose to take each other's measure.

"Is that the best you can do?" Robert spoke tauntingly, but he did not underestimate his enemy. Reese was strong and surprisingly swift. Balancing himself on the balls of his feet, Robert sprang forward, and this time blood spurted from Reese's arm. Then he closed for the attack.

Gwenyth heard the grunt of effort as the two powerful fighters met, sword to sword. A prayer had formed within her, inarticulate and almost unconscious. Please, God, let Robert live, please. Over and over she repeated the litany. Then she cried out, agonized, as she watched the castle lord swing his heavy sword with such deadly accuracy that it slid off

Robert's shield and glanced off his shoulder. A sigh went up in the hall as they saw blood drawn again.

"No-o!" Her wail was full of pain as if she herself had been wounded, and Robert heard it as he parried Reese's murderous thrusts. He knew that he wasn't fighting only for his life but for hers as well. If he failed her, Reese might prevail on Glendower to let him marry her. Only the man's death would make her safe.

There was a gasp in the hall as Robert Gavin's sword beat like rain against Reese's shield. Back went the burly castle lord. A lightning-quick blow, another—and Reese's sword was knocked from his hand. Next moment Robert had his foot on the blade.

No one was prepared for what happened next. Huw ap Reese dropped his shield and extended his arms. "You've bested me," he said. He was smiling, but Robert noted the cunning in the broad face as Reese continued, "Well, supposing we end this?"

"Look to yourself, the bastard has a dagger!" Dafyd's bellow cut into the silence. It seemed impossible for anyone to move so fast, but as Reese's hand went back, Robert leaped for his throat. Next moment the dagger fell to the floor, and Reese went down also. Robert raised his sword for the death-blow.

"Hold, minstrel, I yield." Reese's voice was choked but clear and it shivered through the muttering hall. "You cannot kill a man who yields."

Robert hesitated and Dafyd said sternly, "You are forsworn. You entered the hall with a concealed weapon, and that cancels all laws of hospitality and combat." To Robert he snapped, "Kill him."

Reese screamed from the floor, "No, wait! If you do, my men will fight, and many lives will be lost. Better to listen to me, Owen Glendower. You have an enemy within your walls, but it's not I." The man's voice was frantic.

"Hold your hand, Master Gavin," Glendower decided. "Let him talk." He rose from his dais and strode down the hall until he loomed over the still-prostrate Reese. "What do you mean, there is an enemy within my walls?"

"What I say." The crafty light in the russet eyes blazed into triumph. He threw out an arm pointing at Robert. "But your so-called minstrel can tell you more than I."

Almost stumbling with hurry, Gwenyth ran from her place near the dais toward Robert. Impelled by a fear she couldn't understand, she reached him, felt his bracing arm support her. "He lies, he has always lied. Why should we listen to him now?"

"Ask your champion if I lie," Reese retorted. "Ask him if he isn't an English knight and a spy for the English king!"

Chapter Nine

"WHAT!" DAFYD ROARED. WITH HIS UNWOUNDED hand he seized Reese by the throat. "I'd like to tear out your lying tongue. This man saved my life."

"And the life of my son." Glendower's voice was cold. "You had better explain—and quickly."

Other voices rose in angry protest, but Gwenyth heard none of them. Her eyes were riveted on Robert Gavin's face. Why wasn't he denying this ridiculous charge?

Reese was shouting, "He's an Englishman, I tell you! He's a knight in King Henry's pay sent to infiltrate Eyri by any means he could. I have proof—unless you're afraid to hear it."

"What kind of 'proof' could you have, you forsworn cur? Take your lie to hell."

Robert raised his sword, but before it could arc down, Glendower caught his arm. "Wait, Robert. If Reese is lying, you can kill him. But these are grave charges against you, and they are best refuted beyond doubt. Let him get up. We'll hear his so-called proof."

Again Gwenyth felt sickened at the cruel gloating in the castle lord's smile. "You know that my men and I ride often to ravage the lands of great English border lords for booty. Often there are prisoners I hold for ransom. Those who can't pay, I kill."

Disgust flickered in Glendower's eyes. "Get to the point," he snapped.

"I brought one of those English prisoners with me. My men will bring him here into the hall now, and he'll tell you more about your precious Master Gavin."

Gwenyth darted a look at Robert. She could read the telltale signs of tension in the line of his jaw and an unnamed fear filled her. Almost frantically she turned to her father and cried, "That's all he has—the word of a captive Englishman who's been tortured into obedience! Surely you can see that this is revenge. He cannot best Robert Gavin with his sword, and so he resorts to lies."

Golden head held high, her lip curled in scorn, she was magnificent, a fighting Welsh princess, and her championship gladdened Robert. His voice rang with authority when he said, "The lady speaks truth. How could the testimony of some dog of an Englishman affect me?"

Gravely the master of Eyri considered this and

then made his decision. "You may bring in your prisoner, but I warn you, Reese. If you're lying, I'll let Robert Gavin cut you to pieces."

As he spoke, two of the castle lord's followers came into the hall dragging a third man along by a rope around the neck. He was a small fellow, obviously terrified, and through the rents in his ragged tunic, angry whip marks were clearly visible. When one of his captors tugged at the rope, he cried out in pain and fell forward on his knees.

The others looked on unmoved, but English though this man was, Gwenyth could not help feeling pity. "What are you called?" Glendower was asking in English. "Whom do you serve?"

"Thomas Carpenter," the little man quavered, "and, if it please Your Lordship, until I was made prisoner, I was a man-at-arms at Stoake Castle."

"He follows the cruel earl of Stoake." Dafyd almost spat the words, and Gwenyth saw murder glint in his eyes. "The whoreson Englishman who bribes Welsh brigands to war on their own people. We've all lost loved ones to this bastard's master."

Reese now spoke. "I've raided Stoake Castle many a time and been rewarded with the English milord's goods and livestock." He reached out, seizing the rope around Thomas Carpenter's neck, and yanked. "Fellow, look around you and see if there are any other Englishmen here."

The small man peered around the room. Then his eyes bulged. "By the rood, Sir Robert!" he exclaimed. "Then you, too, were taken prisoner."

There was a deathly silence into which Reese

spoke. "Point this Sir Robert out." The man hesitated. "Obey me, or die here and now."

Slowly the prisoner raised a shaking pointed hand. There was a ringing in Gwenyth's ears. Sweet Lord, it couldn't be true. She heard her voice speaking as if from far off. "He's been bribed by Reese. He's been terrified into lying."

"He's certainly been well beaten. It's like you, Reese, to torment a helpless man." The contempt in Robert Gavin's voice was replaced by savage anger as he added, "I don't know this poor bastard, but English or not, I'd not treat the sorriest dog as you've treated him."

Sternly Glendower interposed. "Your so-called proof does not convince me. A man with a rope around his neck will swear to anything just to save his life."

"Then he's no use to me any longer." Reese turned to his men. "Take him outside and kill him."

The prisoner let out a wail of horror. As he was being dragged out, Robert stepped between Reese's men and the door, barring their way. "My lord Glendower, this is murder," he protested.

Glendower's eyes narrowed. "Why are you so concerned? The man is Reese's prisoner. These are times of war, Master Gavin, and bad times make hard laws." He gestured. "Step aside."

As Robert hesitated the prisoner wailed, "Sir Robert, Sir Robert Marne, help me. In the name of God, don't let them kill me." He twisted around, clutching the rope around his neck and babbling, "I swear I speak the truth—he's English, like me, and

Prince Hal's great friend. Don't let them kill me, Sir Robert, I beg of you . . ."

As the man's words died away into incoherent sobs, Gwenyth saw Robert lower his sword. For a moment she thought he was going to allow Reese's men to take the Englishman out. Instead, he spoke quietly.

"No need to kill the man for telling the truth. I am Robert Marne."

Utter and complete silence swept the hall. Into it Dafyd swore. "Sweet blood of Christ," he whispered. "Then it's true. You're an Englishman. . . ."

The damning word spiraled away into deathly stillness. Robert felt as if an iron band had been clamped across his chest as he looked across the hall at Gwenyth's pale face. Her eyes were enormous with horror and betrayal. He took a step toward her, but before he could take another, Dafyd had barred his way. The elderly soldier's face was twisted into a grimace of anger and outrage and misery.

"I knew I should never have brought you to Eyri. I suspected you from the start—Englishman." He spat the word out, then added, "Your sword."

Silently he handed over the blade. "So all this time we harbored a spy in Eyri," Glendower was saying. "God above, the sight of you sickens me."

Gwenyth heard the rage in her father's voice. She knew she should be furious herself, but she felt nothing. It was as if she had gone numb, as if her blood had turned to ice. From far away she heard Robert say, "Will you at least listen to my reason for being here?"

"What other reason could an English dog have for coming here?" Glendower's voice was icy. "Take him away and throw him in the prison pit below the armory. Guard him well. He'll tell us many English secrets before we're done with him." With an effort he calmed himself and turned to Reese. "One thing I do not understand. How did you know that the English spy was here?"

"A lucky guess." The burly man's voice was smug. "News travels, and I heard about a minstrel who had brought Lady Gwenyth back to Eyri. Then from my prisoners I learned of an English knight who could sing like an angel and fight like the devil himself. I put two and two together. What better way for a spy to breach Eyri's security than to become the champion of Glendower's own daughter?"

Listening to the damning words, Robert searched Gwenyth's face. He could not bear the devastation there. She looked bruised, and her eyes were full of numb horror. Strange, he mused, that with his life hanging by a thread he could only think of her. He tried to tell himself that she would survive as she had survived everything else, that now he was named an enemy, she would cut him out of her heart and forget what had passed between them, but he knew he lied. He only faced torture and death, but she would live each day with the memory of what she thought was his betrayal of her love. Somehow he must find a way to tell her that his love for her had not been a lie.

She raised a shaking hand to brush back her hair,

and that small gesture brought back painful memory of the day they had spent by the enchanted lake. Memory—and something else. There was a way!

Addressing Thomas Carpenter, he spoke clearly, almost cheerfully. "Don't grieve, man. We're soldiers, and we took our chances. Fortune is fickle— '*Slaisan verta nei,*' as the ancients say."

He heard Gwenyth's gasp and saw her start and turn to look directly at him. He met her glance without flinching, willing her to understand what he'd said in the secret language she'd taught him by the lake. He had only a moment and then Dafyd signaled his men-at-arms to take the two Englishmen away, and as he walked the length of the suddenly hostile hall, he heard young Ivor say in a subdued voice, "What will you do with him, father?"

Glendower's reply was grim. "What the earl of Stoake would do to any Welsh spy. First he'll talk and then he'll die."

"But he did save my life—and Dafyd's. And no matter if he used Gwenyth to get to Eyri, he helped her as well." Ivor sounded troubled.

"Aye, and we'll pay our debts. When he has told us all he knows, he'll die quickly. It's more than he deserves."

They were going to kill Robert Gavin—no, not Robert Gavin, Sir Robert Marne. Into Gwenyth's confused mind came that one coherent thought, and on its heels came another: Before he was led away he had asked in her mother's secret language to see her. All reason forbade her honoring such a request. He was an Englishman, a spy, and he had used her cruelly to further his ends.

I will not go, she told herself bitterly. I hate him, this Englishman. Let him die as he deserves.

The prison was dark. Outside it might be day or night—Robert had no way of knowing. Here in this earthen cell there was no trace of light and the mud walls and floors held a sour, bone-chilling damp. There were several such prison rooms. He had seen this when men-at-arms had marched him and Thomas Carpenter down the stone steps that led from the armory and rudely shoved the Englishmen into separate cells. There was no way out except for the solid wooden door, no possibility of escape. The earthen walls were thick and ended in the stone floor of the armory above—he had seen this also. So had the guards who brought him there. "Make your peace with God," they jeered. "You'll never see England or King Henry again."

Strangely that did not worry him. There were things he regretted, of course, and they came to him as he waited in the dark: misty mornings over an English countryside and the feel of a good horse under him as he rode across broad green fields. And he would miss laughter and song and good companionship, and the heady adventure of risking capture in the service of his prince. But these faded like mist before the thought of Gwenyth's frozen horror.

He knew what she thought. To her he was an enemy, a traitor who had come to Eyri to destroy her father and her country. Worse, she must think that he had kissed her with a sneer in his heart. The thought of dying without making her understand was unendurable.

There was the sound of a door opening upstairs, and he went swiftly to the door, listening to footsteps on the stairs. They were coming for him, either to question him or to kill him. Well, he had known the risks before consenting to play Prince Hal's game. He listened to the steps drawing nearer until they stopped at the door, but there was no sound of a key rasping in the lock. Instead, a doubtful male voice spoke. "My lady, are you sure that this is wise?"

My lady . . . his heart leaped as a low, sweet voice made reply. "Don't worry, Clydach, I know what I'm doing."

"But to be alone with that dog of an Englishman may not be safe," the guard persisted.

"My lord father sent me. Clydach, it's important that the man talks—important for Wales." Her voice was earnest. "The man has knowledge we need."

"Yes, but—"

"You know I have ways to make men talk," Gwenyth interrupted. "Do you think that this English dog could lay a hand on me? I'd blast him into pieces with my magic." Her voice became stern. "Obey me, Clydach, and open that door."

"Aye, my lady." There was superstitious fear in the man's voice, and metal squeaked against metal. Then ruddy light from an oil lamp flooded the cell. "If you need anything, you need only call."

Murmuring her thanks she stood for a moment silhouetted in the doorway, and then holding the lamp high, she stepped inside. "Be careful not to hurt yourself, the ceiling's low." She heard his deep voice first, and then saw him coming out of the darkness toward her. "Thank you for coming," he was saying. "I didn't know if the words were right—"

"Stop there—don't come closer." He stopped, and she drew a bracing breath that smelled not of damp earth but of the clean, vital scent that she remembered. With effort she asked, "You wanted to see me. What do you want?"

She looked so pale that she seemed to be made of ice. Her eyes were emerald hard, her lovely mouth was stern. Every line of her rigid body spoke of hatred for an enemy, and the sight was chilling. Abruptly he asked, "First tell me why you came."

Her answer was so prompt it sounded rehearsed. "You saved my life and honor. I owe you this."

"You owe me nothing." Her faint scent was of roses and sunlight, and he was tormented with the memory of the mountain and the enchanted lake. Regret twisted knifelike in his heart, and he fought an urge to gather her into his arms and kiss the frozen look from her eyes. He turned half away from her so that he could collect his thoughts and remind himself why he'd asked her to come. "I need to explain something to you," he told her. "I must tell you the reasons why I am here."

Her reply was swift. "I know why. You're a spy for Henry of England."

"I'm not here at Henry's bidding. Prince Hal sent me here—he that is Prince of Wales."

Eyes narrowed, she snapped, "My father is the Prince of the Welsh—Englishman! And in spite of you and those like you, he will throw off the English yoke." She began to turn toward the door, but he caught her by the wrist, restraining her. She glared at him, trying to fling off his hand, but his clasp was too strong. "Let go of me!" she cried.

Steadily he said, "Prince Hal and I met in Oxford years ago. He was the friend with whom I shivered at Queen's College. We became close friends." His deep voice grew warm with conviction. "Gwenyth, he wants only justice for Wales."

"I refuse to listen to you," she snapped, but the hand on her wrist held her fast, and the warm press of his fingers brought shameful memory. "You used me to get into Eyri. To spy—"

"Sweet Christ, girl, it's not to spy that I came." In the dim light of the cell her eyes were almost black, the pupils enormous with emotion. "Prince Hal sent me here to learn more about Owen Glendower—"

"About Eyri, you mean! About the secret way to get here and the sentries and the fortifications and the names of the lords in the alliance—"

"No." Even now the sound of his voice caught at her heart, weakened the anger with which she had armed herself against him. "Henry of England might want such information, but not my prince. He wanted to learn about Owen Glendower as a man, about his life, his way of thinking. He respects your father. He hoped that by learning all he could about him, he could find a way to forge peace with him."

"I don't believe you." Her voice was low, riding on unshed tears. "You lied to all of us—to me."

"Gwenyth, I didn't lie to you." She threw up her head to defy this and looked into his eyes. Smoke-gray, intense, they held hers when she would have looked away. "God knows that I did not hold you in my arms because you were Glendower's daughter. This I swear. Nor would I have let any harm come to you or yours."

If she listened to him any longer, she would begin to believe him. She was wavering already as his nearness and his voice worked their subtle magic. She had come here not to hear his excuses but to tell him of her hate and her contempt. She had come resolved to exorcise his memory from her mind and heart before his just execution. And yet now, look-ing at him, she pictured that death.

The guards would come to the prison cell and take him out and march him outside the fortress. There they would throw a hemp rope over the nearest tree. She closed her eyes but the merciless image per-sisted. She could see the lean, powerful body she had caressed and kissed struggle in its death throes and grow still. The thought brought such pain that she was dizzy from it.

He saw her sway and moved swiftly to catch her in his arms. She lay still against him, and the walls of the cell seemed to disappear along with any reality except that of the fragrant slenderness that he held in his arms. He could feel her heart beating wildly against him, and a surge of passionate tenderness wiped away all thought of wisdom as he buried his lips in the gold of her hair. "Do you believe me?" he asked her. "That is all I want or ask, that you believe me."

The arms around her were strong and sure. In spite of herself, in spite of everything she knew, she could not stop from clinging one more minute to the warmth and strength she had never thought to know again. For that instant she registered all that she had remembered and would always remember—strong arms, unyielding wall of chest, lean male belly, and muscle-taut thighs. But even in that moment she knew that she could no longer believe him or anything he said.

"Let me go." As he heard her low voice, he knew with despair that he had lost and that she did not believe him. His arms loosened around her and he watched as she pulled clear of him and got to her feet. Then she said, "I don't believe you, Robert Marne. But neither can I bear to see you killed. I once told you that Merryn taught me that all life is sacred—" She broke off to add, "I'll help you get away."

"How?"

The eager light that filled his eyes made her realize what she should have guessed, that his protestation of love was just another ruse. He was playing for his life, and he'd known she could not resist his sweet words. Dishonor and shame filled her, but greater than both was the knowledge that she could not bear to see him die.

Her voice was wooden when she said, "I am going to tell the guard that I have made you confess and that I am taking you to my father. You must pretend that my magic has taken away your wits. Once outside, we will walk toward the house, but you must stumble along in such a way that you veer toward the stables."

But he was shaking his head. "You will be blamed for letting me escape, Gwenyth."

"No harm will come to me. I'll tell my father that you tricked me and swore to answer all his questions. I'll say that you overpowered me and ran."

His eyes narrowed, and she knew he was going over each phase of the escape in his mind. "What time of day is it?" he demanded. "Near to sunset—then the gates of Eyri still will be open, and the stableboys will be rubbing down the horses and feeding them for the night. It could be done if I reach the woods near the lake before the gate guards shoot me down."

Listening to him, her heart nearly failed her. He knew so much about the habits of Eyri—he knew the mountains, too. And yet, she was going to help free this enemy of her people. Then he added, "One thing more—I must take Thomas Carpenter with me."

He meant the English soldier. Surely he knew that taking the frightened little man with him would imperil any slight chance he had? He seemed to read her mind, for his firm mouth relaxed into a smile. "Would you leave a Welshman in English hands? No, not if it meant your own death."

Mad—insane—and she was mad, too, or bewitched, to do as he asked. "You must say that you're both ready to confess," she told him. "I'll call the guard now."

Turning from him she called for the guard and instructed him to get the other English prisoner. "This one's agreed to confess, and I want the other to verify what he says before my lord father. You're to escort us to the great hall, now, Clydach."

The guard stared hard at Robert, who stood with bowed head and loose-hanging shoulders, and then with awe at Gwenyth. Hurriedly he loosed Thomas Carpenter from his cell and prodded both men before him as they climbed up into the armory and then proceeded outside.

Shambling along in a half-witted way, Robert looked quickly about him. As Gwenyth had said, the sun was about to set, and thick, ruddy gold bars of sunlight lay across Glendower's mountain home. For all that men-at-arms walked patrol on the great wooden walls, the place was peaceful. He could see several horses being rubbed down before the stables near the gate, while a few others were still saddled and waiting their turn. If they could manage to get close enough . . .

"English dog, get back into line," the guard snapped. Robert pretended that he did not hear but lurched closer toward the horses. As he did so he spoke in a low voice to the bewildered English soldier beside him.

"When I say ride, get atop a horse and follow me. Ride as if the devil himself were after you. There won't be a second chance."

Thomas Carpenter merely gaped at him. Robert wasn't sure that the little man understood him, but he couldn't chance another whisper. As he lurched toward the stables again, Gwenyth gave a mocking laugh. "My faith, but I have put too strong a spell on him. No harm. In a few moments he'll stand before my lord Glendower and tell all he knows."

As she spoke, Robert lunged. His powerful back-handed blow caught the guard on the side of the head and the man went sprawling. Next moment he was running toward one of the saddled horses and vaulting into the saddle.

Out of the corner of his eye he saw the little Englishman following him, and then he was bent low over the back of his mount and making for the gates. Behind him a startled babble rose and Gwenyth's despairing cry. "The prisoners are escaping. Stop them—shut the gates!"

The gateman leaped to do her bidding, but it was too late. She saw Robert and Thomas Carpenter spur their horses over the wooden bridge and toward the trees near the lake. Arrows and a hail of spears flew after them, but before any could do them harm they had disappeared into the woods. She closed her eyes and let pure relief flood her.

"Gwenyth."

Relief died as she saw Glendower standing only a few steps behind her. His face was rigid with anger and betrayal. She began to give her prepared excuse, but he cut her short. "You helped the English spy escape," he told her bleakly, and in his black eyes she read understanding—and damnation.

Chapter Ten

"YOU ARE SUMMONED BY YOUR LORD FATHER." GWEN-
yth flinched at the hostility in the guardsman's voice.
"You're to hurry, too. Those are my lord's orders."

In this man's eyes, in the eyes of everyone in Eyri,
she was a traitress in league with the enemy. Glendower had confined her to her herb room immediately following Robert's escape, but before the
guards had marched her away she'd had a glimpse of
Margaret Glendower's face. There had been hatred
there.

"Am I to be taken to the great hall?" she asked.

"You'll see when we get there, and keep well
ahead of me. None of your witch's tricks," the man
snarled.

When she got to her feet, she felt cramped and
weak. Though her father had sent her food and

wine, she had touched nothing. Instead she had sat immobile on the narrow bed, listening for sounds that would tell her of Robert's capture. When none came and the unsuccessful searchers returned in the dawn, she hadn't been able to check shameful relief.

"Our lord will know what to do with you." The venom in the guard's voice prodded her through the stillroom door and down the stairs to the solar and Glendower's study. Her heart lifted slightly. Instead of sitting in judgment of her in the great hall, her father was at least seeing her privately.

But her first sight of him was disheartening. She had never before seen her father's eyes so stern or so unforgiving. He was seated by the window, and the noon sun shone down on his stern face without in any way lessening its severity. He was dressed in a stark black cotehardie over black hose, and there was no color in his pale face, either. He watched her without speaking as she crossed the threshold into the room, and made no motion to stop her as she sank down onto her knees. "My lord father," she began.

He cut her short. "Don't ask for pardon, Gwenyth. Your actions yesterday were basest treason. Didn't you stop to think that Robert Marne knows many of Eyri's secrets? That you were setting free a dangerous enemy?"

"Father, he swore—"

Bitterest contempt filled his words. "You listened to the promises of a spy? Or perhaps he paid you well to listen."

Her head went up and her eyes widened. "You cannot believe that!" she cried indignantly.

Their glances locked and then Glendower sighed. Defiance crumbled inside her at the sadness in his voice as he said, "I know you were deceived. Robert Gavin was a handsome man and he was charming—by St. Cynog, didn't he charm all of us? Besides, you were lonely. I know well what loneliness is, my daughter."

Instinctively she knew that he was thinking of her mother, and when she raised her head to look at him she saw him staring away from her and looking back into the past. The remembering look took her back into her own memories. In spite of all he had said last night, honesty compelled her to admit that Robert had probably never loved her. She had been lonely, and because of this she had compromised her country's safety and her father's precious alliance.

A knot formed in her throat, making it hard for her to speak. "Father, I'm so sorry. If I could undo what I did by dying, you could kill me now. Whatever you say, I will do it."

He got to his feet and walked to a large table in the center of the room. "Come here," he ordered. Surprised, she followed him to the table where a map of the British Isles had been spread. "Marne knows the names of my allies, and he's privy to many of my plans. King Henry will attack soon—no doubt of it. I need you to help me strengthen my position again."

"I'll do anything," she promised.

He tapped a northwest corner of Wales. "Here is

where I'm weakest, and Robert Marne knows this. I'm sure that Henry will launch a sea invasion of the northwest coast, so it must be fortified at all costs. Gwenyth, you must marry Reese."

"No!"

He spoke as though he hadn't heard her involuntary cry of dismay. "Reese was right when he said he'd be a better ally than an enemy. I know what you are going to say. He's a cruel man. He's also tricky and in any other matter I wouldn't trust him. But he loves wealth—and he hates the English. They fear him with reason, for no man has made so many raids on border castles and taken as many English prisoners. Once married to you and given a high position in the alliance, he'll be invaluable."

"You can only blame yourself," a new voice said, and Gwenyth realized that Margaret Glendower was standing near the door of the study. Her fine features were twisted with anger as she went on, "You'll do as your father tells you."

"Please, my lady, you know what he's like—" Desperately she ran to her father's wife and caught her sleeve in pleading hands. "He doesn't want me. He wants my so-called magic. When he learns I don't know any spells or sorcery—"

A stinging slap cut short her words, and Margaret Glendower snatched her sleeve away. "If I had my way, I'd have you beaten to an inch of your life. Hillwoman's brat! We took you in and treated you well, and in return you betrayed us and your country." Her eyes were stony cold. "You aren't fit to live."

"Margaret—enough." Glendower's voice was angry, but Gwenyth knew that his mind, too, was made up. He said, "Prepare yourself, Gwenyth. You will marry Reese and return with him to his castle within the week."

Later, Gwenyth would think back and wonder how time could pass so quickly and yet be so leaden with hopelessness. As Glendower's subdued household prepared for her marriage, she felt as though she were strangling in silence. No one spoke to her. Glendower had ordered that she be kept to the herb room under constant guard, and both the tight-lipped Lady Margaret and her half brother and sister avoided her. Dafyd and his family kept away, and even the servants who brought her meals and saw to her needs tried to avoid speaking to her.

Her one consolation was that Reese also kept his distance. Mostly this was because he and Glendower spent many hours discussing mutual defense, but his avoidance had also something gloating and cruel in it. It was as if he knew how his bride-to-be felt about the coming marriage and was playing with her as a cat toys with a doomed mouse.

Even knowing this, it was a relief not to see him or be near him. She tried not to think of him at all and instead busied herself with packing the herbs she would take with her to her new life. Sometimes as she worked, she thought of her mother and the happy days spent in the hills near Cader Idris, but there her memories ended. She would not—did not dare—think of Robert.

Her wedding day dawned gray at the end of the week, and silent women of the household helped her dress in her wedding clothes. The open-necked, tight-sleeved gown of blue frieze was a handsome garment, but she knew that she had been given this fine raiment only because Glendower did not want to appear discourteous toward his new son-in-law. When the women led her toward Eyri's small church and she saw her bridegroom waiting for her, she had to fight an impulse to turn and run.

Reese was in high good humor, his beefy frame resplendent in a crimson cotehardie and parti-color hose. He took her hand in his hot one, and russet eyes burned triumphant as he leaned closer. "I vow you look as eager as I am, sweetheart. It's a pity I have to wait to bed you until we reach my castle."

Fighting an urge to scream, she walked with him into the church and stood erect beside him and spoke her vows. But when he kissed her, his mouth deliberate and insulting, she could not bear it. "Now you are mine," he told her softly. "Mine to command."

She pulled back from him there at the altar. "I'll never be yours," she spat.

His face darkened with anger, but he let her go. It was a small victory, and she knew that she would pay dearly for her defiance. All through the wedding feast that followed, his russet eyes followed her, and though he and his men drank heavily of the heavy, spiced red wine that was served with the roasted rabbits and lamb, stuffed capons, and elaborate pork pies, she herself couldn't touch a morsel. Neither did the people of Eyri seem to have much appetite. In sharp contrast to Reese's followers, the knights and ladies of Glendower's household sat in dispirited silence. No one here was celebrating this marriage.

At last Reese got to his feet and thanked his host, adding, "Say your farewells, wife. It will be some time before you come to Eyri again."

A long time, and perhaps never—though she had no second sight, some inner voice told her that this was the last time she would set eyes on this mountain refuge. She forced back tears as she knelt to kiss Margaret's cold hand and then her father's. He gripped her hand for a moment. "Remember that we are nothing, Wales is everything," he whispered. "Forgive me, daughter."

"Gwenyth!"

The sudden cry surprised them all, and still kneeling before her father, she turned to see Bronwen running across the hall to her. Eluding those that tried to stop her, the little girl flung herself into Gwenyth's arms. "They wouldn't let me come to see you before," she sobbed. "I don't want you to go. Please don't go."

Her heart felt as if it would break as she held Bronwen tightly to her, and the same eerie sense of foreboding whispered that she would never see the child again, or Dafyd—she glanced at the old warrior standing at attention with his men, and saw that tears were streaming down his face. Tam and his mother Ethelwyn were weeping, and Olwen had covered her face with her hands. Their sorrow filled her with renewed resolve. If marrying Reese could ensure Eyri's safety, she'd gladly pay the price.

They left at once, with Reese and his new bride riding ahead of the men and the packhorses that would carry her few belongings down the mountain. Riding through most of the day, they passed through the cave in the Cliff of the Old Ones and reached the valley beyond by sunset. Gwenyth had thought that they would make camp here, but Reese had other plans and they continued to ride through the night. He did not inquire once as to her welfare, so Gwenyth gritted her teeth and kept up with the men.

Hard and skilled riders they were—she had to grant them that—but though they obeyed their officers without question, there was none of the kindness or camaraderie that Dafyd had instilled in his men. Nor was there any kindness in Reese. When he halted his followers to water the horses, he did not even offer to help his new wife dismount. Instead, he jeered, "A pity there's no place here to camp. Are you eager to see what a proper man can do?"

"You sicken me," she told him coldly.

"I like your spirit," he said, and she could hear him laughing softly in the dark. "I'll enjoy taming you."

In spite of her resolution, thoughts of escape filled her mind, but there was no such possibility. Not only did Reese's men keep her under close watch, but she also knew she could not break faith with Glendower. "We are nothing, Wales is everything," he had said, and through the long, weary night the words became a litany. They were still turning wearily in her mind when dawn came and showed her that they had reached the coastal road.

This was not a part of the coast she had seen before. Here narrow beaches marked with rippling tide flats were interspersed with juts of limestone that pushed out to sea. Here the dawn wind flattened rough gorse and sea grass that fringed the beaches and surrounded her with the rank, damp smell of brine, while below, in the gray water, rubbery brown seaweed floated like the hair of the dead.

Reese's voice spoke beside her. "We still have half a day's ride to Castle Reese, but you'll soon see it, sweet wife. You're not inclined to forget your first glimpse of your new home."

She knew he was right when the castle hove into sight some hours later. So weary was she by now that at first she saw that it was part of the Lleyn Peninsula that protruded far into the water, but soon she could make out the building. From this distance she could see little beyond the limestone bulwark and the barbicans above the gates, but even so, it filled her with a sense of despair.

"The castle was built in 1290 by my great-grandfather, and it has withstood Atlantic storms and invasion. It's wild country, this. I've heard tell that the traitor Vortigern fled here after betraying his country to the Saxons, and lived near Hell's Mouth at the tip of the peninsula." Pride of possession filled Reese's rasping voice as he added, "Now, with Welsh magic to aid it, Castle Reese will be stronger still, and richer than any other in Wales."

She did not answer him, but her heart sank as the sea road broadened into a narrow strip of tilled land. This land was planted with wheat and oats, but Gwenyth saw that the crops were sparse and poor in quality and wondered how such a meager harvest could feed a castle full of people.

Her question was answered as they rode through the open gates and past semicircular barbicans thick with archers. A great, square building of stone stood in the center of the castle yard, and near it a storehouse was filled to bursting with armor, weapons, cattle hides, and sacks of grain. Some distance away a wooden pen held fat cattle and sheep, horses, goats. The noise and the stench were incredible on this hot June afternoon, and Gwenyth felt her empty stomach churn.

"Loot, my dear." Reese had ridden close to her again and was looking about him with satisfaction. "You can see that my raids over the border are worth the while."

As he spoke, there was the sound of voices some distance from them, and the door of another stone house opened to show a dozen or more men. They were dressed differently from Reese's men, but this was not what made her stare. Her tired ears had caught a foreign language that made her start. "They're Englishmen!" she exclaimed.

He grinned. "Not all my prisoners are treated like that miserable Thomas Carpenter. Many of these milords have relatives who'll pay sacks of gold for their return. If not, they provide sport for my men before their throats are slit."

"You're despicable!" she cried.

His smile faded, and rust-colored eyes narrowed. "You're overfond of Englishmen, I think." He reached across his saddle and gripped her arm, and as she cried out at the fierce pressure, he snarled, "Robert Marne was eager to defend what he called your 'honor.' Was he your lover? What did you give him, eh?"

She had given him her trust, her love—a love that had made her betray the faith of her family. "I gave him nothing!" she cried.

"That's easily discovered. If he's taken your maidenhead, I'll make you the sorriest woman in Wales."

Before he could say more, a new voice spoke nearby, and Gwenyth saw an elderly, sour-faced woman who stood on the step of the great house. Her eyes were cold as she looked Gwenyth over. "So you're home, master," she said ingratiatingly. "And this is your bride, yes?"

Grunting assent, Reese dismounted and tossed his reins to a groom before coming to help Gwenyth. Much as she loathed his touch, today she could not move from her saddle without his aid. Her muscles had cramped to the point of screaming pain, and each separate joint and bone seemed to be on fire. She swayed on her feet and he put an arm about her shoulders to support her. "This is Tegwen Williams, my chatelaine. She'll help you to the solar." Turning to the woman, he ordered, "Get her what she needs. And make sure there's food for the rest of us in the hall."

Smiling ingratiatingly, the woman curtsied low. "There's food, master, and wine as well. It'll be brought to the main hall at once." Then her smile died away and she said to Gwenyth, "I'll help you to the solar, now."

Tegwen was none too clean, and the expression in her eyes was cold. Gwenyth forced herself to walk unaided and painfully climbed the steps into Reese's great hall. Unlike the clean, well-lit hall in Eyri, this massive stone room was filthy with neglect. New rushes had recently been strewn on the floor, but the stench of rotting food, stale wine, and vomit was overpowering. An army of servants who hurried about appeared terrified but incompetent.

Perhaps it was better upstairs—but Gwenyth soon found it was not. The solar had been a fine room once, but now it was unkempt and almost empty except for a large wooden chest and a massive bed. The room's one window was shut, and the room held a musty, mildewed smell. She glanced once at the high-posted double bed in the center of the room, and her stomach roiled again.

"The servants will be bringing in your things. Will you be needing anything?" The woman's words were civil enough, but the tone in which they were uttered was faintly mocking. "Perhaps if there is, you could magic it up," Tegwen continued.

It was too much. Gwenyth folded her arms across her chest and raised her chin imperiously. "Yes, you can do something. Those windows are to be opened immediately."

The chatelaine hesitated. "Opening windows brings in foul night air that is poisonous to the body. Everybody knows it."

"Nevertheless, you'll do as I say and at once." Muttering under her breath, the old woman complied, and a breath of fresh sea air billowed into the solar. "That's better. And now, please bring me water. I would like to wash."

The woman had started to leave the solar, but now she turned. Malice sparkled in her eyes, and her lip lifted in a sneer. "High and mighty, aren't you? Maybe you were somebody where you came from, mistress, but here you are nothing. Like the rest of us, you're under the master's heel."

When the woman had gone, Gwenyth walked painfully toward the window. It fronted the sea, and she could see the pale sheen of first moonlight over the water. She leaned against the cold stone wall and stared blindly into the distance. What Tegwen said was true, she thought. Here I am nothing.

"We are nothing, Wales is everything . . ." The litany filled her mind again, but now it did not seem to help. She could find no trace of resolve or courage left in her, and what was left was raw panic. If Reese came through that door now, she would scream until she went hoarse. If he tried to touch her, she'd throw herself from this window. And yet, what would her death accomplish but the ruin of all of Glendower's hopes? She was trapped, had been ever since she'd helped Robert Marne escape.

Suddenly he seemed to be there with her, not the Robert whose memory she had tried to suppress, but the man who had rescued her on the rocks, who had drawn his sword to face overwhelming odds in her defense, who had been her champion always. She closed her eyes and instead of the muffled sounds of the sea she heard him singing to her. She could taste his mouth on hers, and feel the strength of his arms. Weariness altered, changed to honeyed fire, and she thought, God pity me. No matter the shame to her, she could only be glad that he lived.

"Haven't you readied yourself for me yet?"

At the harsh voice the vision shattered, and reality flooded back as Reese swaggered into the chamber. He stood framed in the doorway for a moment and then approached her, his footsteps drunken and unsteady.

"You've not yet undressed. No matter. I'll soon have you where I want you."

She spoke without thought of the consequences. "Don't touch me. On your peril, don't touch me . . ." Then her words fell away. She had no dagger, no weapon of any kind with which to defend herself. How he would laugh at her pitiful defiance.

But he didn't laugh. Instead, the drunken lust in his eyes changed. His gaze sidled away from her, and he licked his lips. "You can't do a thing to me, witch," he slurred.

Like the sea wind, understanding flooded her. He was still terrified of her magic. Had he thought that now that she was married, she'd submit to him? Gathering up all her courage, she turned on him. "Do you think so? You had a charm, didn't you, when you kidnapped me on the road from Rowyn?

But I got away from you. My powers enabled me to find Robert Marne, and when he faced your men, they were helpless before him."

Surely he wouldn't believe such nonsense. But he did. There was glazed fear in his eyes. "You're lying," he mumbled.

"I didn't want to marry you, I only did so to preserve peace in Wales. You wanted my magic, not me. Our marriage is one of convenience, and well you know it. In every other way I'll do your bidding, but if you put one hand on me, you'll die—and not a clean death, either." She narrowed her eyes to green slits. "I can make your skin erupt into loathsome boils. I can make your manhood shrivel and fall off. If you want to know more about what I can do, try touching me."

He cursed her and called her filthy names, and listening to his shrieking rage, she tried to still the hammering of her heart. She must show absolutely no fear, or she was lost. She managed to stare him down until he said sullenly, "If I leave you alone, you'll ride with me and the men? You'll bring your magic to help me in whatever I do?" She nodded, and he snarled, "Damn you, then, sleep alone. There are enough willing wenches, and it's your magic I seek, not your body. But play me false, woman, and witch or not, you'll wish you were in hell."

He stormed out of the solar and slammed the door after him, leaving the chamber silent except for the whistle of the sea wind and the moan of the surf.

Only then did she let go her pent-in breath, and it came out as a sob. How long could she keep him at arm's length? How long before he realized that she had no magic? Not long. Not long at all.

You'll wish you were in hell, he'd said. She knew she was already there.

Chapter Eleven

GWENYTH SAT BY THE WINDOW AND STARED AT THE sea. It was almost shrouded in mist today, and yet from the solar she could see bare-legged fishermen launching their round coracles for a day's catch. She envied them their freedom.

In the two weeks she had been in this place, she had effected minor changes. The solar had been scrubbed and aired, and fresh linen covered her bed. Though Reese's slovenly chatelaine had complained about the extra work, a wooden bath had also been constructed, and it now stood in a corner of the solar. But these were small victories, insignificant beside the fact that by law she belonged to the brutish castle lord.

She felt familiar tension as his footsteps sounded

on the stairs and he swaggered into the solar. Today he was booted and spurred, and he held a whip which he slapped against his beefy thigh as he said, "Get on your riding things, mistress. It's time to prove your worth."

"Do you want me to ride with you?"

He sneered. "With all your magic, can't you tell a simple thing like that? You'd better do better than that against Castle Pryse."

Had he gone mad? "Merdyn Pryse is one of my father's most trusted allies," she protested.

His scowl deepened. "Maybe he was once. Now he's a traitor. Apparently the English spy you turned loose has been bribing your father's staunchest supporters. One of the damned Englishmen I took prisoner on my last raid told me of Pryse's defection."

She flinched at his words but spoke defiantly. "He would not sell their country for gold!" she cried.

He shrugged. "Everyone has a price, Gwenyth. My price was you—remember?"

Her mind went back to that moment in Robert's prison cell when he had promised never to hurt her or hers, and the memory cut like a knife. Dully she said, "Castle Pryse is well fortified. I saw it only once but I remember that it was built to withstand siege. And anyway, it is not up to you to punish the man. The alliance—"

He snorted. "The alliance will mumble and mutter long enough to give Pryse time to wiggle out of it. That's not my way. He's a damned traitor and must be punished, and Glendower will secretly thank me for it. You'll know a spell to open the gates so that we can get inside without a fight."

When he had left the solar, she went to her chest of clothing and reluctantly drew out her riding habit. As she unlaced her bodice and stepped out of her clothes, she wondered how much Merdyn Pryse's defection would hurt the alliance. Now a crucial portion of north Wales lay in a traitor's hands. . . .

There was an intake of breath behind her, and she saw that Reese was standing in the half-open doorway of the solar watching her. His eyes were narrowed as they devoured her bare arms and shoulders and the proud rise of her breasts, half exposed by her linen shift. He licked his thick lips, and seeing their wetness, she felt both fear and disgust. Hastily she pulled the riding habit over her head. "Do you not know to knock on a door?" she demanded.

"Since when must a husband crave his wife's permission to enter their room?" Lips drew away from teeth in a smile that was almost a snarl.

There was nothing she could do but dress and follow him outside. Their horses stood saddled and ready, and his men stood by their mounts. A great cheer rose as the master of the castle pushed Gwenyth forward.

"We've got Owen Glendower's magic on our side," one of Reese's lieutenants shouted.

"Aye—magic that'll make us rich. There's booty waiting for us in Castle Pryse," he bellowed back.

She knew that if Merdyn Pryse was a traitor and

had accepted English gold, Reese was within his rights as a member of the alliance to ride against Castle Pryse. Even so, the greed in her husband's eyes disgusted her. Even worse was the way his hands lingered on her knee after he had helped her mount her horse. If she couldn't help him get into Castle Pryse, she would really be in his power.

She *must* get into Castle Pryse. But how in God's name was she going to accomplish that? She thought desperately of this as they rode away down the sea road. From what she remembered of the castle, it was a smallish but very rugged fortress of stone and protected by the Conwy River on which it was built. Only true witchcraft could get them inside those walls.

Absorbed in her dilemma she was blind to her surroundings as they crossed dreary marshlands and then followed a rutted road toward the northern interior. It took them up a steep hill tufted with summer grass, then led away into forest land. Here, in spite of her problems, Gwenyth's spirits began to rise. The scents of crushed grass and new wood, the sound of birdsong and late June insects, were wonderfully sweet after weeks of being penned up in the castle, and she looked about her with pleasure.

Her husband seemed to sense her change of mood, for he reined in beside her. "Don't think to escape me into these woods, Gwenyth," he warned. "Remember the bargain we made."

The trick was how to fulfill the bargain. As she racked her brains to think of some way, one of

Reese's advance scouts came spurring back along the road. "My lord, there's a convoy up ahead," he reported excitedly. "An English convoy."

"English?" Reese's eyes darted to his wife. "How could you tell, sirrah?"

"There were English soldiers, my lord, and there was also a knight in armor. He had his helm off, and I saw him as clear as I see you. A big, fat knight with a black beard, he was. I heard him shouting orders in English."

All of the men had gathered around, and one of his lieutenants, a thin-lipped man called Evan Williams, asked, "Could this be the start of invasion, my lord?"

The scout took it upon himself to reply. "It wasn't a military convoy. The knight and soldiers were guarding horse-drawn carts loaded with sacks. If you ask me, those sacks were full of gold."

"Gold!" As the greedy murmur rose, Gwenyth saw Reese exchange a look with Evan Williams and his other lieutenants.

She had an inspiration. "This must be the English gold brought in by spies to bribe Welshmen. Instead of going to Castle Pryse, why not waylay the convoy and take the gold?"

The men nodded amongst themselves, and one of them cried, "Your lady speaks true, my lord! Easier to capture this convoy than Pryse Castle—especially since we've got magic on our side."

She had expected Reese to leap at the idea, but he seemed curiously hesitant. He frowned at his men and then at Gwenyth. "I make the decisions," he growled.

"But, my lord"—bewildered, Reese's scout spread wide his hands—"Castle Pryse will be there tomorrow or the next week or even next month, and this gold's so near us we can almost smell it."

Again the castle lord and his lieutenants exchanged looks. Then Reese said, "It lacks an hour to sunset, and by that time the Englishmen will be close to the forest of Nant y Coed. That's where we'll surround them and attack them." He paused to level a finger at Gwenyth. "You will stay out of it, mistress. I know how fond you were of a certain Englishman, and I want you to cast no spells against us. Do you hear?"

She breathed a silent prayer of thanksgiving as he ordered one of his men to stay close to her and keep her back from the fighting. Now that the attack on Castle Pryse had been postponed, she had won some breathing space. She was also glad that they were going to attack the English convoy and divert gold that would otherwise be used to lure Welshmen away from the alliance.

They stalked the convoy as the day turned to ruddy afternoon. Near sunset Reese's scouts brought word that, as he had predicted, the convoy was halting in front of Nant y Coed. He now deployed his men, sending several of them ahead to slip around the convoy and infiltrate the forest. "Stay there until I blow my horn," he ordered them. "That's the signal for us to fall on them. And remember—I want prisoners as well as that gold. Strike to stun, not to kill, and if they surrender, stop fighting at once."

Ordered to one side, Gwenyth sat her horse beside the glum guardsman detailed to stay beside her. She watched as Reese's men readied themselves and then, on the given signal, charged forward. Her companion swore unhappily.

"By God's bones," he cursed, "I never thought I'd see the day when I was forced to play nursemaid when there was booty to be had just yards away." He frowned down at her, adding, "It won't hurt if we at least see what is going on."

"Your lord ordered me to stay here!" she cried, but he'd already seized her bridle and was urging her horse and his up the road and onto a grassy clearing. It was full of noise and mounted men, and she could hear Reese's roars as he demanded that the English knight surrender. This knight, a fat, black-bearded fellow on a tall horse, was urging his men to surround carts laden with bulging sacks.

"The gold," the soldier beside Gwenyth breathed. As he leaned forward to get a better look, there was a flash of light, and a spear buried itself in the ground a few feet away. Gwenyth's horse shied nervously and, before she could control it, cantered directly into the thick of the fighting.

She called to the animal in Welsh, and as her clear voice rang above the noise of battle, the leader of the convoy stared at her. "The Welsh witch!" he bellowed in English. "They've got the Welsh witch with them. Lay down your arms. No use to fight them when they have the devil on their side."

How could anyone believe such idiocy? But they did believe. The English soldiers dropped their arms, and with a shout of triumph, Reese's men surged forward. Some of them disarmed the sullen Englishmen while others hurried to open the sacks on the carts. One of them cried, "My lord, there's enough gold in these sacks to pave the way to the castle!"

"A good day's work—English gold and prisoners." The last of the sunset reddened Huw's eyes as he addressed the leader of the English convoy. "What's your name, and are you able to ransom yourself? Or will my men amuse themselves by seeing how long you take to die?"

Gwenyth felt sickened, but the black-bearded Englishman said, "I can ransom myself and my men," in bad but recognizable Welsh. "Our families will get the gold to free us." Then his eyes darted to Gwenyth. "But we'd not have been caught so easily except for your damnable sorcery. The spells you shouted froze my sword arm and stopped me from fighting."

"It's plain that the lady has her uses." She didn't like the way Reese stared at her. He moistened his thick lips, and his narrowed eyes stripped her for a long moment before he turned back to his men. "No need to go farther after booty, so we'll make camp here the night. The horses need their rest if they're going to pull the gold safely back to Castle Reese tomorrow." Again his eyes came back to her. "Besides, my lady must rest. Erect a shelter for her at once."

Why was he so solicitous suddenly? Perhaps it was because in spite of his orders she had worked her so-called "magic" for him. She got down from her horse and wrapped herself in her cloak, withdrawing to the farthest corner of the clearing as camp was set up and praying that he'd be so pleased with the gold and his ransom-paying prisoners that he'd forget about her.

It seemed that she was in luck. As his men busied themselves building cooking fires and assembling shelters for the night, her husband sat down with a wineskin and the English prisoners. Apparently he was negotiating terms of their ransom, for he seemed to be in high spirits. While he drank and even passed the wineskin around, she heard him laughing as if at some great jest.

He didn't request her presence when the rough wayside meal was prepared, and instead two of his men brought food and drink and made haste to set up a makeshift tent for her near the edge of the woods. "My lord felt you'd be more comfortable away from the rest of the camp," one of them explained as he spread blankets on the ground. "You'll be far enough from the men to have your privacy, but you'll be safe, too. A few of us will be watching the woods to make sure no enemy creeps up on us."

And to make sure that she didn't escape. She

could hear the warning note in their so-called reassurance, but though she knew Reese was taking steps to see that his "Welsh magic" was safe, she was grateful for even the small comforts given her. She ate sparingly of the tough, fire-blackened meat, and then lay down on the blankets. They were rough against her skin and the ground was hard, but when she lay down on them, weariness claimed her almost at once. The noise of laughing and drinking men, the flicker of ruddy campfire, the choking smell of woodsmoke and grease from burning meat grew fainter, disappeared as she slid into sleep.

In that sleep she dreamed that she was back on the mountain by the enchanted lake. It was daylight, and a meadowlark sang its heart out in the blue and gold sky. She was waiting for Robert, and she sang a lovesong as she walked through the thick green summer grass. "I need no longer be alone, my love, now that your arms hold me . . ."

Then her singing stopped as she saw him coming toward her, and she ran to him. But then her dream changed. The lush green of the mountain grass became quicksand that caught her ankles and mired her in mud. And as she foundered, Robert changed. Before her disbelieving eyes he was transformed into the black-bearded leader of the English convoy. With drawn sword he barred her way, and it was then that she saw that his hand was covered with blood.

She started awake screaming as the bloody hand grasped her, and waking she screamed again. Reese was bending over her, his hand heavy on her arm. He grinned. "I fear I've wakened you from pleasant dreams."

Caught in remembered horror, she did not hear the mockery in his voice. "No pleasant dream," she whispered. Yet, it had only been a true one. Robert was behind Merdyn Pryse's defection, and his hands were truly covered with Welsh blood.

As she thought this Reese rasped, "I missed you by the fire, sweetheart."

"It was you who suggested I keep away from the rest of the camp." She tried to pull loose from him, but he would not let go and she added, "I'm very tired. Please leave me to rest."

"So tired from working magic, sweetheart?" It was dark here, but starlight and a new moon picked out the leaping lights in his eyes. He pushed his shaggy head closer. "My men are saying that I neglect my pretty bride. I think they speak truly."

There seemed to be an icy knot in her throat. "We have an agreement," she reminded him.

He spat in the dust. "That's how much I care for our agreement," he snapped. "Willing or not, you're my wife and tonight you won't deny me my rights."

Blood pumped painfully through her, but she forced her voice to cold calm. "Be careful. You saw what I did to the English knight today. You heard him say that at my word his sword arm grew weak. You wouldn't want that to happen to you."

To her surprise he began to laugh. "I saw you work your magic." Then his laughter died, and his face turned coldly cruel. "I'll take my chances with your sorcery, witch."

She pulled free from his clutching hand and rolled away from him. Then she jumped to her feet and ran. He cursed her loudly, but before he could get to his feet, she had darted into the shelter of Nant y Coed and the forest closed about her. There was no path here, and it seemed to her that she was running full tilt into a wall of trees. Brambles slashed her and tore at her clothing, and a branch lashed her face as she stumbled forward.

She had no idea where she was going, no thought except to get away from him. She heard him shouting for men to help him chase the witch, and then his crashing pursuit through the underbrush. "You bitch," he was snarling, "when I catch you, you'll scream for mercy."

Sternly she forced terror away. Make a plan, she urged herself, think! Reese might be stronger and swifter, but she knew more about the woods. There must be a place where she could take refuge. Desperately she searched as she ran, and as if in answer to her prayer, she saw a huge oak tree that had been split by lightning. In that crack was a space barely large enough for her.

There was no time to lose. Hastily wedging herself into the split of the ravaged tree, she strove to still her breathing. Nearer he came and nearer still, until he was almost upon her. Fighting an urge to scream, she closed her eyes and said a silent prayer. Mother, help me. Don't let him find me.

A rush of footsteps, and he had passed her hiding place. She could hear him crashing onward, held her breath as his curses grew fainter with distance. Merciful God, she thought, I've done it. I've tricked him . . .

"Damn you, witch, I see you!" His roar came from a point just feet away, startling her. Involuntarily she moved—and then realized by his triumphant shout that he'd tricked her.

She began to run again. Panic blinded her, turned her into a mindless, clumsy thing. Her lungs felt as though they would burst. Behind her, Reese had gone quiet like a hound settling in for the kill, and she could almost feel his hot breath at her shoulder as she burst through the woods and into a clearing.

It was a small glade surrounded by aspens and thick pine, and burnished to a pale silver by the moon. She darted across it, and as she did so, something slipped under her foot. As she fell forward she cried out in despair.

Her cry became a scream as rough hands clamped down on her shoulders, forcing her down to the ground. She kicked at him, and Reese cursed and loosed his hold on her. Rolling away from him, she nearly gained her feet before he threw her down, this time pinning his entire weight on her. One steely hand clamped down on her throat, the other caught her struggling hands.

"Stop it, or I'll beat you bloody." Then he taunted. "Go ahead and curse me. Blast me with your spells. Raise some woodland spirit to defend you, Gwenyth."

Almost as he spoke, a large, dark shape loomed against the greater darkness of the woods. For a moment she thought that Reese's mockery had roused some ancient Druidic forest god, and then Reese was jerked forcibly away from her and a human voice hurled a command. "Go!"

Snarling, Reese flung himself at this unlooked-for adversary. Gwenyth tried to get to her feet, but her knees had gone rubbery. Not taking her eyes off the swaying combatants, she dragged herself on her hands and knees to the edge of the clearing. Then she saw something flash in Reese's hands and she cried out in warning. "Be careful! He has a dagger—"

She was interrupted as a horn sounded in the woods nearby. Taken by surprise, the newcomer hesitated for a moment, and in that split second Reese whirled and disappeared into the tangled woods behind them. They could hear him yelling as he ran. "Over here, curse it. Williams, get your men over here."

Gwenyth's rescuer began to follow Reese, then checked himself. Faint moonlight flared against the blade of a sword as he said, "No time to chase the swine now. I've got to see you safe."

At the sound of his voice she went rigid. He couldn't be here, she thought wildly. But then he moved toward her, and faint moonlight caught the glitter of hard gray eyes and the shadowed, unmistakable features of Sir Robert Marne. Gwenyth felt as though a hand were squeezing her heart. "So Reese was right!" she cried. "You did come back to try and destroy the alliance."

Chapter Twelve

"YOU CAN TELL ME WHAT REESE SAYS ON THE WAY."
Moving with the powerful swiftness she remembered, he crossed the glade and caught her by the
arm. She hung back.

"I'm going nowhere with you, Englishman." But
before she could protest further, he had lifted her
into his arms. She struggled, but he held her easily
against the hard wall of his chest. "Let me go!" she
cried. "Put me down."

"Do you want your loving husband to catch up to
you?" That thought silenced her, and he began to
run through the trees toward a horse tethered nearby. As he lifted her into the saddle, she glared at
him.

"I've told you that I'll go nowhere with you."

The words were wrenched away by the wind as the horse plunged forward. She was thrown back against him, the curve of her back pressing against the solid muscles of his chest and belly. The impact left her shocked and dizzied, and when she tried to draw in oxygen, his remembered, vital scent seared her lungs.

"You act sorry that I stopped Reese from raping you." He sounded angry. "Perhaps I should have let you be."

She shivered involuntarily, and he sensed the horror of her life with the Welshman. If he'd had one more moment, that bastard—but it had been more important to get Gwenyth to safety. Instinctively his arm tightened around her.

She tried to pull free. "You're as bad as he is."

As she spoke they rode out of the woods and onto a broad, marshy meadowland that lay between two low, round hills. Robert momentarily slowed his mount, and in that split second Gwenyth began to slide from the saddle. Before she could touch ground, he had caught her by the waist and pulled her back. "What in hell do you think you're doing?"

"I told you that I wouldn't go anywhere with you." Defiantly she turned to glare up at him. His face was inches from hers, and in the depths of his eyes she could see a raw, angry flame. "Can't you just let me go?"

In spite of the danger of pursuit he halted his horse and studied her in the faint light. The loose tumble of her hair framed a face that seemed thinner. She was paler, and there were shadows under her eyes. Marriage had done this to her. His fingers itched for Huw ap Reese's throat, and anger made his voice harsh. "Go where? You can't go home to Eyri, and unless I'm mistaken, you'd scarcely want to return to Castle Reese."

"It's no concern of yours where I go."

"If your fond husband's men find you wandering nearby, they'll know I'm near at hand, too," he retorted. "You see why I can't have you falling into his hands. I've a liking for life."

"You mean you've got to finish bribing Welsh lords to betray the alliance," she charged hotly and then added, "Let me go. I know this country, and Reese's men won't catch me. I can live in the mountains until they stop searching for me."

"I doubt you'd reach the mountains." He spurred his horse again and urged it through the meadow and into the shadowy woods between the hills. As he did so she heard pursuing hoofbeats echo nearby, and a dozen horsemen appeared on the fringes of Nant y Coed. Shouting to one another, they fanned out across the meadow and up the slopes of both hills.

"Your fond lord's men are looking for you," he said. "I still can't believe that Glendower would give his own daughter to the brute."

"He had no choice. He needed an ally on the northwest coast."

Anger rode his voice. "Before I gave anyone I loved into that man's keeping, I'd have cut my own throat. Be honest. It was punishment because you helped me escape."

You aren't fit to live—Margaret Glendower's bitter

words filled her mind for a moment before she denied this. "It was my choice. I serve my country in every way I can."

He was silent for a moment and then nodded to the hills. "Reese will see to it that this way is blocked. We'll need another way to get to the border."

She turned to glare at him. "The English border?"

"Where else? If we go before Prince Hal—"

"Never!" she cried.

Swiftly he covered her mouth with his hand. "One more outcry like that, and we'll have your loving husband's men all over us." She wrenched her head free of him and he gritted, "Where do *you* want to go?"

She answered immediately, for she had often thought of this way of escape during her long days at Castle Reese. "To my half sister Mairi. She lives in Cadwen Castle in the Dovey River Valley."

His eyes narrowed in thought. "The best way to get there is to follow the coast and then turn inland at the mouth of the Dovey River, but Reese may guess your plan and be watching the sea road. We'll have to go the long way, inland across the mountains."

She hesitated before saying, "There's another way. My father and his allies know of the Monk's Trail which begins in the heart of Nant y Coed. If we're lucky, we may find it."

"We'll find it." He began to guide his horse back the way they had come. As they entered the woods, Gwenyth heard her husband's horn again, its raucous loudness a threat in the darkness. As if reading her thought, Robert said, "Be easy. He won't harm you."

The words recalled Glendower's great hall, the clash of swords, and the memory of love. But there was no tenderness in his deep voice now, and she reminded herself that his concerns for her safety lay rooted in fears for his own skin. The thought that she was helping him in any way made her writhe, but she had no choice but to guide him toward the center of Nant y Coed. But though they easily came to the place Glendower had described to her, finding the trail itself was another matter.

They both dismounted and searched, but here the trees grew so thickly as to block out light and underbrush, and vines tangled so tightly together that they seemed to make a solid, living wall. Robert looked about him doubtfully. "Are you sure you're not mistaken? There seems no sign of a pathway."

Resisting an impulse to give way to despair, she said, "I know there is. Some years after I came to Eyri, I helped my father map all the little-known roads in Wales. This was one of them."

"Roads which would be used to transport fighters and supplies across the mountains," he said thoughtfully, and she could sense that he was turning over this new bit of information.

"My father spoke of two large, round rocks that marked the beginning of the Monk's Trail," she told him coldly. "They lie somewhere among these trees."

They searched together until she found the two

rocks. Near them was the path itself, narrow and overgrown with brambles. "You see, I was right!" Gwenyth exclaimed.

He pointed to a large oak tree that spread its branches above them. "I think that the old gods of the Druids had a hand in the discovery. Oak bears mistletoe, and that's sacred, isn't it? Even mortal enemies share a kiss of peace under the holy plant."

Involuntarily she took a step backward away from him. Next moment something clutched at her cloak. Reese—with a gasping cry of remembered terror, she shrugged out of the mantle and ran forward into Robert's arms.

The remembered strength of his hard body was a bulwark against all the terrors she had endured in the past weeks. Though she knew that she should pull away, she could not bear to do so. Then it was too late. His arms went around her and she felt his cheek against her hair, heard him murmur her name, and without her conscious will her head tipped back for his kiss. And when it came—warmth and sweetness, firm, sure touch of lips and teasement of tongue—memory roared through her like riptide that swept her from reality into giddy madness. She sobbed, deep in her throat, as his mouth took hers.

He kissed her quiet. It was as if he were drinking from her lips as a thirsty man drinks from a clear fountain. Dazedly he thought that she was sweeter even than his memories of her, and every fear he had felt for her during the weeks they were apart became now transformed into longing. But this was not the time. She was still in danger.

His voice was husky with control as he said, "We have found the path and appeased the old gods with a kiss of peace. Now we'd better be on our way."

A kiss of peace—she bit her lower lip hard, but it wasn't only the pain that brought tears to her eyes. Fool, she called herself, fool to forget even for a moment that there could be no peace between them.

Wordless now, they followed the path on foot and in a silence that pressed close to her as they walked. His brief kiss had awakened all her senses, and she was acutely aware of his nearness and of the night around her, of the rustle of grass underfoot and the noisy song of insects in the fragrant woods. She was glad when he broke the silence to ask, "Did monks truly make this trail?"

"It's said that long ago some holy men came this way from their monastery in Strata Florida. They crossed the Snowdonia Mountains, hoping to build a monastery hereabouts, but the way was so long and hard that they abandoned the idea."

"But they left the trail for us to follow. It widens here. Time to ride again, Gwenyth. We've a long way ahead of us."

They rode through the night and by first dawn had left the forest of Nant y Coed behind and were following the trail up a shaggy hill. Morning showed that there was no sign of Reese pursuing them, and in her relief Gwenyth realized how tired she was. She tried to keep awake as they crested the hill, but her eyelids grew steadily heavier. They had almost closed when she heard Robert's exclamation.

Jerking awake she blinked at the view that spread

before them. From their vantage point they could see a silvery river wind through a wide valley before disappearing between round hills. Beyond the hills rose the Snowdonia chain and the faraway Hebog Mountains.

"It's a fair valley to which your Monk's Trail leads." Robert looked down at her and added, "You are too weary to go any farther, so we'll stop beside the river for a few hours."

Though she knew that they must put as much distance between them and Reese as possible, she was too exhausted to protest. He rode his horse down the side of the hill and into the lush, waist-high grass of a valley that was noisy with birdsong and the cry of summer insects. The valley nearest the river was half marsh, but after traveling some distance they found a stretch of ground covered with fine sand that was shaded by a small grove of trees. Here he dismounted and reached up to help her. "Come," he told her, "time to rest."

Her features were drawn with exhaustion, and it was not her beauty that he admired this time but the spirit that made her force herself to fight tiredness even now when she was scarcely awake. She slid from the back of the horse into his arms, and for a moment he held her before lifting her off her feet and carrying her into the shade of the trees, where he spread his cloak on the ground as a makeshift bed. "Sleep," he told her. "I'll watch to make sure your rest is not disturbed."

She wanted to protest that he must be as weary as she, but before she could even think the words, she was asleep. As she slipped six fathoms into sleep she held one strange waking thought—that here with this English knight she felt safer than she had ever felt in her life.

Perhaps it was this odd sense of security that made her sleep deeply, for when she awoke it was close to noonday. Nearby she could hear the horse cropping contentedly, and the warm summer air was full of birdsong. A sense of ineffable content filled her.

"You've slept well." She sat up and looked around and saw Robert seated nearby. He had a map spread over his knees, and though there were lines of fatigue in his face, he smiled at her protests that he should have awakened her. "You slept so contentedly that waking you would have been a sin. I have enough on my soul without adding more."

The deep voice made her wary. She'd been tired and vulnerable last night and this morning, but no more. She glanced at the map he had spread out on the grass beside him and saw that it was a map of Wales.

"You have been busy marking the Monk's Trail on your map," she said dryly. He didn't answer and she added bitterly, "No doubt your king will be glad to know about my father's secret road. Perhaps you'll even use it to ferry gold to the next traitor willing to leave the alliance."

"So you believe Reese." There was something in his voice that made her look at him sharply.

"Why else would you have been with the convoy?" she demanded.

Without answering, he folded his map and slid it

into saddlebags that lay nearby. "If you'll watch for your loving lord and his henchmen, I'll sleep for an hour," he said brusquely. "You'll wake me at the end of that time, agreed?"

She watched him settle his cloak away from the sun and stretch his long limbs onto it, saw how he laid his sword hilt under his hand before he slept. Then she walked down to the river and longingly looked toward the mountains. Once there, she would be safe. She glanced back at the sleeping English knight and then the thought came to her. Supposing she went on now—alone?

She was rested, and there was food in his saddle-bags to last her until she reached the mountains. She'd need to take his horse, but that could not be helped. After what he had done against Wales and the alliance, taking his horse need not bother her. And there was something else she would take as well.

Softly she crept past the trees where he slept and up to his saddlebags. Very carefully she removed the map of Wales. This she tore in several pieces which she threw into the river. Then she walked quickly toward his horse.

It whickered when it saw her, and she caught her breath for fear that Robert would awake. "Be still, horse, good horse," she soothed as she mounted the animal and guided it down the trail toward the mountains. For a while she rode without thought except that of putting as much distance as she could between her and the English knight, but after a while doubts came. Supposing Mairi did not help her—suppose she and her husband insisted she go back to her husband?

The thought tormented her. She would rather face death than return to Reese. And yet, with the Welsh in peril thanks to English bribes, did she have the right to think of herself? "Wales is everything, we are nothing," Glendower had said when she dared to love an Englishman.

Involuntarily her eyes swung back to the grove of trees where she had left Robert asleep, and her heart almost stopped. Six horsemen were riding down the hillside toward the river. Did they know about the Monk's Trail, she wondered, or had they come into the valley by another route? She could not see their faces from this distance, but sunlight flashed on weapons they carried slung across their backs. Spears and bows, she thought, and short swords. These were Welsh soldiers . . .

Reese's henchmen! Her first instinct was to spur her horse and put as much distance between herself and the approaching men as possible. Then she forced herself to look again with her hill-trained attention to detail. These were certainly Welsh soldiers, but they weren't wearing Reese's colors or the kind of clothing she'd seen at his castle.

They weren't after her, she thought, and her relief was so great she was dizzy with it. They would not bother her, especially not when they found Robert Marne, alone, horseless. After all, all of Wales knew of the English spy who had escaped Glendower and so they'd be wary of strangers. She'd like to see the supposed bard talk his way out of this situation. She started to spur her horse onward and then a question formed in her mind. Supposing he couldn't explain his presence—what then?

"They'll kill him." Her lips felt dry as she spoke the words aloud. It would be six men against one. She swallowed hard and tried to tell herself that he was her enemy, an English spy, that without him Henry of England would have less chance of ruining the Welsh alliance. It was no use. Before the words were past her lips she had turned her horse and was pounding back the way she had come. Enemy or not, he'd saved her from Reese last night and let her sleep while he watched this morning, and she couldn't abandon him to certain death.

The Welshmen were by now riding down the side of the hill, and as she rode she formed a plan. She would catch the men's interest and draw them toward the marsh away from Robert. The noise would wake him, and he could take cover. As for herself, she wasn't worried. If the soldiers caught up to her, she would explain who she was and they would treat her with respect, for no Welshman would offer harm to Glendower's daughter.

Now they saw her. She saw them stopping to stare, and then they spurred forward toward her, shouting at each other. Though she couldn't make out the words at this distance, she hoped that Robert was by now awake. She started to ride away from them, and the shouting grew louder. The tone of their voices was full of male triumph, and remembering Reese's clutching lust, she was suddenly chilled.

Sternly repressing that prickle of fear, she spurred

away into the marsh grass. As she had planned, they followed her. But here her plans went awry, for the men separated and surrounded her. One of them, a big man with a thick red beard, was shouting endearments as he came, while the others grinned and leaned forward on their saddles.

She drew herself up in her saddle and forced every bit of strength and courage into an imperious challenge. "I am Gwenyth, daughter of Owen Glendower ap Gryffth Vychon. Tell me your names and the master whom you serve."

She thought that would stop them, but they only howled with laughter. Didn't they believe her, or—God above, were these men renegade Welsh? She looked about her for a way to break free of them, but the laughing men had her surrounded. Now all of them except Redbeard dismounted, and she could hear the sigh of the long grass brushing their thighs as they sauntered toward her. "Come, little dear," one of them invited. "We'll have some fun."

Sun flashed on steel, and Gwenyth screamed as the man who'd spoken fell, clawing at his belly. Next moment Robert had erupted out of the high grass. The remaining four soldiers fumbled for weapons, but before they could reach them, two more men had been slashed down by the Englishman's sword. The remaining two ran for their horses and galloped away, followed by the mounts of their slain comrades.

Redbeard did not follow. Instead he yelled loudly and spurred his horse toward Robert. Sun flamed on his spear as he circled his foe, but in looking for an opportunity, he came too close. Yelling loudly, he was pulled from the saddle.

As he went down he threw his arms about his opponent and took him to the ground, also. Over and over on the grass the two men rolled, sword and spear forgotten, until the Englishman managed to catch his opponent around the throat. "Don't kill me," Redbeard croaked.

Gwenyth started violently. The man hadn't spoken in Welsh but in English. "Who are you? Why are you here?" Robert exclaimed in like astonishment.

He must have loosened his grip on Redbeard, for the man suddenly rolled away and snatched up Robert's sword. "Die, Welsh pig!" he yelled.

Robert acted instinctively. As Redbeard sprang forward he grabbed for the man's discarded spear and lunged upward. Transfixed on his own spear point, the bearded man crashed to the ground.

"He's dead." Gwenyth's voice shook. She was still seated on his horse, and Robert noted that she looked sick. He retrieved his sword and wiped it on the long grass before returning it to his sheath. Then he walked over to her.

"He's certainly dead, and so would I have been had they found me asleep," he told her coldly.

She was too stunned from the sight of death and blood to note the tone of his voice. "I saw them coming over the hill, and I—I thought they were Welsh soldiers. Were—were they really English?"

"This man certainly was, so the others probably are—or were, also." He looked about him at the bodies on the valley floor, and she had never seen him look so angry. "Of course you thought that they were Welsh, otherwise you wouldn't have led them to me."

Now she knew what he meant and she faced him defiantly. "I did take your horse to ride on alone, but when I saw them and knew they would kill you, I came back to lead them away from you."

From his expression she could tell he didn't believe a word she'd said. "Ironic, isn't it, that in your defense I've killed my own countrymen? I don't know how they came to be here or why, but you've just caused four Englishmen to die. No doubt you think that's cause for celebration."

His voice was bitter, and she cried, "I should have left you to their mercy! I should have let them kill you."

He caught her wrist in a painful grip. "I'll say this so that we understand each other. We'll travel together until we cross into the mountains, and after that, I don't care where you go. Is that understood?"

They glared at each other. "Understood, Englishman," she snapped.

Chapter Thirteen

THEY TRAVELED THROUGH THE AFTERNOON AND INTO twilight, Robert leading and Gwenyth following on Redbeard's horse. Now Robert was even more careful to cover their tracks, often doubling back to make sure no one followed, even though the valley seemed empty of human life. It was only farther along that they found shepherds grazing their animals on the marshy meadowland, and later they came upon a small village consisting of a handful of rude stone cottages. It appeared deserted, but as they rode past, there was a rustle in the tall grass. Robert drew his sword and wheeled his horse around, but Gwenyth checked him.

"Look, it's only a kitten." As she spoke a small white cat ran out of the tall river grass and was followed immediately by a little girl. The child was in rags and obviously terrified. "Don't fear, we'll not harm you," Gwenyth reassured her.

Now a thin, snarl-haired woman ran out to put her arms around the child. "God be praised, you're Welsh. We were afraid you were the English come again."

Slowly other villagers appeared. Robert sheathed his sword and noted that except for a few old men and very young boys, the village was made up of women and children. "Are your men hiding?" he asked the ragged woman.

She answered fiercely. "No, gone to fight with the prince against the English." Then the fire died from her eyes. "English soldiers have come this way before. They took our cows and pigs, though we managed to hide some of our sheep, and they stole three of our children. That's why we hid when we saw you coming."

"We met some Englishmen disguised as Welsh soldiers on the way," Gwenyth warned. "Don't trust anyone. If a group of men or even one man rides by, hide your sheep and your children. No one is safe until the English are beaten."

She did not look at Robert as they went on again, but when they had left the little village behind she could no longer keep silent. "I've heard that the English steal children, that it's a game with them, but I didn't think it could be true."

"It's true enough." His tone was curt. "In a war like this, there are foul deeds done on either side. If no peace is made, this will go on for years."

A hard knot of anger churned within her as again

she saw before her the thin, terrified faces of the villagers. How could he pretend to speak so reasonably when it was his fault that the Welsh alliance was crumbling?

He was saying, "It's getting too dark to travel now, and we are both weary. Tomorrow we'll cross into the mountains."

And then they would part company, she thought as Robert chose a place for their camp on high ground near water that beavers had partially dammed into a rippling pool. Here he perfunctorily explained that he would rather not risk a fire. "Not only for our sakes but for the villagers'. I'm certain they want to remain hidden."

"You can say that even when you're helping to ruin their country!" she cried. "At least Reese is no hypocrite. He doesn't hide his villainy under a show of concern."

He shrugged. "A villain and a liar—sweet words, my lady. But then, I never stooped to kill a sleeping man." As she stiffened he added more insult. "Did your hillwoman mother school you in such tricks?"

She had never struck anyone in her life, but she threw all her unskilled strength into the blow. He sidestepped it easily, and next moment he had caught her by the arms. "Damn you," she seethed, "let me go."

For answer he jerked her still closer until she was pressed full-length against him. The hammerblows of her heart impacted against his hardness, and against the soft curves of her body she registered the muscled flatness of his belly, the powerful tautness of his thighs. "Let you go so you can hit me again? That much of a fool I'm not."

She struggled again, but he held her easily, feeling under his hands the delicate bones of her shoulders and the heat of her body. Even in the darkness he could sense her anger and hatred for him, and an answering fury rose within him. She had tried to have him killed, she had named him knave and villain. He had put his life at risk for her again and yet again, but she had forgotten this or else she did not care. Why then should he care what became of her?

She cried out in pain as his restraining arms tightened yet more, and when she tried to breathe, the still, warm summer air was full of his scent. That clean, vibrant male fragrance seemed to fill her lungs as his mouth bent to hers.

She started to scream protest, but speech died as his mouth covered hers. One of his hands rose to clamp itself against the back of her skull, anchoring her for his pleasure. His strong thighs straddled hers, imprisoning her as his other hand flattened against her hip. Dazedly she felt her softness pressed against hard masculinity. She could not breathe or move.

"No?" There was grim mockery in the deep voice. "But I feel your heart beating tenderly against mine." He was cupping her breast in his hand as he spoke, his touch not loving but still expert, still evoking sensation as he stroked the proud slopes and found the tender peaks. "It's more fun to kiss than to kill, Gwenyth."

"Please," she heard herself whisper, but inexorably his mouth covered hers again. Parting her lips, his tongue plundered the inner softness of her mouth, and desperate for breath, she drew oxygen from his lungs. The taste and texture of his mouth, the skillful touch of his hand on her breasts—they dizzied her, and she scarcely felt him unbuttoning the front of her riding habit until his hands cooled her hot bare skin. When he took his mouth from hers to cover her upthrust nipples, her moan was no longer one of anger or despair, and as his mouth savored her sweetness, as his tongue nudged and licked and teased the tender rosebuds of her breasts, honeyed fire filled her blood.

He sensed the change in her even through the heat of his blood. Want for her hammered through his veins, and every nerve and muscle in his body shouted for possession. He had dreamed often of this—of the soft firmness of her breasts and her smooth, satin belly and her parted white thighs. His own body was a vast, fiery ache that could not be slaked, and he sensed an answering need in her. If he lowered her to the grass, she would be as sweetly willing as she had been beside the enchanted lake. . . .

The lake—memory of it shivered through his mind, and suddenly he felt chilled. The heat within him still blazed, but now he could think of what she had risked and given up for him. Was it any wonder that she had turned against him? Besides, he thought despairingly, he'd come to help her, not hurt her.

Loosening his arms around her he stepped back so quickly that she was unbalanced. Instinctively she reached out to him for support and found that under her questing hands the muscles of his arms had gone to steel. For a moment the harshness of his breathing and her own ragged breath were the only sounds that broke the silence, and then he said, "I apologize for this. The fault was mine. We were both too angry to think."

Empty desolation filled her and then swiftly shame and anger rushed in to fill the void. "It's no more than I could expect from an Englishman." She tried to sound defiant, but the words came in a shaky whisper.

"I should have left you with that good Welshman, Huw ap Reese," he retorted, and then was immediately sorry. A welter of conflicting emotions flooded through him, and he wondered bleakly why one slender, green-eyed girl could so complicate his life. "It's late and we are both exhausted. Tomorrow we'll need to ride hard and long. I suggest you sleep."

"And will I sleep undisturbed, Englishman?" The question was scornful, and he answered in kind.

"I've never needed to force a woman." As she winced he made himself remember how she had tried to engineer his death that morning. "And lest you be tempted to ride away tonight, I don't intend to sleep. I mean to stay alive until we reach the mountains."

Pride stiffened her spine and she retorted, "I

cannot wait until we get there and I am free of you."
And she had to be free of him, she told herself.
Otherwise, she was lost.

Sensing that the weather would turn mercilessly
hot, she rose before dawn and bathed. She was glad
of this later, for the sun beat down on them as they
set out again into changed scenery. Now the river
soon became narrower and wilder, seeming to push
aside the steep-sided hills. The river valley here was
no green-meadowed plain but a steep, narrow place
of forbidding beauty, and no houses or stone shepherds' cottages marked the lonely trail. Farther on,
the path left the river and began to lead up the side
of a steep hillside. The trail was narrow here and
overgrown with grass that had been burned brown in
the summer heat, and Robert dismounted to guide
the horses over terrain that was often treacherous
with rocks and grass-hidden crevices.

He whistled as they came to the crest of the hill.
"So that's what we have to cross."

The mountains were some distance from them,
but from this vantage point the thrust of the nearest
peak loomed ominously high. It was separated from
them by a narrow, tree-choked gorge, and trees also
grew thickly up the side of the mountain and almost
to the top. There dark, naked rock formed a flat
scarp.

"Does the Monk's Trail lead us up the mountain?" Robert asked, and Gwenyth shook her head.

"Somewhere along the way up is the Black Pass.
My father never came this way, but he had heard of

men who did. The Black Pass is said to be perilous, but it cuts the way in half."

And she would be grateful for anything that would shorten this journey, she thought as they rode down into the gorge and across it into the shadow of the mountain. But here the Monk's Trail suddenly ended, disappearing into thick underbrush. They searched along the foot of the mountain but found no trace of its resuming, and finally Robert called a halt. "This is futile," he said. "What would happen if we followed the gorge?"

"That would take us days. The Black Pass cuts right across the side of a mountain. Once on the other side I could ride through hill country toward Cadwen."

"Then we have to find the trail again. Since it was a trail for holy monks, perhaps heaven will help us and lead us to it."

But they weren't so fortunate. In spite of all her own training and the nature craft she had taught him, it took them half the day to locate the trail again. It was choked with brambles and gorse, and their climb up the side of the mountain was slow. They rode single file with Robert in the lead, and it was turning to sunset when he checked his horse. "Sweet Christ," he exclaimed, "is this what you mean by the Black Pass?"

She urged her mount forward until she could see. No pass, this, but a narrow ledge hacked into the rocky side of the mountain. It snaked across dark, barren rock for about five hundred yards, then descended toward woodlands on the other side.

"Once we get across, the going will be easy," she said stoutly.

"The trick is to get across." She followed his gaze downward to the gorge, now several miles below. "It's almost a straight drop down the side of that cliff," he went on. "It might be best to backtrack and follow the gorge."

"Supposing the men who escaped yesterday have carried the tale?" she parried. "They'd certainly be waiting for us along the gorge."

She could sense him turning the thought over in his mind before he dismounted and came around to help her down. "I'll go ahead with the horses," he told her. "When I get them across, I'll come back for you."

She protested this at once. "I can walk across as well as you can, and I can lead my own horse."

He frowned. "Christ preserve me from obstinate women. I will go first with one horse, and be back for the next. Or do I have to tie you to that tree?"

Bitterly she held her peace, and yet, when he started across the narrow ledge of ground, she found herself holding her breath. Against the black rock that had given the pass its name, he seemed suddenly dwarfed and vulnerable, and in spite of herself a familiar prayer formed in her mind. Please, let him be safe.

Apparently he needed no prayers. Amazingly surefooted, he walked across the narrow pass. She could hear him soothing his horse as he went, calming the beast as if they were walking down a country lane. Then they were across and he and his horse momentarily disappeared into the woodlands beyond before he returned along the ledge.

"I could feel the rocks sliding under my feet," he warned her. "Even if you're as surefooted as a Welsh goat, be careful."

There was real concern in his voice, and when she looked up she saw in his eyes the same look that she had seen many times in Eyri. Then he turned his back to her and began to guide the horse across the ledge.

Sunset colors beat against them and turned the rock face to flame and crimson, the colors of blood. She felt the dying heat of the sun against her face as she walked carefully after Robert. "Don't look down," he warned her as they walked. "Keep your eyes on the woods at the end of the pass."

They had reached the halfway point before she first felt it, the crumbling of stones under her heel. In spite of Robert's warning she looked downward and saw that the rock of the path had eroded until only loose gravel remained. A terrible place, she thought as she hugged the hard wall of the mountain, carefully seeking a toehold before she set down her weight. A step. Another. Still another. One more, and she was almost at the woods and safety.

She could see Robert leading her horse into the woods and turning back for her, and relief made her careless. One moment she was stepping down onto the sand and rock of the pass, the next she felt the ground slide from underfoot. She tried to get her balance, knew she could not. She had only time for one cry as she fell sideways into space.

There was a whistle of wind and she felt the scrape of rough rock against her body. Instinctively her outstretched hands clawed for a fingerhold and miraculously found something—an out-thrust tree root that had grown under the rock. Sobbing with effort, she clutched at the root with both hands.

Through her sobs and the rattling sound of sand and rock falling into the gorge below, she heard Robert's voice. He was leaning over the edge of the pass, and through her driving terror she heard him say, "Be as still as you can. I'm coming for you."

How? she wanted to cry, but he was already gone, and an eternity of seconds crawled by until he returned. He had wrapped one end of a rope around his waist, the other around something she could not see. Now he tugged the rope taut and lowered himself over the edge of the cliff. Shooting pains tormented her arms, and her shoulders felt as if they were being ripped from the sockets, but this wasn't what tortured her the most. She could feel the root she was clutching give way, and she knew that her weight was straining it to the breaking point.

Through her pain and fear she heard him say, "I used to climb rocks as a boy, and it's a skill you don't lose. I dreamed of doing heroic things with my knowledge. Of course, I never knew I'd be called on to rescue a princess in distress."

She knew he was talking to calm her, knew from the tension under the jesting words that he realized that they both could die. The edge of the rock against which the rope rested was sharp. If it cut through the rope, he would fall to his death.

As she thought this he launched himself into space, then swung back so that his feet impacted with the rock. Another swing, and he was almost beside her. Through the pain of her arms she looked up and saw the rope sawing on the edge of the pass. She cried, "Go back before you die, also! The rope is fraying . . ."

He ignored this. "I'm going to swing behind you and take you by the waist. When you feel my arms around you, let go of that root."

If he failed—but he was already pushing off from the rock wall. For a second she felt the weight of his body pressing her into the cliff wall, and then his arms clamped around her waist. "I have you."

She could feel the strain of his muscles as they swung back into space, and at his instruction she turned and wrapped her arms and legs tight around him as he began to haul them both up on the rope. "Don't worry, love," he then said, "I won't let you fall."

His voice was tense and harsh, and she knew that he wasn't even conscious of speaking. His words were only an extension of his deepest thoughts. Rather than let her fall he would have died with her—might still die with her. She clung to him, feeling the friction of rock against her body as he grunted with the last effort it took to haul them both to the ledge of rock. Then she was lying on the hard path, and he was beside her.

For a long moment they lay silently together, and then he asked, "Are you hurt?"

She shook her head. Strangely there was no pain

at all. Instead she felt curiously numb and cold. "I'm all right," she tried to say, but her teeth chattered so that she could hardly form the words.

Now he saw the numb blankness in her eyes. He'd seen that look in the eyes of men after battle, and he knew that her mind was retreating into shock. Lifting her into his arms, he carried her the last few feet of the Black Pass and then into the woods. Against him, he could feel the tremors of her unnaturally icy body. "I'll soon have a fire to warm you," he told her.

His words seemed to come from a distance, but he was the only reality she could cling to. When he set her down on the ground and wrapped her in his cloak and blankets, she murmured a protest. Through her daze she heard his voice telling her he'd be back, and there was so much anxiety in that voice that she struggled to answer. "You mustn't fear—about me," she whispered, and though her teeth chattered, she tried to smile at him. "All right now. Just cold."

Any other woman would be screaming and crying out for him not to leave her, he thought as he gathered firewood and cleared the wooded mountainside to make space for a fire. But then, Gwenyth wasn't like other women. She shone above them like the evening star. The thought that he had almost lost her back on the pass was like ice in his guts, and when he had the fire blazing, he carried her near to the warmth and set her as close to the flame as possible. "Is that better?" he asked her.

She tried to nod, but she was still shaking, and her

cheeks were as white as new milk. He stripped away the cloak and blankets and began rubbing her arms to try and restore her circulation. There were bruises on her wrists, and her hands were raw from clinging to the branch, but when he looked down into her face, he saw with relief that she was losing that dazed, numb expression.

He realized then how tightly he'd been holding her, and he loosened his grip. "If you're better, I'll water the horses. Luckily, there's a mountain stream nearby—"

She couldn't bear the thought of him leaving her. With the memory of death so close, she spoke before she thought. "Please don't go," she begged, and then she whispered, "Hold me."

Chapter Fourteen

RESPONDING TO THE YEARNING IN HER VOICE, HE DREW her back into the circle of his arms. For a moment he held her close, and then she whispered, "I was so afraid."

Her voice trembled. When he looked down into her face, her eyes were shut, and the dark lashes made smudged circles against her cheeks. She had been close to death, he thought. No wonder she wanted the comfort of his arms. He cradled her more gently against him. "There's no more danger."

"But there is." She opened her eyes and he could see reflected firelight dancing gold in the clear emerald of her eyes. Some color had returned to her face, and her mouth curved softly.

"From whom?" She could hear the change in his voice. "Do you mean those Englishmen we met yesterday? I doubt if any Englishman knows about the Black Pass."

"You do," she reminded him sadly.

He drew away from her then and turned to the fire, so that his back was to her. "You really think that I'm here to bribe Welsh lords into leaving the alliance? I'm here because I heard you were being married to Reese."

"But I thought—"

"Thomas Carpenter and I reached the castle of the earl of Stoake a week after we left Eyri, and there I learned the news of your coming marriage. I was sure you weren't a willing bride. I'd have liked to ride up to Castle Reese with a band of Stoake's soldiers behind me, but I was afraid that one of your husband's men would betray the location of Eyri to save his skin, so I came alone."

Something in the starkness of his words told her he spoke truth. She had tried to flay Robert Marne from her mind, and yet he had returned at peril to himself to help her. He was saying, "When I crossed the border, I learned I was too late. You'd already been wed. Though I knew it was folly, I went on to Reese's castle, but when I reached it, it was only to see you riding away with your husband and his men. I followed you hoping for a chance to see you, get you away. When Reese ambushed that convoy, I was tempted to fight on the English side, but I held back because my concern was all for you."

That was why he'd been there in Nant y Coed. She leaned forward so that her cheek rested against his broad back, and her voice was riding unshed tears as she said, "I should have known you'd come. I thought of you always. And though I wanted to stop loving you, I could not."

Wordless, he turned to her. He did not crush her to him but enfolded her against him, kissing her hair and her forehead and her eyes. And between those swift kisses she heard him whisper the lovesong of his heart. "My lady, my darling, my love—" and then the song was stilled as his mouth found hers.

None of their kisses had ever been like this. As their lips touched, something deep and elemental in her yearned toward him and she knew that here in his arms was not just love, not just completion, but homecoming. Through danger and suspicion and even across the brittle lines of loyalty, they had found each other again.

As if he had read her thought, his kiss changed. As tender but more passionate, his mouth seemed to drink from hers, and his tongue tasted hers, sought the satin of her inner mouth. Possessively his hands relearned each curve and hollow and line of her, and he stroked her back and her arms and the ridges of her spine down to her rounded hips and then up again to caress her breasts. She pressed against his questing hands, her body aching with a delight so intense that it was almost pain.

"For you, a man would give his chance for Paradise." His voice was low, husky with desire, and aching tenderness. "Yet I fear to hurt you. Love for me has brought you too much sorrow already."

"And without your love I'd know nothing of joy." He heard the lilt in her voice as her eyes smiled tremulous welcome. She shook back her loosened hair, then reached to unfasten the buttons of his tunic.

He helped her with her riding habit and she with his clothing. Now when he gathered her close, she registered the warm, crisp-furred hardness of his chest and bent to kiss the flat male nipples before he lifted the linen shift from her shoulders and caressed her breasts. "As proud as the peak of Snowdon, but much warmer," he murmured, and she murmured with pleasure as his knowing fingers worked their magic. "And as sweet as honey, my love."

She caught his dark head to her breast as he adored the aching buds, circling the pale areolas with his tongue and then covering the nipples with his warm mouth. He sucked gently, then with more force, and she felt as if her body were an open flower full of wild honey. His mouth seemed to draw the very heart from her, and she ran her hands over the smooth muscles of his back, the strong shoulders and arms, then up to the hard line of his jaw. She kissed his hair and then his neck. "Robert, you make me die of pleasure."

He stripped away their last garments, then lowered her to the blankets and pillowed her golden head with his cloak. In the firelight her eyes shone with love and passion, but the curve of her mouth was tremulous. The desire he felt for her was matched with an aching tenderness and a need to please her. He caressed her lovely body, her arms and her breasts and her slim belly, the soft golden rise of her womanhood and between her thighs.

His touch was like firebloom, and she moved against him with an urgency she could not control. Clasping her arms around his neck, she sought his mouth with hers. "My love," he whispered against her lips. "Queen of my heart. None else but you, now and forever."

Hardly could he contain his passion for her, but he held back, loving the feel of her slender body and the way her slender hands stroked his face and his chest and the backs of his thighs, and when her eager hands roved over his manhood, he knelt between her parted thighs. But at his first thrust he heard her gasp and realization hit like a hammerblow. "Sweet Christ, you're a maiden. But how, when you were forced to marry—"

"I wouldn't let him touch me. It was you, always you."

Astonishment turned to joy, but now he held back, afraid of hurting her, until she circled his neck with her arms and drew him down to her. He began to court her again, kissing her nipples and her hands and touching her in the ways that made her moan with pleasure. Then, raising her hips to meet his thrusts, he began to move inside her again.

He tried to be slow, to be careful, but she arched against him with such eager joy that his control shattered and his body became only the instrument of his love and his adoration. They moved slowly together and then faster, faster still to the drumbeat of their blood. And as they burst into flame together, as Gwenyth felt the shattering of her body and her soul, she knew that this was where she had always longed to be, had always meant to be—with him.

"My lovely lady of flowers." It was his voice that awakened her. Long before the trill of morning birdsong filtered through her dreams, she heard his murmur. "My love, my dear love . . ."

Eyes still closed, she tried to cuddle closer to him. It was hard to do. His big body already curved about hers and his arms cradled her while along her back she felt the tender stroking of his hand. His touch, his nearness brought back remembered loving, and her body hummed with ineffable content as she opened her eyes and looked up into his smiling face.

"Good morning." As he bent to kiss her she watched her reflection shimmer in his eyes and wondered how joy could be so great that it could almost hurt. The same happiness softened his features, made him look again like the lighthearted minstrel she had met at a wedding in Rowyn. He kissed her again, his mouth lingering on hers. "I've wanted to do this since earliest dawn, but you slept so soundly I did not want to awaken you."

Lifting her arms from the blanket that covered them, she caressed the hard line of his jaw and ran light fingertips along his mouth. "You should have," she chided. "There was no need for you to keep watch this time, sir knight."

"It was time well spent. You are a beautiful sleeper, my heart." The vibrance in his deep voice made her shiver from want. But one hunger awoke another, and she realized that she was ravenous. He seemed to read her thought, for he kissed her once again and then threw off the covering blanket to sit up. Early sunlight lit his lean strength, and she caressed him with her eyes, loving the broad shoulders, the strong, furred chest, and muscled belly and loins and hard male power. The fact that he so obviously wanted her stirred both her desire and a sense of mischief.

"If I am beautiful asleep," she murmured, "you are beautiful awake. And I see that you are full awake, lord knight."

Laughter silvered his eyes, but he only clicked his tongue at her. "And you brought up to be a dainty princess. Such thoughts, such thoughts, my lady." With swift and powerful grace he got to his feet and began to pull on his clothes. "If you keep looking at me like that, neither of us will get our breakfast." She glanced toward the saddlebags, but he shook his head. "You don't think that I'd offer stringy dried meat and hard bread to the queen of my heart? Fresh coney gives a man strength."

She sat up, wrapping herself in his cloak against the morning chill, and watched him pull on his boots. "You seemed strong enough last night," she told him, and when he bent and kissed her, she licked the cool, sweet morning air from his lips. She felt weak from want of him, and she whispered, "Don't be too long."

"Do you think I could?" He bent, and for an instant touched lips to her much-kissed nipples.

Then he was striding away from her into the woods, and she heard his deep voice singing as he disappeared. The song was a promise of joy to be renewed.

She got to her feet and stretched. She felt changed, renewed, gloriously alive. Her naked body was still warm from his caresses, and she remembered each loveword that he had spoken in the night. This was what love meant, she thought, and suddenly she understood the loneliness that Merryn had hidden deep in her heart throughout the long years. She prayed that Merryn had known mornings like this if only for a little while. Love such as this was worth a lifetime of loneliness.

A cool wind brushed its fingers over her bare skin, and she shivered. Then she put such thoughts hurriedly away. Nothing must darken this morning. She was so full of energy that she wanted to run, to leap, to sing, but these things could be postponed until after she began preparations for breakfast. She dressed quickly and began to gather firewood, then remembered Robert speaking of a nearby stream. She had only to find it to fill his waterskin.

It was not hard to find the stream, and when she saw it, she stopped in delight. Though it was only a mountain brook, it was deep and clear and shone gold in the early sun, and downstream from her it widened just enough to form a pool of swift-flowing water. It was fringed with fern and starred with dandelions and marsh marigold, and velvet moss cushioned her knees as she knelt to test the cool water. It was like the rivers that had flowed near Cader Idris where she and Merryn had bathed and washed their clothes—the thought formed in her mind for a moment, and then she smiled. Well, why not?

The woods around her hummed with birdsong, and she knew instinctively that there was nothing to fear. She undressed and carried her clothing to the lip of the natural pool, and using sand and a stick to pound the clothing, she washed busily, humming happily to herself. The sunshine and cool wind on her naked body felt good, but it was nothing compared to the feeling when, clothing all washed and spread to dry, she slipped into the pool herself. Shivery, delicious cold greeted her as she washed herself and her long hair and then swam blissfully back and forth in the confines of the bubbling little pool.

"If you don't come out, you'll become as wrinkled as a dried apple." Blinking golden waterdrops from her eyes, she saw Robert sitting on a rock by the little pool. She had not heard him come up, but then any noise would have been drowned out by her splashing.

She smiled at him mischievously. "Welsh women don't wrinkle, but Englishmen shrivel and turn blue. It's common knowledge."

"I have a mind to test that old wives' tale. Is your pool wide enough for two?"

Before she could answer, he was pulling off his clothes, and the splash he made as he entered the water made her sputter, but he stopped this by catching her around the waist. For his pains she caught his dark head and ducked him and then swam away, laughing. "English knights cannot swim very well, either."

Her laughter enchanted him. It shimmered like gold sunlight over the water, and when she turned to look at him, the green eyes under the tangle of wet golden curls were merry. To make her laugh again he pretended to chase her and let her swim joyfully away, but when she brushed against him, enticing him to still more water games, he caught her in his arms and pulled her close to him.

Instantly her arms circled his neck. He drew her legs between his and held her within the hard cradle of his thighs. "Time to show you that an English knight can do more than swim," he told her between kisses.

Her chuckle was warm and sensuous, and her mouth opened eagerly under his as he kissed her. The tip of her tongue teased his, and her hands stroked his shoulders and back and thighs, then curved about his taut muscled loins to caress his hardness. "Show me," she whispered.

He had meant to carry her back to the sun-warmed bank, but when he looked down into her eyes, they were almost black with passion, and when he moved to lift her in his arms, she stopped him. "No, here. Love me here."

She heard the deep male growl of pleasure as their mouths merged, touching, tasting, sucking with a passion that was almost primal. Then his mouth left hers and he lifted her clear of the water to taste her breasts, his tongue flicking the waterdrops from her nipples until she cried out with yearning. Instinctively her body moved against him, mimicking the ancient dance of love. This was madness, and she knew it and gloried in the draw of his mouth on her nipples, and the rough tenderness with which his body invaded hers. Swaying together against the current of the running water, he held her joined to him, and they kissed and touched and moved together until she cried out his name and drew deep within her the honey of his seed.

Even then he held her, and she leaned her forehead against his, feeling his warmth in the cool water until he began to carry her toward the shore. His cloak lay on the ferns and moss, and onto this he lowered her, then sat beside her to look down at her. Water glistened on her smooth young body, and her eyes were like emeralds. "Never did I believe you could be so lovely," he told her.

Her voice seemed to catch in her throat, and her mouth trembled. "Nor I that love could be so sweet," she whispered. As if unable to be apart from him even for a second, she began to stroke his arm, brushing away water droplets as she caressed him. "I never knew what loving meant," she told him softly. "Not until I met you. There is no joy in my life but you."

There were no words for what he felt. He kissed her, his mouth lingering on the sweet, much-kissed curve of her lower lip, and then he lay back on one arm, looking out across the golden brook. "This is what it feels like, then. I didn't know."

Understanding that he thought out loud, she rested her cheek against his arm and did not ask him what he meant. So close she felt to him now that there seemed no need of words between them. But in a moment he said, "To be happy, content, at peace, and yet alive and strong and glad of life. Now I know how it was to be alone before you came and filled my life."

"*'Dy chaun dy uda dy unic'*—it's said that God will provide for the lonely man. And for the lonely woman, too, my love." She had spoken without thinking, but as the old Welsh proverb left her lips, the brilliant gold of the day seemed to fade, and she felt suddenly cold. She looked swiftly up at him and saw that a shadow had also darkened his eyes, and cruel realization swept her that though everything had changed for her and for Robert, all else remained the same. He was English, she Welsh. "Wales is all, we are nothing : . ." God above, why should she remember this now?

"Gwenyth." The new note in his voice shattered her thoughts, but she did not dare look at him. "There's need to talk," he was saying.

She shrugged her slender shoulders helplessly. "What use? We are from different worlds, and even if we can forget it here, we can't continue to ignore it when we reach the real world."

"We'd have no need of the world if we were together. I have lands given to me by the king himself. There's a manor house and a hill there and ponds and broad meadows. We could be happy there."

Yearning, she listened to him, but she shook her head. "You know that can't be. In the eyes of the law, English and Welsh may not intermarry. But even if we scorned the law, there is another barrier between us. I'm Reese's wife."

"That could easily be mended." His voice was suddenly harsh.

She could read murder in his eyes, and fear for him caught her heart. "Promise me you won't seek him out!" she cried. "If you do, he'll lay some trap for you—I know the kind of man he is. He won't rest until he has killed you by some foul means."

He sensed her real terror and began to stroke her golden hair. "But I cannot let you go, my heart, so what can we do?"

A huge gold and black butterfly had settled beside Gwenyth, and she watched the fluttering velvet of its wings as she spoke. "Would you have me go with you to England?"

Understanding that to her England was an alien land full of cruel men who hated her people, he answered stoutly, "If not to England, then to France. Charles of France is your father's ally, isn't he? You'd be welcomed there."

"You would even leave England for me?" When he did not answer, she searched his face and saw the struggle etched harsh in his features. Yes, she thought, he would exile himself for her. He loved her that much. Her voice was even lower as she whispered, "I cannot let you do it, Robert. How long would you love me if I made you turn your back on your country and your prince?"

She saw the pain in his eyes, but his voice was firm. "You speak foolishly. I would do anything rather than lose you."

Fighting the tears that flooded her eyes, she threw her arms about him. Her voice was broken as she whispered, "Let's not talk about this now. We have each other and love and days and nights until we reach Cadwen Castle. To us the future doesn't matter. Today must be enough."

He heard the hidden tears in her voice, and he drew her hard against him to kiss her and call her every name of love he knew. When she grew still against him, he began to kiss her more passionately. Her breathing grew swift and shallow as she met his love with hers. "When you hold me like this, nothing matters," she told him, and he heard the echo of her cry: Today must be enough.

She had thought to have spent her passion, but now it filled her like the waters of the swift-flowing stream beside them. Her body sang and melted with his kisses and his touch. He knew her body so well already, and with exquisite care and skill he brought each sense alive. Her breasts, her flat, velvet belly, and her inner thighs, the honey of her womanhood, each was adored. But she would not let him have all the pleasure. She kissed his hard jaw, his throat, the flat male nipples, and the muscled belly, caressed his taut thighs and male desire. And when they came together, body against body and heart pounding against heart, she smiled up at him with adoration golden in her eyes and forced silent the fear of sorrow to come.

And then the pleasure of his body's invasion took away all thought.

Chapter Fifteen

GWENYTH BUSIED HERSELF CLEARING AWAY THE EVI-
dence of their camp. This dawn, mist hung over the
valley where they had spent the night, and it clung to
her clothes and turned her hair to dull gold. As she
worked she sang the song he had taught her in the
moonlight a few nights ago. "When my love is far
from me, my heart is as heavy as the stones on the
mountain . . ."

The song died as she heard his muffled footstep,
and she turned to him eagerly. As he caught her in
his arms she accused, "You left me as I slept. It was a
churlish thing to do, my lord knight."

"Not easy, either—as I've said before, you're
lovely sleeping." He stroked the fine line of her
cheek and forced cheerfulness into his voice. "I went

to reconnoiter. Now that we're away from the mountains, it's possible that Reese's men are on the lookout for us."

"Let them look. We will vanish into the mist." She chuckled as she rubbed her cheek against his shoulder, and he marveled at the difference in her. They had had six days together, long golden days and star-spangled nights, and in that short span of time he had seen Gwenyth become a woman full of laughter and confident happiness. They had stretched the days as long as possible, taking their time as they crossed the mountains and passed within sight of great Cader Idris itself. "You know that the great Merlyn is supposed to be sleeping here in Wales, don't you?" she was asking now. "Perhaps we can find him and he'll teach us real magic."

"I have no need for magic when you are with me." His arms tightened around her, and she sensed trouble. Drawing a little apart, she looked questioningly up into his face, and abruptly he said, "From that hill I saw the landmarks. Cadwen is very near. Another half day's journey, and you'll be with your sister."

"I've known these few days." The brightness went from her voice and she sighed. "I'm foolish. I did not want our time together to end."

Six days of talk and laughter and song, six nights in which to grow closer, love more. Six days and nights during which she had forced herself to forget what lay before them both—in the circle of his arms she told herself that nothing could take this time away.

But now he stepped away from her. "I see you've broken camp," he said in a carefully neutral voice. "We'd best start now while the mist shields us from any sentries Reese may have posted near Cadwen."

"Would you not like to eat first?" she asked, and he shook his head. Well, she was not hungry either. Silently she followed him to the horses and helped him saddle them. Usually he kissed her as he helped her mount, but today he did not and she knew why. He was preparing for the parting ahead of them, and so must she.

They were silent as they spurred their horses away from their camp and then followed the valley for several miles. But when, after an hour's ride, they began to climb one of the round hills that edged the valley, she could keep silent no longer. "These last six days have passed so very quickly," she began.

For Robert the words lacerated an already raw wound. If she were really happy to go to her sister, if he knew she would be protected, cherished as she deserved, he knew that it would not be such anguish to part from her. But her voice was unhappy, and he could not keep from asking, "Supposing your sister won't help you? Supposing she returns you to Reese instead?"

"Mairi has always been fond of me," she protested.

"But she is married, and her husband might not want to antagonize a powerful man like Reese." He knew he was being deliberately cruel, but he hoped that this might make her see the helplessness of her position.

Her voice was low. "Where else could I go? There is no one . . ."

"You know that isn't true." In spite of himself his voice filled with pain. If she listened to him, she would do as her treacherous heart bade her and go with him to the ends of the earth. She could almost feel the words of consent rising to her lips, words in which she wanted to tell him that she would turn traitor, become English, forget her loyalty to Glendower just to stay with him. And to add to her confusion he was saying, "I swear that I'll honor and love you and that my sword will protect you as long as there is breath in me."

His deep voice weakened her will still further, and afraid to stay and listen, she urged her horse forward and cantered up the side of the hill ahead of him. She blinked back unshed tears and told herself that she must think not of herself but of Wales—and of Robert. Sir Robert Marne was the crown prince's friend. He could be rich and honored in his own country providing he did not become entangled with a married Welshwoman who could bring him nothing but grief. If she knew it was for his sake, she could bear today's parting.

By the time she had reached the crest of the hill, she had her emotions under control again. As she waited for him to catch up with her, the sun broke through the mist, dazzling her with a scene of rare beauty. The summit of the hill was full of summer-green trees, and some distance away from them a small lake shimmered dreamily. Far below in the rolling countryside, the Dovey curved like silver ribbon.

He had come up beside her and reined in his horse, and they were both silent, watching butterflies ride shafts of sunlight and listening to the busy birdsong and to the drone of summer insects in the hill grass. She could not bear to have this last morning she would spend with Robert be so lovely, and she began to spur her horse forward so as to leave the place, but he stopped her. "From here we can see everything that moves or crawls below us or on the hillside," he said. "It's a safe place to have breakfast." The thought of food nauseated her and she said so, but he persisted. "There may be no other chance to eat. You'd not want to appear at your sister's castle fainting with hunger."

She knew he was right and silently followed him to the rim of the small lake. But when they neared the water, she exclaimed aloud, "Look at those stones in a circle! Robert, it's a fairy ring."

Eyebrows raised, he followed her pointing finger. "I thought you didn't believe in magic."

She reproved him. "Don't laugh. It is near Midsummer's eve, that most magical of nights. The people of Eyri believe in the power of the little people, and even Dafyd puts out a saucer of milk for them so that they won't rust his armor or take the bright sharpness from his sword."

He couldn't help grinning. "I can see old Dafyd tiptoeing about with a saucer of milk. But you didn't answer my question. Do you believe?"

She hesitated. "I believe in the magic of these hills. There's a power here that was old when Arthur ruled in Camelot. I think it sleeps now while Wales is torn with war and violence, but one day it will make the country bloom again."

He dismounted as she spoke and came around to stand by her stirrup, looking up at her. "Perhaps the power will let us rest, too. That is, if you dare to stay here near the fairy ring."

She leaned down into his arms as he helped her from the horse, and for a long moment he held her pressed tightly against him. This time it was she who drew away, saying, "I think we had better eat before it gets much hotter. By noon this hilltop must sizzle with the heat."

While she took out a portion of cold hare left over from last night's food and then searched along the grass-lipped lake for young leaves of dandelion and other greens to go with their meal, he saw to the horses and watched the remnants of mist clear in the valley. His thoughts were clear and precise until the moment when he must escort Gwenyth up to her sister's castle, but he could not bear to think past that moment of parting. It was like being sentenced to eternal damnation.

"Robert, look!" She sounded pleased, and when he turned he saw her hurrying toward him with hands brimful of wild strawberries. "I found a patch of them by the stones. Perhaps the little people mean them as a gift."

He wanted nothing more than to kiss her berry-red lips, but he held back. "Cold coney will be tasteless next to your berries. Let's see if the lake will yield us some fat trout instead."

The waters were well stocked and the fish eager to nibble on the cold meat he used for bait, and while she picked more strawberries, Robert caught four fair-sized fish, and they grilled them over a small fire. Later they ate by the edge of the lake, and as they divided the strawberries Gwenyth said, "This place reminds me of the hills near Cader Idris. It was a little like Eden there. I wish that you could have seen it."

"Perhaps I will someday." He kept his voice under tight rein. "You may return there also."

"I don't want to go." She whispered. "No one I love lives there anymore, and there would be nothing left for me. No Eden, no glory, only the empty valleys and the lonely mountain."

Now he couldn't hold back the words. "Don't you think there'd be loneliness in my life also?" he asked. "The only thing I fear is to live my life without seeing you or touching you or holding you in my arms. God knows that I do not have the courage."

He jerked to his feet and moved away from her with the stiff-limbed slowness of a wounded man. "Love," she mourned, "you know there is nothing else either of us can do."

Swiftly as thought he turned to catch her by the hands, pulling her up into his arms. Her unresisting body melded against his, and without her conscious will, her head tipped back for his kiss. Their mouths met with aching force, and she clung to him as he held her so tightly that she could hardly breathe. Nor did she need to breathe to delight in the familiar textures of his lips and tongue. The world around them vanished in a vortex of desire.

Then he stepped away. Loosening her hands from around his neck, he held them very tightly for a moment and then returned them to her sides. "We'd better go," he told her.

She nodded, but neither of them moved. Standing apart, they looked into each other's eyes with the bleak, lost look of starving people. Gwenyth knew that in that moment they were both trying to store enough for a lifetime of memory. And she would remember—her eyes followed lovingly the thick wave of his dark hair, the arch of his brows, and the intensity of his gray eyes. She held him with her gaze until he shook his head as if to clear it. Now she knew he would walk away from her. "Not yet," she pleaded. "My love, not yet."

"We must." But when she threw her arms around his neck, his own closed around her fiercely, and he lifted her up and carried her to the grassy edge of the lake. Kissing her eyes and mouth and throat, he went down on one knee and took her with him, cradling her against him before he lowered her to the sun-warmed ferns. And while he kissed her soft mouth and worked loose her clothing and his, one thought formed in his mind. This would be the last time that he would love her. The last time he would ever love.

She knew it, too, and her mind was filled with sunshine and shadow, joy and pain. Today she did not try to filter out the sadness but let it come, let her heart swell with love for him and the bittersweet knowledge that this love must last throughout her life. "Let this be enough," she whispered against his lips. "Make it last, my only love."

They were as deliberate as possible. When their clothing had been discarded and they lay together in the fragrant sunshine, he did not begin to caress her until he had drawn the heady honey of her lips for long, delicious moments. Then his hands began to touch the sensitive, secret parts of her body, to caress the smooth slopes of her breasts without yet touching the erect nipples, to stroke the long line of her thighs and legs without trespassing farther. With each touch and kiss he loved her, and she in turn returned this love, smoothing the musculature of his back and his hard buttocks, letting butterfly-light hands rove over the backs of his side and over his chest and loins.

"My lady of flowers." She smiled as he spoke his name for her, and then cried softly with pleasure as at last his fingers brushed her nipples. "Your breasts are honeyed roses." Closing her eyes, she felt the descent of his mouth, the sensuous curl of his tongue on her areolas and then the ardent draw of his mouth. Then lower, kissing, tasting, his mouth drew tendrils of fire over smooth belly and concavity of navel to the secrets of her womanhood.

She would shatter against him, crumble into a thousand pieces of desire. Her hips were moving against him as she tugged weakly at his crisp, thick hair. "Not yet," she begged him. "I must love you, too."

Sun glimmered in her eyes and the dark shadow of wind-kissed trees swung above. She knelt above him as he lay on the grass beside her, and she kissed his eyes and his lips, his throat, and the tickling crispness of his body fur, the coolness of flat male nipples, the hard play of muscles that ran from broad chest to lean belly. Passionately, tenderly, she tasted the salt of his skin and gloried in his male beauty, and then bent to the strong, tense thighs and hard male power, letting her eager mouth express her love.

His arms trembled with the effort of control as he lifted her to sit astride him, and she took him deep within her, her body welcoming and sheathing his hard strength. Then they stayed still together, kissing and touching, and she knew that she would remember everything about this last loving. His hard fullness in her, the touch of his hands and the sweetness of his mouth. This she would remember.

Their bodies moved together slowly at first and then faster and then swifter still. And as they shattered together and soared together into the heat of the sun, she heard him echo the words in her heart. "I will always love you. I will love you till I die."

As though they could not bear to linger where there had been so much joy, they left their hilltop within the hour and made for Cadwen Castle. They made good time. The sun was directly overhead when Gwenyth caught her first glimpse of the high barbican that protected the castle gate.

He reached across the distance that separated them and took her hand. No words were needed, and as they rode they smiled at each other. Sorrow they would know, but not quite yet, and each moment they spent together must be savored. They rode close together as furrowed fields now came in sight.

"Mairi said that their people planted wheat and oats," Gwenyth explained, "but closer to the castle walls there are fields of flax. It's because the soil is fertile and moist from the river nearby, I suppose, but I remember thinking it was the flax made the fairest green I had seen."

But not as fair as her eyes, he thought, and wondered almost dispassionately if everything he saw from this moment of parting would remind him of her. Aloud he said, "Tell me about Cadwen Castle."

"It is a grand place. The manor house is half timbered and there is frosted glass in the windows. The outbuildings are made of stone and brick. Mairi has planted a garden full of roses around the manor, and there is also a place for herbs." She tried to force enthusiasm into her voice, knowing he asked about Cadwen Castle so as to reassure himself about her future life. "There are meadows full of livestock —sheep and small lambs, and cows and pigs. We should see them as soon as we pass the fields."

As she spoke they came up to the first tilled plot of land. Wheat stood in rows of summer wealth, and farther on oats bowed their rich, tasseled heads. Robert looked around him in surprise. "Where are your sister's peasants?"

The fields were still. She could hear crows cawing in the distance but nothing else. "Perhaps they have stopped to eat their noonday meal," she said uncertainly.

"They'd be resting under the trees." He reined in his horse and looked about him, noting that willow baskets filled with drying strips of fruit were upset and that hoes and wooden buckets lay scattered about as if their owners had flung them down in haste. "Something's wrong."

They spurred their horses forward past tilled fields which lay deserted in the sun. Now they could see the barbican gate clearly. "No one on the walls and the gate is open. Besides—sweet Christ!"

On the exclamation he caught Gwenyth's reins and turned her horse around but not in time to stop her from seeing how the fields nearest the castle had been ravaged, trampled into the ground. A fire had been set in one wheatfield, and the smell of fire and soot clung to the place. But this was not all. Beyond the burned fields a hoard of crows were cawing and flapping their wings over the bodies of slaughtered sheep and cattle. Sickly Gwenyth saw that the grass was sticky red with their blood.

"The people who did this may be nearby." Robert's hard voice jerked her back from the horror before her. "Quickly—we must ride back to the hills."

"I can't—I must find out what's happened to Mairi and the baby."

Pulling her reins free from him, she wheeled her mount around and galloped back toward the castle, but he,was beside her at once saying, "Let me go first, and if there is trouble, ride back the way we came and don't look back."

She was too horror-struck to argue, and as she followed him that horror mounted even higher. Among the trampled flax fields and around the wooden bridge that linked the castle to the road lay the bodies of the castle guard and of men and women. So many bodies—all lying still in the hot sun. Her brain reeled. Had everyone from the castle been killed?

She followed him across the bridge and then they both stopped just inside the wide-open gates. The once stately manor house had been gutted and burned. Each window had been smashed, and glass littered the charred ground. The outbuildings were smoldering ruins also, and there was no sound beyond the crows' cawing and the brittle crack of broken glass under their horses' hooves. The place seemed deserted.

"They can't all be dead, they can't." Frantically she guided her snorting horse farther into this scene of devastation. "Mairi," she called, "Mairi, are you here? It's Gwenyth . . ."

There was no answer, and Robert dismounted and with drawn sword began to check the nearest buildings, praying that he would not find the bodies of

Gwenyth's half sister and child. She dismounted also and followed him, and he said, "Perhaps they were warned and escaped."

As he spoke there was a rustling noise nearby. Pulling Gwenyth behind him, Robert challenged, "Whoever you are—come out—at once, if you want to live."

This time there was a sob. "Mercy—have mercy, your lordship, don't kill me."

Gwenyth gasped as an old woman crawled out of the shadows on her knees. "Dear heaven—it's Mairi's old nurse, Blodwen Rhys." She fell on her own knees beside the sobbing woman. "Blodwen, tell me what has happened here. . . ."

Blearily the old woman's eyes focused on Gwenyth. "Oh, my lady, I was sick and in bed and could not run away fast enough when they came."

Robert's voice was stern. "Who are 'they,' old woman?"

Blodwen Rhys's voice was so low that Gwenyth had to bend to catch it. "The earl of Stoake and his men came last night, killing and looting and burning. May the English burn in hell for it forever—it was they that did this."

Chapter Sixteen

"THE EARL OF STOAKE!" HOW MANY TIMES HAD THE people of Eyri cursed that cruel name? "Where is Mairi and the babe?" Gwenyth cried.

The old woman groaned. "They managed to escape with the lord and some of the servants while the men-at-arms fought. But there were too many of the English. I heard our people screaming and running. Some got away, but many were killed. Others were taken prisoner. Children, too."

Robert's knuckles were white as they gripped the hilt of his sword. "And you're sure they were Stoake's men?"

Blodwen nodded. "I heard them boasting that their master could not be beaten now that there was someone on their side who was strong in Welsh magic."

"What did he mean by that?" Gwenyth demanded. Through the horror she already felt, a new and insidious fear was spreading. "Why would they say such a thing, Blodwen?"

The old woman shook her head helplessly. "I don't know, my lady. I just remember the soldiers bragging that they had a spy who knew all of Glendower's plans. They said that this man was working behind the scenes to destroy Wales . . ."

He saw the dawning horror in her eyes and, taking her suddenly cold hands in his, drew her some distance from Blodwen. "What are you thinking?" he demanded.

Unhappily she said, "You told me that you had gone to the earl's castle after your escape from Eyri. And you are the only Englishman who knows my father's secrets and his 'Welsh magic.'"

Deny it, she pleaded silently, but instead his eyes turned to gray ice. "My thanks for your trust in me," he told her bitterly.

"You are English—your allegiance is to England." When he still did not deny this, something in her heart seemed to shatter. She turned away from him thinking of the names of her father's allies, the secret passage to Eyri through the Cliff of the Old Ones. Had he given away all these secrets? A moan of desolation was wrenched from her as she realized that he must have done so. Had it all been a lie, then?

She didn't realize that she'd spoken aloud until he caught her by the arms, drawing her some distance from the old woman. "Blood of Christ, girl, have sense. Why would I have brought you here if I'd known Stoake's plans to attack the castle?"

Some note in that deep voice could yet make her hope. "You didn't want to bring me here. You wanted me to go to England with you." She saw his eyes grow wary, and her last hope died. He had sworn to love and honor and protect her all his life. Lies—all lies. "You see," she told him bitterly, "you do not deny that you are an enemy of Wales."

Naked emotion hardened his face for a moment, and she read anger and savage hurt in his eyes. Then his features grew impassive and his hands fell away from her shoulders. "You cannot stay here, whatever you believe. I'll take you and the old woman to a place of safety."

Before she could answer, Blodwen gave a cry. "My lady, hide! The English are coming back."

Several riders were coming down the road. Sunlight flared against steel helmets and armor, and the colors that waved above them were those of the earl of Stoake. "Blodwen, we must hurry!" she cried. "Mount this horse and I will take the other and we'll outrun them."

Robert caught her arm and pulled her back. "If you run they'll shoot you down." She struggled to escape his hard grip as he added urgently, "Cover your face with the hood of your mantle. You and the old woman must remain silent whatever they say. Let me do the answering. These men know me."

She wanted to tell him she'd had enough of his help, but she realized that she and Blodwen were helpless, that they must do as he said and trust that he would not give them up to Stoake's followers. She instructed Blodwen to do as Robert ordered and from the shadow of her hood she watched the hated Englishmen ride over the bridge and through the ruined castle gate. There were fourteen of them, twelve men-at-arms led by two knights in full armor, and when they saw Robert and the two women they stopped and stared.

One of the knights, a middle-aged fellow with sandy hair and drooping eyelids, spoke haughtily. "Fellow, what do you here? This land belongs by law of conquest to the earl of Stoake."

With an effort of will Gwenyth remained silent and motionless, but Blodwen glared at the knight and muttered curses under her breath as the other Englishman, a pleasant-faced, chubby young man, protested. "That's no 'fellow,' Ulrick, it's Sir Robert Marne. He always has managed to appear unexpectedly and in fine company." He cast an admiring and curious eye toward Gwenyth, adding, "You remember that he rides far and wide on the prince's business."

"Then why isn't he with Prince Henry?" Ulrick retorted. "You and I both know that the crown prince is visiting the castles along the border." He paused and added, "What's your business here, and who's the woman with you?"

Insult was clearly meant. "I'll ignore the first question," Robert retorted. "As for the lady, she is with me and that is enough."

The sandy-haired knight frowned, but remained silent, obviously cowed by the steel in Robert's voice. The cheerful young knight chuckled. "Do not mind Sir Ulrick. Tell me, what adventures have you had in the name of the prince? They must be fine ones to involve so lovely a lady."

"Later, friend Andrew, for I must leave at once." Robert gestured toward the horses, adding, "Mount your horse, my lady. Your servant can ride with me."

Gwenyth turned to gesture to Blodwen, and as she did so, the hood of her mantle slipped. As she hastened to pull it back over her face, one of the men-at-arms swore loudly. "I know who the woman is!" he cried, and she looked up into the incredulous face of the little guardsman, Thomas Carpenter. "She's Glendower's daughter."

There was a moment of almost total stillness, and Robert thought fast. He could throw Gwenyth into the saddle, mount after her and ride. Perhaps he would take them by enough surprise to make it through the gate—but there the odds turned against him. It would not help Gwenyth if he were felled by an arrow and she left alone and defenseless in the power of the earl.

"The witch!" Sir Ulrick's sleepy eyes seemed ready to pop out of his head. "But how did you accomplish this, man? To catch a witch is not an easy task." He added suspiciously, "But why didn't you tell us this at once?"

"You forget that I'm on the prince's business and need not tell you anything." Robert could feel Gwenyth's outrage as he added, "I was taking this prize of war to His Highness."

Again he began to walk toward the horses, praying that she would understand what he did and would play along. But before he could put this to a test, Sir Ulrick spoke sharply. "So fine a prize should be taken to the earl. He will know what to do with her."

Taken to the earl of Stoake—to the man whose name filled all Welshmen with rage and fear. "The cruel earl," she heard old Blodwen groan beside her. "My lady, if we go to his castle, we're lost. He'll torture the both of us to learn more about your father, the prince. Can't we do anything?"

What could they do? In a whirl of fear and revulsion, she heard Robert's deep voice protesting, "She is not Stoake's prisoner, Ulrick. The prince has ordered me to bring her to him."

Sleepy eyes narrowed. "Is there some reason that you want to spirit this woman away? Perhaps you want to keep her to yourself, eh? Does she warm your bed?"

With effort, Robert kept his hand free of his sword hilt. Nothing could be gained by confrontation now. The plump Sir Andrew was saying peaceably, "It may serve your purpose to bring Glendower's daughter with you to Stoake Castle, Robert. It's rumored that the prince will be riding there soon to parley with the earl."

It cost an effort to smile, but he did so and even forced relief into his voice. "In that case, you're right. We'll take the woman to the earl and await the prince's pleasure there." He turned to Gwenyth. "You must ready yourself to ride, my lady."

To have trusted him again and again been played false . . . In a low voice she said, "I'll never forgive you for this. I should have tried to escape. Better to die than be betrayed again by you."

"What of the old woman?" Sir Andrew was asking doubtfully.

Robert shrugged. "She's old and not quite right in the head. Why burden ourselves with a servant of no importance? Let her go."

Blodwen fell to her knees, and Gwenyth tried to smile down at her. "You'll be safe when you find my sister's people. And—and they may come back and need you." She bent to kiss the weeping woman. "God be with you."

But there could be no God, Gwenyth thought numbly as she mounted her horse. No God could watch unmoved as scenes of such horror and devastation were played out in the world. She tried to curse Robert in her heart as two men-at-arms fell in to guard her, but she could not find words in the empty desolation that filled her. She had felt this way after Robert had saved her from the Black Pass. Why had he saved her then only to betray her now?

The answer came to her as they rode away from the ruined castle. Watching him riding and laughing with Sir Andrew, she knew that he had kept her safe because she was important to his prince, because she was one more weapon to use against Owen Glendower. Had it been his intention all along to hand her over to Prince Hal? Within the freezing numbness, she felt as if she would go mad.

They rode southward through the rest of the day

and long after dark. They did not stop for rest or water, but Gwenyth didn't care. Sick horror made her deaf and blind even to discomfort and exhaustion. Nor was she aware of the falling darkness or the fact that they had come to the English border until one of her guards shouted. Then, looking up, she saw in the near distance the massive walls and barbican gate of Stoake Castle.

"We're almost there and you'll be able to rest." She had not heard Robert ride up beside her. "You look weary," he added, and she heard the concern in his voice. "I'm sorry for this long ride, Gwenyth."

Anger such as she had never felt seared her. "What need for concern, lord knight?" she cried at him. "Aren't prisoners meant to suffer—especially Welsh prisoners?"

"Listen to me—" But now he heard the guardsmen mutter about him and fell silent, cursing the fact that he could not speak to her alone. The men-at-arms were all listening, and Thomas Carpenter leaned forward.

"Just a few short weeks ago, Sir Robert, it was you and I who were prisoners of the Welsh. I can feel the lashes on my back still."

The men around her muttered, and one of Gwenyth's guards said, "Hanging's too good for Glendower's daughter."

"Remember that she's the prince's prisoner." Robert's voice was hard. "She's to be treated with care—aye, and with respect. She'll help end this war with Wales."

"Never, Englishman," she spat at him. "Leave me, now. I do not wish to ride with you."

As she spoke there was another shout, and now she saw that above them towered massive black walls on which torches glimmered like feral eyes. The ominous, threatening shadow of the enemy stronghold's donjon loomed dark in the shadows, and she repressed an involuntary shudder as the barbican gate opened and a drawbridge creaked down to let them in. For a moment she drew in the stench of smoking torches, the sour smells of metal and wood, and then her horse's hooves echoed on the wooden drawbridge and the great gate shut behind her with a clang. God help me now, she thought.

Knowing she must not show fear before her captors, she reined in her horse with the others and looked about her. Here was not the disordered wealth of Reese's holdings but a castle and outbuildings laid out with military precision. The place bristled with men-at-arms, and she could see them standing guard on the walls. As grooms ran to seize the knights' horses, the captain of the guard saluted and then bawled orders that the earl was to be told of the noble knights' return.

"Say also that we bring a prisoner. Tell him we have the Welsh witch." Sir Ulrick's voice was unctuous with self-congratulation. "Aye, it's Glendower's daughter that we bring back with us."

Instantly there was a commotion in the castle yard. "Her sorcerer father killed my brother," a male voice hissed. "Hang the witch or burn her before she can work more of her evil."

A babel of voices rose at this, and someone threw a handful of small stones. They struck Gwenyth's horse, who snorted and reared, and as she controlled it she saw torchlight flash red on Robert's sword. Riding his horse between the soldiers and Gwenyth, he snapped, "The next man who raises his hand dies." Steely-gray eyes went from man to man. "She is the prince's prisoner, and any man who tries to harm her will answer to me."

"Enough." The new voice was the coldest she had ever heard and sliced through the tumult. Gwenyth saw a tall figure limned in the open entrance of the castle and knew this was the earl. "So, my knights have returned with guest and booty." Though he stood in silhouette and his face could not be seen, Gwenyth had the impression that he was watching her avidly. "Sir Robert Marne, you and the prize you bring are most welcome here."

"My lord." His deep voice was courteous but noncommittal. "I had not hoped for the honor of your company. I'd intended to ride on to meet His Highness the Prince of Wales."

"Nevertheless, I am glad you are here." Now her keen ears noted the gloating pleasure which accented the coldness in the earl's voice. "Come in, noble knights," he then added. "And bring your prisoner with you."

He strode back into the building. Robert would have helped Gwenyth dismount, but she forestalled him by accepting the aid of one of her guards. Nor did she look at him as she walked, still escorted by her two guards, in front of the other two knights. Prisoner she might be, she thought bitterly, but she wanted no part of her captor.

Eyes straight ahead, she climbed the steps that led to the entrance of the earl's stately dwelling place and into his huge stone hall. It was hung with richly worked tapestries and lit with a hundred blazing oil lamps, and inside as out everything was clean and orderly. The rushes that matted the floor were fresh and sweet-scented, the huge wooden tables were scrubbed down and polished smooth, and on the walls weapons and armor blazed with reflected light. Several knights and attendants stood or sat in this hall, and at one end of the room, on a raised dais much like the one her father had had at Eyri, sat the earl.

Somehow she had pictured him to be in the prime of his youth, but now she saw that he was an old man, silver-haired and gaunt. He was dressed in the height of fashion in black hose and a velvet cote-hardie with dagged sleeves cut back to show a scarlet tunic. Both coat and tunic glittered with gems, but above the finery his face was narrow and intolerant with a high, flaring nose, a narrow gash of a mouth, and pale blue eyes that were fixed on Gwenyth.

"So this is the Welsh witch." Long, nervous fingers tapped the arms of his gilt chair. "An earldom should be yours, Robert Marne, for capturing accursed Glendower's daughter."

"I act only on my prince's orders and for his pleasure." Robert spoke with great courtesy, but the

underlying firmness in the words was unmistakable.
"It is for him to decide what to do with the lady, my
lord earl."

Angrily the old man leaned forward. "Do you
bandy words with me, sirrah? Here my word is law,
and I order you to surrender your prisoner to me.
There are many questions I would put to this fair-
haired sorceress. Before I have done with her, she
will tell me all the secrets of her father."

There was no misinterpreting his meaning. It took
all of Robert's control to bow and pretend regret. "I
do not seek to flout your authority, my lord. I only
bring to your attention the fact that the lady is the
prince's prisoner."

"'Lady' you name her? Foul witch, I say.
Woman," he then added sharply, "on pain of the
torture that awaits you, confess what you know of
your father's alliance. I need to know how many yet
hold true to Glendower's mad scheme to unite
Wales."

Answering anger rose in her. Remembering all
those from Eyri who had died at this man's hands,
remembering the stolen children and the slain servants and the poor people at Cadwen Castle, she
forgot to be wise. "The scheme is not mad, my
lord," she retorted. "All loyal Welshmen believe in
their prince, Owen Glendower ap Gryffth Vychon."

Her voice was clear and gave no quarter. Robert
knew she little cared for her peril, and he felt both
fear for her and admiration as she continued, "My
father is the true Prince of Wales, and he will

succeed one day in ridding the country of you English invaders. That is all I have to tell you."

A terrible silence echoed through the hall. Behind her, she could hear young Sir Andrew's gasp of surprise and see the uneasy looks of the other knights. A dull red crept under the earl's haggard cheeks and stained his forehead as he commanded, "Take her to the dungeon. See that she talks—and quickly—or kill her. I care not which."

With God's mercy, she would die quickly, she thought, but before the men-at-arms could take her by the arms, Robert sighed. "But, my lord," he protested, and the change in his voice was so great that she turned to stare at him. He sounded peevish, aggrieved. "My lord earl, I beg a moment. You say, 'kill her,' so easily, but do you know the miseries I have undergone to find this woman for our prince? The pains with which I managed to infiltrate Glendower's Eyri—and the misery of digesting several weeks of Welsh food." Sir Ulrick gave a nervous little titter and Robert continued gloomily, "Food, my lord, that you would not feed a good English pig. My belly was seized with pains for days. And on top of this, since I was supposedly a minstrel, I was forced to sing—in Welsh."

Sir Andrew was grinning. "But you enjoy a song, do you not? And have a good voice, Robert."

"Maybe so, but no one can sing in that foul country."

Gwenyth glared at him, but his humor was causing laughter. Sir Ulrick grinned and even the earl was smiling. "You are much to be pitied, Sir Robert. Then it was your duty to turn songster?"

"I was so commanded by my prince. I swore to His Highness that I'd deliver the woman unharmed. But," he added hastily, "I relinquish her to Your Lordship. It's enough that I don't have to play the minstrel for Welshmen who stink of goats and sheep."

A guffaw rang through the hall and the earl actually laughed aloud. Now beyond indignation, Gwenyth listened in disgust as Robert continued to jeer at Eyri, its people, the mountains, and especially the Welsh speech. "One cannot speak it without a potato in the mouth, my lord. Where else in all the world could one find words and names like *Merysydd, Hela* or *Ogof ddu?* And the songs—blood of Christ, it's enough to make a man plug up his ears. If you'd like to experience a tenth of what I've suffered, you should hear one of those Welsh ballads."

By this time the company was shaking with laughter, and the old earl had forgotten Gwenyth for the moment. "Sing one of these songs to us now," he commanded. "It would be rare entertainment."

Robert bowed. "Gladly, my lord. My harp is in my saddlebag, but a servant can get it." At a nod from the earl, one of the servants ran out quickly and returned with the familiar five-stringed harp. "Now you'll hear the kind of drivel I was forced to sing."

He broke into a Welsh ballad extolling the deeds of ancient heroes, but today he parodied the words, mispronouncing, twisting, to make the English laugh. Gwenyth wished she did possess magic for one moment so that she could silence him. But as she stared hatingly at him, she started. There was no mockery or merriment in the depths of Robert's eyes, only a steely resolve she knew well. And as her own eyes widened, she realized that the Welsh words had changed to Merryn's secret tongue.

"Demand to see the prince." That much she could make out, but his pronunciation of the hill language was not expert and she missed the rest. Besides, after everything, did he think she would trust him? But he was still singing. "It's your one chance. Say you'll tell him everything. That if you are not allowed to see him, you will never speak." Then he returned to Welsh and yet his eyes held hers. Trust me, they said.

She would be mad to take him at his word. She looked away from him, but still the smoky-gray gaze stayed imprinted in her mind. She could hear the old earl laughing, and she knew he would rejoice to see her torment. But would Robert Marne's prince be any better?

The song ended, but the hall still rang with laughter. "Music for crows and goats, my lord. Now you see what I suffered to bring this woman to the prince."

The amusement in Robert's voice seemed so real that she hesitated even though she knew that she must decide now or the chance—if any—would be lost. As the old earl nodded, chuckling, she made her decision. Raising her voice she called, "And it is to the prince that he will hand me, lord earl. Only to him will I speak. Otherwise, you may torment me and make me die by inches but I will not say a word."

Her defiant words echoed and died, and inwardly she felt despair. But before it could take root, Robert said, "The Welsh are like that—I was afraid of this, my lord. When I took her prisoner, she swore on the dragon of Wales not to use her magic against me as long as she was the prince's prisoner. But once she is out of my hands, that oath goes by the wayside. . . ." He paused, significantly, and several of the earl's knights surreptitiously crossed themselves. "Surely for the sake of England it would be better to keep her for the prince?"

He was smiling as he spoke, but inwardly he was tensed for action. If the earl refused, there was nothing for it but to fight. He had no illusions as to his chances if it came to that, but at the least Gwenyth would not end her life undefended.

Clearly the earl was not happy. He stroked his thin line of mouth and his eyes were hating. "I command here, sirrah," he snarled.

I have lost, Robert thought. Almost imperceptibly he nodded at Gwenyth to be ready for trouble. But then the earl continued. "Still, I wish to please His Grace the Prince of Wales in everything. If this woman is such an important prisoner to him, let her be kept alive and well until he arrives."

Greatly daring, Robert spoke again. "Alive and well and in comfort, is that not so, my lord? Let the Welshwoman taste real English hospitality. If more Welshwomen felt such comfort, they might persuade their men to surrender to us without striking another blow."

She was aware of how much he hazarded for her safety. Like blood rushing to a heart long numbed, it began to hurt again. Did she dare believe in him with the horror of Cadwen Castle still fresh in her mind?

The earl was laughing. "You are a saucy knave, Sir Robert Marne, but your song amused me and that puts me in a mood to grant you what you wish." He turned to Gwenyth's guards. "Take her to the room in the turret and let some servant bring her food and drink."

Robert did not dare look at her as she was led away, but his fingers still strummed lightly on the harp and he sang a few more outlandish words as if for the company's entertainment. But Gwenyth, walking down the hall, heard and understood. Above the laughter in the great hall he sang to her in Merryn's secret tongue: "The game is not yet played out. Trust me, my lady of flowers. I love you more than my own life."

Chapter Seventeen

HORNS BLEW IN THE FAR DISTANCE AND WERE AN-
swered by those within the castle walls. From the
turret where she was imprisoned, Gwenyth watched
a small troop of mounted men approaching from the
southwest. Even from this distance, her keen eyes
singled out one man on a gray horse who wore no
armor and who rode slightly ahead of the others. She
guessed that this was England's crown prince.

A blast of trumpets far below in the courtyard
signaled the opening of the castle gates, and the
magnificently dressed earl of Stoake rode out with
his knights to greet Prince Hal. Robert rode with
them, and she leaned over the lip of the window to
see him better. As she did so he turned toward the
turret and looked up.

Even at this distance she could feel the intensity of

that gaze. "I love you more than life." The words he had sung to her last night formed involuntarily in her heart as he rode past the turret and out of the gates, and she watched his progress in a turmoil of emotions. She had Robert's word that she could trust the Prince of Wales, and she had no choice but to believe him.

The prince's party was nearer now, and she could clearly make him out. He was a tall and well-built young man, and to her surprise he was dressed simply in buff-colored riding clothes. Gwenyth watched the prince gesture to Robert to ride at his side as the earl led his royal guest back to the castle, and she told herself that now all she could do was wait.

She didn't have to wait long. Before an hour had passed, the dour old woman who had attended her since her imprisonment entered the turret room. "His Grace wants to see you," she told Gwenyth. "The earl commands you to ready yourself for an audience with the prince at once."

Gwenyth sighed. "There's little I can do to get ready." Last night she had begged for and been allowed water in which to bathe, but there had been no way to wash or mend her dusty and torn riding habit. "I hope that the prince will forgive my lack of proper clothing."

Grudgingly the old woman placed a bundle on the narrow bed by the window. "This was sent to you by order of Sir Robert Marne. He sent for these clothes yesternight."

After so long it was a delight to dress in new

clothes. First came fine linen undergarments and over these a long, gored gown of pale green silk. Next came a sleeveless hip-length cotehardie of deep emerald satin, and the old woman clicked her tongue in disapproval. "Only fine ladies are allowed to wear silks and satins," she complained. "I never heard of a prisoner being allowed such luxury."

Gwenyth thought of the woman's words as she braided her long hair and wrapped the thick golden plaits about her head. It was true that she was still a prisoner of the English, and she had been summoned before an English prince. This fact was further brought home when two ar..ed guardsmen escorted her to her audience. She sensed their hostility as they led her down the winding stairs and paused near a large solar. "The prince will see you in this chamber," one of them stiffly informed her.

Her heart had begun to beat loudly as she stepped into the room and found herself bathed in sunlight. The windows had been flung open to the golden afternoon, and sun streamed in, together with the scents of July: ripening wheat, late roses, the green fragrance of woods and meadows. For a moment she could only blink at the brightness in the room, and then she saw Robert standing by the window.

Sunlight found the coppery highlights in his dark hair, and she had a moment to note that for the first time she saw him dressed to fit his rank. His broad shoulders seemed to strain the elegance of a wide-sleeved cotehardie of gray frieze, and matching gray hose outlined the hard-muscled length of his legs. A jeweled chain around his neck flashed with light as he strode across the room to take her hands. "You've been treated well?" he asked her worriedly.

So close to him, she found it was hard to speak. Hard, too, to think, and she could only nod as his eyes caressed her. "There's much to say and little time when we can be alone. Do you trust me, Gwenyth?"

Wales is everything, we are nothing. The old words filled her mind as she replied, "Yesterday, I was sure that you were the spy of whom Blodwen spoke."

"And now?" Looking down into her troubled eyes, he saw that she tried to smile.

"I don't know," she answered honestly. "I only know that I love you. And yet, I—I fear for Wales."

He lifted her hands to his lips. "I rejoice in your love."

His gentleness confused her further. She wanted to throw herself into his arms and tell him that she trusted him without reserve, and yet the memory of Cadwen Castle ravaged by his countrymen held her back. As she hesitated, there was a new step in the solar, and a tall, brown-haired young man walked into the room.

Robert bowed deeply. "Your Grace," he said.

There was a dry humor in the young man's voice. "Please, Robin, no more of these 'Your Graces.' I have been subjected to such pomp and ceremony by Stoake that I think I will never recover." He added, "So this is Gwenyth of Wales."

His hazel eyes were smiling, and so was the mouth above the cleft chin. She sank into a low curtsy, and he took her hands and lifted her to her feet, saying, "I beg you, no. There is no need for Owen Glendower's daughter to bow to me."

He wasn't mocking her. He meant what he said. "I thank you for seeing me, Your Grace," she began.

"Robin requested it, and I seldom question his judgment." He turned to smile at the silent, gray-eyed man. "We've been good friends for years, have we not, Robin Marne?"

"I wanted you to hear the truth concerning Wales from her lips." Dropping royal protocol, Robert spoke earnestly. "Glendower has no magic, Hal, and neither does Gwenyth. I want you to hear what holds the Welsh alliance together. She'll explain to you that the only magic in Wales is that of love of freedom and country."

As he had done last night, he held her eyes and willed her to understand. He saw misgivings and then surprise and finally realization flood her face as she understood what he asked. Joy filled him as she nodded firmly. "I'll do my best," she promised.

The prince said, "Then start on this point of magic. For years I've heard about Glendower's powers. How his forces melt away into morning mist and then come screaming down from the hills to attack and conquer—how he causes floods to inflame rivers that swallow up our knights and their supplies. I've heard such tales from many hard-bitten veterans."

"If my father possessed such powers, don't you think he would have driven the English out of our country? Sir Robert is right, Your Grace. That kind of magic doesn't exist. My father and I, too, understand things about our country—the terrain, the changing weather, even the way rivers flood at certain times of the year. He uses this knowledge to his advantage, that is all."

The young prince sighed. "It's hard to swallow the fact that we English have been beaten by nothing more than a knowledge of nature. It would be easier for our pride to find him a real sorcerer. But tell me, how did you come to be so wise, Lady Gwenyth?"

Somewhat unwillingly, she began to explain about the lessons she had learned from Merryn. As she spoke, her words began to take on a lyrical eloquence, and she told the prince about walking over sun-splashed hills, bathing in clear, cold springs, and about watching the seasons come and go over the snow-capped mountains and fair green valleys. "Wales is so beautiful," she told him. "And again, Sir Robert speaks truly. The love we have for our country and our willingness to fight for it is the only 'magic' we know."

"I, too, love your country. Did you know that I spent much of the happiest times of my childhood there and that a Welshwoman was my nurse?" Thoughtfully the prince added, "You've spoken freely and so must I. Gwenyth, I, too, regret my father's war with the Welsh, for I feel it wrong for one man to impose his will on another. If by God's grace I become king, I will do my best to set things to rights."

Robert said, "There is another reason why I asked

for this audience. I want you now to listen on a matter closer and dearer to me." His deep voice turned formal. "Before Your Grace I own that I love Gwenyth, daughter of Merryn and Owen Glendower, and that my life is dedicated to her service."

The sun-filled solar seemed to drift away. For a long moment their eyes met to the exclusion of all else, and then Prince Hal shook his head. "Impossible," he said. "The lady is married."

"Her husband in name," Robert retorted. "The marriage was one of convenience only."

Unhappily Prince Hal said, "Still, in the sight of Holy Church she's a married woman. And there is the law against intermarriage. You'd be stripped of your lands, Robin, and you and the lady would be imprisoned. I say all this without pleasure, but it's true."

"It's also true that I have pledged Gwenyth my word," Robert shot back. "I've never gone back on that. And the laws against intermarriage are foolish and unjust—as is this war against Wales."

Frowning, the prince began to pace about the solar. "You're a fine one, Robert Marne, to bully me in front of the lady. Nevertheless, I must admit to you that I've always hated war. It only enriches unscrupulous men on both sides of the conflict. Greedy fellows like this Reese and cruel men like Stoake. There will be peace if I can help it. A just peace."

"And my love for Gwenyth?" Robert persisted.

The young prince glared at him. "Would you have me make promises I can't keep? No matter whether

the laws change, she is still a married woman."
Gwenyth slid her hand into Robert's big one and felt
it close tightly around hers as the prince added,
"Besides, there's every likelihood that the Welsh
may be crushed before I reach the throne."

In spite of the warning squeeze of Robert's hand
on hers, Gwenyth could not check a cry. "What do
you mean, Your Grace?"

The prince was silent, but Robert answered.
"Stoake has been commanded by the king to set a
trap for your father. He's going to burn one of the
towns across the Welsh border, and he's also going
to besiege a castle nearby. He hopes that your father
will come to the defense, and when he does, a huge
army made up of English border lords and knights
will attack him."

She stilled instinctive fear. "My father will know
it's a trap."

"Stoake will bait the trap well. Besides, Hal just
told me that there's a Welshman helping from within
the Welsh alliance," Robert said.

"You mean the man of whom Blodwen spoke is a
Welshman?"

At her exclamation the prince interrupted. "Now
that you know so much, you may as well know the
rest," he said somewhat peevishly. "This Welshman
—no one knows his name save Stoake—has been
smuggling English soldiers into Wales so that they
can attack Glendower from the rear. While Stoake
and his allies thrust from the front, there will be
another attack from behind Welsh lines. Caught
between the two forces, Glendower may very well

be forced to surrender. If he does, you know that it's the end of Wales."

And Henry of England would grind the country under his foot. Men and women would be slain and children sold into servitude. The fair land would lie torn and bleeding, and a Welshman—not Robert Marne or any Englishman but a Welshman—would be to blame. She remembered what Reese had told her about Merdyn Pryse. But surely by now her father would have been warned about Pryse and the other castle lords who, Reese said, had been taking English gold. So who could the unnamed traitor be?

Robert spoke into the jumbled confusion of her thoughts. "Glendower is resourceful. Supposing he escapes this trap?"

"What would you have me say?" Prince Hal demanded hotly. "You know that I'll never go against my father's orders. For your own sake I'm going to take you with me when I leave the castle tomorrow, Robin." Robert began to protest but the young prince threw up a suddenly imperious hand. "It is to save you both from pain that I take you with me, and indeed I have need of you. It will be a hard journey, parleying with the border lords and making certain that they join Stoake in this offensive against Glendower."

"As Your Grace wishes." Robert's voice had never been so cold, and the young prince frowned unhappily.

"I know how you feel, and I sympathize. I can offer you only one consolation, Robin. *If* Glendower is not crushed this time, I will do my best to counsel my father to make peace. Unfortunately, he seldom listens to such talk." He turned to Gwenyth. "I will instruct Stoake to treat you with all courtesy until my return. This much at least I can do."

She sank to the floor in a deep curtsy and Robert bowed as the young man left the room. They could hear him issuing orders outside the solar and then his footstep on the stairs. A moment later the two guards who had escorted Gwenyth earlier hovered at the doorway, and one of them asked, "The prince says you'll take the woman back to the turret, Sir Robert. Is that true?"

He nodded. "I must continue to question her there, and so I'll assume responsibility for her. You are dismissed." Then, as they left the solar and climbed the steep stone stairs, he added in a low voice, "Hal is a good friend. He's given us time to be together before I go."

He was leaving. He would soon be gone. She felt a bruising ache that only his arms, his nearness could take away, and the moment they were in the turret room and the door closed behind them, she went into his arms. Almost desperately she clung to his hard strength and drew in the clean, vibrant scent of him. "I love you," she whispered.

"Even when you feared I'd betrayed you?" But when she tried to explain, he cut her short by seeking her lips in a kiss of aching intensity. Her mouth trembled under his, and the taste and touch of her was worth more than life. At that moment he did not care for anything that happened in the world about them, and he held her closer, caressing the softness of her bare white throat with his lips, cupping the high, firm peaks of her breasts. Want of her was like a flame, and he desired more than anything else to lift her in his arms and carry her to the narrow bed beside the turret window. "My love," he called her. "My dear love."

"You mean more to me than anyone on this earth." Reality came crashing back, for she had spoken in Welsh. He knew what it would mean if Glendower was captured. Stoake would have no further need of Gwenyth then, and in spite of the prince's orders, he was afraid for her. Worse, if he were with Prince Hal, he would be too far away to help her. His arms tightened about her as his mind skimmed through his options, but he could only think of one.

As if reading his thoughts, she spoke with sad resignation. "There is nothing that can be done. There is no way to warn my father about this nameless traitor."

"There is one way." His tone was grim. "We can take him the news ourselves."

"We!"

At her wide-eyed incredulity, he forced a smile. "I pledged myself to your service, remember? No true knight would let his lady cross the mountains herself." She began to speak but he silenced her by saying, "Tomorrow, when the prince leaves the castle, I'll plead illness and remain behind. At nightfall, I will make a dramatic recovery and follow him. But as a knight cannot travel without an esquire, I will ask that Thomas Carpenter go with me. He's the only guardsman about your height."

Incredulous joy gave way to a bruising sorrow within her. In pledging himself to her he was risking so much—his lands, his freedom, his life. No, more than his life, for what he did would be called treason. "What of your friendship with the prince?" She saw grief darken his eyes and added sorrowfully, "Nor will you be welcomed by my people, either. You are thought to be a spy . . ."

He kissed her quiet. "We must take this one step at a time."

"But—"

"The prince wants peace between England and Wales, not massacre and bloodshed. He also knows that I pledged you my word and he will understand." And if he did not—he held the thought for a moment and then put it firmly away. "Will you trust me to see you safe?" he asked her.

Tears shimmered in her eyes, but her voice was clear and sure. "Yes. Now and for always, I trust you with my country and with my poor life. I trust you and love you, Robert Marne, and I pledge to you all that I have to give. Marriage or no marriage, law or no law, I am yours forever." He drew her back into his arms, and her voice broke as she whispered, "And now, love me. Love me, my heart, while there is still time."

Chapter Eighteen

Her cloak drawn tightly around her in spite of July heat, Gwenyth watched the lurid eye of the sun sink into the western hills. From where she stood by the turret window, it looked like a congealed drop of blood.

For the hundredth time she went over the plans that she and Robert had rehearsed yesterday. Under her cloak she was dressed as a man. She might pass for Carpenter in the darkness if they were not stopped or questioned too carefully. But that was a big *if*. She did not need magical powers to know that the earl's trained soldiers would be watching the castle gate carefully, and if anyone suspected, if anyone looked too closely, the game was lost.

The sun had disappeared, leaving the world in

semidarkness. This was the time for evil things—for the demons and spirits of legend. Demons and treachery—she shivered.

There was a light tap on the door, and Robert entered. Her eyes leaped questioningly to his. "Thomas Carpenter?"

"He had no suspicions. I called him to my chamber to discuss our travel plans and he came eagerly, glad of the chance to leave the castle. He's bound and gagged and stuffed under the bed where his friends will find him in a few hours, and by that time we will be gone." He paused. "Are you ready?"

For answer she let the cloak fall away and spread her arms, and he couldn't help smiling at the picture she made. She frowned at his amusement. "Did I put something on the wrong way?"

"If anyone gets a good look at you, we're lost." The short cotehardie barely reached her rounded hips, while her long, feminine legs were revealed by the tight hose. His eyes swept up to the proud curve of her bosom that strained at the dun-colored cloth, and a wave of untimely desire surged through him. "You make a terrible man, my love, for which I will never stop giving thanks."

The light in his eyes took the edge from her nerves, and she realized that she felt better. "I will wrap myself close in my mantle and keep my head down," she promised.

"That's my brave lady." He bent to kiss her, his mouth lingering for a long, sweet moment on hers, and then he said, "Don't fear, everything's been arranged. We'll be outside the castle before you know it, and there are saddled horses waiting for us there." He paused. "I've dismissed your guards, but we must be careful that no one else is about. There'd be hell to pay if I was seen to go in alone and came out with Thomas Carpenter."

She waited as he strode. Then he called, "No one. Come, and don't be afraid. If anyone talks to you, grunt or gesture but don't speak."

She followed him through the door and down the stone stairs. They met no one on the first level, but as they approached the solar where the Prince of Wales had been quartered, two men-at-arms snapped to attention. "Sir Robert," one of them called. "Who is that with you?"

Gwenyth held her breath but Robert only laughed. "You are a jackass, Ralph Hardy," he said banteringly. "Don't you have the wits to recognize your drinking gossip, Tom Carpenter?"

Within the folds of her hood and mantle, she gave her best grunt, and the man-at-arms was taken in. "'Struth, sir, I did not know him with that hood on. But God speed to your honor, and you, too, Tom."

They swung past and she followed Robert's brisk but casual steps down. He told her softly, "Now for the great hall. Remember, let me do all the talking."

"Gladly," she told him.

"This must be the first time that a woman willingly let a man have the last word." Under his joking manner she sensed that he was tense for action, yet he betrayed none of this as he bantered with the

knights in the earl's hall. When Sir Andrew protested that he was leaving just when there was the
hope of battle, he pretended grief. "You were born
lucky, my friend. I'll be riding hell for leather after
Prince Hal while you win glory against Glendower."

Sir Andrew's plump face screwed up in mock
sympathy. "And you have only that sorry esquire
with you instead of that golden beauty with whom
you rode into Stoake Castle. Have you bidden her
good-bye?"

"Perhaps we had better comfort her in her loneliness." Sir Ulrick had come to stand a few feet from
Robert and the supposed Thomas Carpenter. "Now
that you're leaving, you'll not begrudge me your
leavings, surely."

Gwenyth saw a muscle leap in Robert's cheek, but
he shrugged and said. "If you're not afraid of her
magic. Witches can cause trouble—for the wrong
man."

He strode past Ulrick and she followed, feeling
the hooded eyes boring into her back as they went. It
seemed an eternity before they had at last crossed
the hall and reached one of the doors that led out of
the castle. Here men-at-arms stood at strict attention, and Gwenyth tried to copy Robert's non-
challant stride as they walked past them. At any
moment she expected to be seized and questioned.
Her shoulders were stiff with strain, her mouth was
dry, and her nails bit into her palms. It seemed an
eternity before she felt the night air on her face.

"The last hurdle," Robert said quietly. Over the

hammerblows of her heart she could hear a drum being beaten for a change of the watch, and the stamp and snort of two ready horses. "The gray is Thomas's beast. When you mount, fall behind and follow me to the gate."

With a show of boldness she mounted the horse and waited. The smells of smoky torches, sweat, and leather were familiar, but tonight they screamed of danger. At any moment Thomas Carpenter might be found—or one of the guards might get suspicious. The need for speed hammered in her brain as she followed Robert at a respectful distance, and her horse seemed to sense her uneasiness. It neighed and stamped on the cobblestone castle yard, calling the attention of a group of about a dozen men who had just come off watch.

One of them called out to Robert and the supposed Thomas Carpenter. "God speed, lord knight, and to you, too, Tom Carpenter. You're fortunate to be able to serve the prince."

Robert saluted them carelessly, and she sketched a wave such as she had seen Dafyd give his men. But as they reached the gate one of the men shouted, "Tom, how about a little drink before you ride off? No chance to wet your whistle for a long time."

Robert interposed, "I need a man with his wits about him, not one fuddled with drink." Then sharply to the guardsman at the gate he added, "Sirrah, be quick. The prince is well ahead of me and I must catch up to him."

The gateman shouted his command and the gates

of the castle creaked open to reveal the bridge and the road beyond. Gwenyth held her breath as Robert began to ride through the gate. They had done it. They were on their way.

"Sir Robert Marne!"

As the words cracked through the silence, the guardsman at the gate froze in position, and so did Gwenyth. Every drop of her blood seemed to congeal, and she had difficulty breathing. Robert wheeled his horse angrily. "Ulrick," he gritted. "What do you want?"

"The earl has written a letter to the prince." Ulrick came forward on foot, the torchlight dull on his limp, sandy hair. "He sent me to stop you at the gate and bring you to him so he can hand it to you himself."

Gwenyth felt a sense of unreality closing in on her as Robert protested, "Man, I'm already late."

Ulrick shrugged. "Complain to the earl. He's waiting for you in the hall."

Robert knew he had no choice. To leave Gwenyth here was risky, but to take her with him would not only seem strange but would mean almost certain discovery. He snapped, "Very well. Wait here, Carpenter. I'll not be long."

Panicked, she watched him riding back to the castle, and then she forced herself to think rationally. To give in to fear meant discovery, and that would doom Robert as well as herself. Gathering her cloak tight around her, she urged her horse into the shadows near the gate. Perhaps she could wait here, silent and unobserved—but as this hope crossed her mind one of the off-duty soldiers hailed her.

"Now that the knight's gone, come off your horse and have a friendly drink."

She could not refuse to answer, and she forced her voice into a croak. "Can't—Sir Robert'll skin me."

"Don't be daft, man, we won't tell him. And what's wrong with your voice, got a cold?" One of the soldiers detached himself from the others and came forward. "Funny. You sounded as right as rain earlier when we talked."

Again she shook her head and as she did so, Sir Ulrick spoke condescendingly. "Get down from your horse, fellow, and have that drink. I'll make it right with your master."

Without looking at him she knew that the sandy-haired knight stood close by. "Nay, sir," she croaked, "I cannot . . ."

"Now, by the mass, that doesn't sound like Tom Carpenter." The man who had offered her the drink came closer, and before she knew what he was up to had reached up to flip off her hood. "God's feet—it's a woman!" the man yelled.

Before his shout had a chance to die away, Robert's voice rang out. "Ride, girl! I'll follow you."

"Jesu—the Welsh witch! Stop her, you fools—take her prisoner!" Spurred on by Ulrick's bellow, she turned the horse's head and dug heels into its flanks. It leaped forward, knocking aside the guardsman at the gate and thundering over the bridge and onto the road. Here she turned to look over her shoulder.

Robert was not following her as he had promised. Instead, he had ridden his horse onto the bridge and there blocked pursuit. She heard the clang of his sword against the guardsmen's pikes. She should have known, she thought, that he would buy her safety with his life. She started to turn to ride back to him and then remembered why they had planned this perilous escape. Glendower's fate and that of Wales hung in the balance. Sobbing, she spurred her horse again, but as the animal began to gallop down the road she heard Sir Ulrick's yell. "Take him alive. The earl will want this traitor questioned."

She knew what this would mean. Not loyalty, not love of her father, not even Wales itself could make her abandon him to torture and death. She sawed her horse's head around and began to ride back the way she had come.

He heard the thunder of hooves approaching and knew with despair what she was doing. The headlong gallop had torn free her braids, and her lovely hair streamed out on the warm night wind. "Gwenyth, go!" he shouted, but she still came on.

"Let him be—it's me you want!" she was crying. "I bewitched him, made him do what I commanded. Let him free."

There were too many men pouring out of the castle now, and he could no longer hold them at bay. Guardsmen swarmed around him, disarmed and then surged past him to surround her horse. From the ground Ulrick's eyes glared triumphantly up at him. "I knew you were besotted by this Welsh witch, but never did I think you to be a traitor. No doubt the heat between her legs proved stronger than your honor."

"Bastard." Robert lunged out of his saddle and threw himself onto the mocking knight. Ulrick grunted loudly as he went down with Robert's hands around his neck. His eyes popped out of his purpling face as the grip tightened. "This is the last time you open your filthy mouth."

Restraining arms gripped Robert by the shoulders, and blows rained down on him, but he did not loose his hold. Then a cold voice ordered, "Let him go, or the woman dies. Now."

The earl of Stoake stood a short distance away, and he held a hunting knife to Gwenyth's throat. As their eyes met she shook her head and he knew what she asked of him. Better a swift knife's thrust than lingering death. He would have taken that escape gladly for himself, and yet he could not bear to watch her die. Slowly he loosened his fingers around Ulrick's throat.

"Seize him and bind him." In the torchlight the thin face of the old earl burned with rage. "Take them both away. Pen the woman in the turret and let her not escape on pain of death. As for this false knight, take him to the dungeon." He stepped forward, the long knife still in his hand. "You foul traitor, Robert Marne. Are you in Glendower's pay?"

He held the tip of the knife against Robert's throat and pressed a little. Gwenyth saw a drop of blood well from the broken skin and spoke with a boldness she did not feel. "If you touch him, if you hurt him, you will rue it, earl of Stoake. I swore to Sir Robert Marne that I would not use my magic, but now I'm released from that vow. If you hurt him, I'll destroy you, throw your armies into confusion, wither your will to fight. The choice is yours."

The terrible old man hesitated, and Robert saw a fleeting glimmer of hope. Where there was life there could be rescue. "She speaks the truth," he said. "Ignore her warning at your own peril."

"Silence!" But the earl was obviously much disturbed. He chewed the inner wall of his cheek for a moment and then decided. "Do not harm either of them—for now." He whirled on Gwenyth, adding, "If you play me false, you will watch your lover die—slowly. You yourself will beg for his death by the time I am done."

She nodded, but she was not looking at the earl. Instead, she met Robert's eyes with knowledge that was bleaker even than despair. If it were not for her, Robert Marne would not be facing torture and death. She had failed both her lover and her father, and because of her the English would catch Owen Glendower in a trap.

For the next week Gwenyth was confined to her turret room. She only saw the surly old woman who spoke gloatingly of an imminent English victory. To Gwenyth's pleas for news of Robert she gave no answer except that the knight was lodged in the castle dungeon. Nor would she carry letter or message.

At least he lived, and she had to be content with

this. There was little else to content her. From her window she could see preparations for the assault gathering momentum. Several messengers rode back and forth to the castle each day, and at the end of the eighth day after her imprisonment, the first of the earl's allies arrived. Clad in glistening armor, a gray-haired lord and his knights galloped into the castle, while behind the advance party scores of men-at-arms set up camps on the meadows. In the next few days more and more allies swelled Stoake's ranks until the meadowland mushroomed with tents. From her window Gwenyth could hear the neighing of horses and the sounds of men anxious for battle.

She also listened avidly to the talk of her guards, and from overheard conversation she learned that the earl's advance party had wreaked havoc on a small village in Monmouthshire and laid seige to Llanwartwyd Castle near the Wye River. The master of Llanwartwyd was a member of the alliance, and Gwenyth's heart sank as she realized that Glendower would soon ride out to its help. Sickened, she listened as the English guardsmen laughed and jested about trapping Glendower.

Then on the thirteenth dawn of her imprisonment, Gwenyth awoke to shouts and horns, and in the early morning three guardsmen came to her room. "You're to come with us," one of them said.

"To the Valley of the Wye?"

The man nodded, grudgingly. "You're to go with us to watch the battle. The earl wants you to watch your father caught like a rat in a snare."

That was like the cruel earl. She bit back bitter

words and asked, "Where is Sir Robert Marne?"
The men glanced at each other, and terrible fear
made her gasp, "Is he dead?"

Another guardsman now said bluntly. "He's to
come with you to see the battle also, as a surety for
your good behavior. If Glendower isn't taken, he's
to die."

She could tell that the men were uneasy about
this. "Is this the earl's order, too?" she demanded.

The man hesitated and then burst out, "Aye—and
it's not for such as me to criticize my betters. But it
seems hard, for he is a gallant gentleman. But for
him Tom Carpenter would have been tortured to
death, for the earl accused him of conspiring to set
you free. But Sir Robert spoke up and took all the
blame." He shook his head. "Even so, poor Tom
was flogged before being sent in disgrace from the
castle. The earl's a cruel master."

She asked no more questions as they marched her
down to one of the side entrances of the castle, and
here she was urged outside. The courtyard was filled
with sunlight so bright that after the gloomy stairs it
hurt her eyes. She staggered backward only to find
herself lodged against remembered hardness, and a
deep voice said, "Good morning, my lady of flowers."

With a glad cry she turned to him. His hands were
bound in front of him, but he lifted them up and over
her head and held her tight against him. He was
thinner, and a wisp of straw on his clothes told her
he had been penned all this time in some foul hole
under the castle. Yet he managed, for all his two-

week beard and his dusty clothes, to preserve something of ease and grace. In Merryn's tongue he said, "You are very lovely and I have longed for you."

"None o' that gibberish Welsh, sir knight," one of the guards warned.

It was so good to bury her head against his hard chest and feel him near. "Now nothing matters," she told him. "Not our failure to reach my father, or even dying, as long as we are together."

"Perhaps it won't come to that." He spoke a few quick words in Merryn's tongue again, and she stared up at him, astonished. She must have mistaken his words, she thought. He could not have meant that a message had been smuggled out of Stoake Castle. But he repeated that very message. "Carpenter carried word from me to Glendower," he said. "He felt he owed me this for twice having saved his life—and after the flogging, he hated Stoake."

For a moment hope soared, then died. "Even knowing, what could my father do?"

She felt so fragile in his arms that he felt the old, familiar ache of protectiveness become pain. "Forewarned is forearmed."

He would have said more except that now Sir Ulrick rode up. He had been bolted into his armor, but his head was bare and his hooded eyes were full of malice as he said, "This should be a brave fight, should it not? We will reach the Wye by this evening, and battle will be joined as soon as the craven Welsh show their faces. We'll show the swine how to fight."

"You're the swine, Ulrick." Sir Andrew had also

reined in his horse close by. "No true knight mocks prisoners whose hands are bound," he continued angrily. "Do so further and you'll answer to me."

He now turned to Gwenyth and Robert and spoke regretfully. "I'm sorry, but the earl has ordered that you be separated during the march to the Wye Valley. You'll have to go with Ulrick, Robert, but I promise I'll see to the lady."

Surrounded by guards, they were forced to ride in different parts of the earl's assembled army. She strove to catch sight of him as they rode through the hot, dusty day, but she saw only glimpses of him. All through the long march the plump Sir Andrew did his best for her comfort, and in the twilight he drew in beside her horse.

This time he was smiling. "We're coming to the valley now," he said. "Our scouts say that everything is peaceful, so we'll camp there for the night. The earl has given orders to keep you apart during the journey, but he said nothing about this evening, so I'm taking it on myself to let you be together."

She thanked him so joyously that he looked a little dazed and rode off promising to find Robert and give him the good news. She waited eagerly until she caught a glimpse of the deep, green valley where the Wye glimmered white between upthrust hills, and here the earl's allies started to pitch camp. Amid the confusion and the noise of setting up camp, she saw Robert riding toward her. He was surrounded by guards, but that did not matter, and eagerly she rode to meet him.

"How are you, my heart? It was a long journey for you." His bonds had been cut so that he could ride, and now he dismounted and came to her, lifting her down and into his arms. She nestled against him and then he said, "So, this is where the assault begins. It doesn't seem different from any other valley. Why here, I wonder?"

"You say so because you do not know the area. That hill yonder is called the Kymin. From the top you can see the Wye and the Monnow and beyond those the ridge of the Black Mountains. And Llanwartwyd Castle is a beautiful place. In the summer the swans swim nearby—"

"There will be no beauty tomorrow," he interrupted grimly. "As an added inducement to make Glendower show himself, Stoake has ordered that Llanwartwyd is to be burned to the ground. Orders are to kill everyone in the castle, man, woman, and child."

She cried out at this cruelty. Even Reese had ransomed his prisoners. "Why kill them?" she cried.

Before Robert could answer, there was a sudden yell in the distance from one of the sentries. "The Welsh. The Welsh are here—"

The shout broke off in a gurgling death-cry, but now the knights on the valley floor picked up the cry. "By the bones of Christ—they are here!"

She threw up her head and her breath caught in her throat. On the crest of the Kymin waved the proud dragon standard of Wales, and below this the colors of her father. Some distance away other standards blew in the dusk. She could recognize the crest of Kerr, of Vychon from the north, of Hanmer, and of Reese. Fluttering above her were standards of virtually every castle lord in the alliance, and she searched quickly in the dusk for Pryse's standard. It was there as well.

"The traitor—" she breathed. "Then perhaps the other, nameless villain is here, also. Perhaps the message didn't reach my father in time."

Robert said grimly, "Warned or not, he has been waiting for Stoake all along. How did he avoid being spotted by the scouts? Does he indeed have the magic to make his armies invisible?"

There was pain in his voice, and she intuited how he must feel. He was English, and these men were his countrymen. But before she could think of words to say to him, the massed Welsh army burst into battle song. Deep echoes crashed down into the valley like thunder, and then, as one, they raced their horses down the side of the hill and into their enemy's midst.

The battle was unequal. The English forces were tired from the march; they had relied on their scouts and did not expect fighting. As the knights shouted for their armor and the men-at-arms scrambled for arrows and spears, they were cut down like straw before wind. But the Englishmen were brave, also. Grimly they took hold and fought back. They had superior numbers, and they were seasoned fighters. Gwenyth, watching, knew that Glendower might have the momentary advantage of surprise but that he could not hold out against superior forces for long.

As she thought this, she felt wind sigh across her face and, looking up, saw that clouds were rapidly blotting out the pale stars. She tugged at Robert's arm and he followed her eyes. "The weather's changing. No wonder he chose to attack now—tonight." As he spoke distant thunder growled, and a flash of lightning lit the battle.

Around them their uneasy guards muttered and plucked at their swords, but did not dare to come too near to Glendower's daughter, and left alone they watched lightning flare and rain begin to pour from the skies. For a while the storm raged so hard that they could hardly hear the screams of the dying. Then, as the storm's fury waned, a cry went up from the English ranks.

"Where are they? Where have the cursed Welshmen gone?"

Glendower's soldiers had disappeared. Behind them lay the broken remains of Lord Stoake's once great army—dead that littered the valley floor, wounded who cried piteously for help. And as if in final mockery, a horn sounded from the top of the Kymin.

"He has done it," Gwenyth breathed. "My father has beaten the earl of Stoake."

"And you rejoice in it." The old earl sat his horse some little distance away. His helm had been sheared away, and his battered armor was sticky with blood. He bled from a gash in his forehead, and his face was pale as death, but it was the fierce hate in his eyes that held her.

"Sorcery has brought this evil upon us." With his bloodied sword he pointed at Gwenyth. "This is your doing, witch. Did I not promise you that if you betrayed me you and your lover would pray for death?"

Chapter Nineteen

"You will not harm her." Robert's voice mingled with thunder that boomed and died slowly along the sky. "She is the prince's prisoner. You may not lay hand on her on pain of his severest displeasure."

It was empty defiance and he knew it. So did Gwenyth, and the earl knew this, too. Lightning showed the cruel pleasure in his eyes. "The prince is not here, Robert Marne."

Robert held the cold eyes with his own. "I will accept his sentence and no other."

"You are in no position to accept or reject. You are under sentence of death for treason to your prince." Angrily the earl gestured to the guards. "Bring them here before me. I want to look once more on the foul witch and her accomplice before we hang them both."

So this was the end. Strange, Gwenyth thought, that she felt no fear and only a terrible regret that she would never again walk in the mountains with Robert. But he was speaking again. "The matter will not end here. I am the prince's man, not yours. To him I owe allegiance, not to you. If you murder us, the prince will never forgive you."

This shot hit home. For the first time there was hesitation in the earl's fierce eyes. He scowled, his fingers tightening on his sword hilt, then he gestured impatiently to the guards again. Gwenyth could not restrain an involuntary cry as rough hands seized her by the arms and twisted them back.

Robert heard the stifled cry, and it took him to the edge of desperation. "If you kill us now, you will be held an honorless caitiff worthy of scorn." He heard a score of angry voices deny this and realized that many of Stoake's allies had gathered around. Among them he saw Sir Andrew, who looked un- happy as Robert added, "And so will you, noble lords, who stand by and watch him murder us."

"Shut up and hold still," one of the guards growled. Robert felt the jab of the man's spear-butt in his back. "Get going, I say."

He prodded again, and the tall knight stepped forward as if in obedience. Then, he feinted to the left, and the lightning-swift move caught the guards- man unawares. He stumbled and fell to his knees, and next moment, Robert had pulled Gwenyth away from her guards.

There was a general outcry and the earl shouted orders to his knights, who moved forward to block a possible escape. But the gray-eyed knight stood where he was and faced the furious earl. "I demand my right as an English knight," he thundered. "I demand my right to a trial by combat."

This time the muttering was louder. Ulrick snarled, "You've forfeited all your rights—traitor."

Robert snapped back, "Meet me with sword and lance and I'll prove that lie on your carcass."

Ulrick fell back hurriedly and Sir Andrew now said, "Sir Robert is right. He has the right to prove his innocence."

Glowering, the earl turned to the plump young man. "Sirrah, it's best you were silent."

"It is for your good name, my lord earl." Sir Andrew held his ground. "It wouldn't look good if the prince came back and saw that you had ordered his dear friend killed. And, after all, Sir Robert Marne is a knight. It *is* his right to ask for trial by combat."

The earl hesitated. Robert taunted, "Are you afraid that I might win, lord earl?" He saw the earl clench his fingers on the sword hilt as he added, "If you want us dead so badly that you'd have us murdered, you are not fit to lead men."

For a moment he was afraid he had gone too far. The old man's face turned an ugly, dull red, and his mouth worked convulsively. Then the earl snarled, "So you demand trial by combat, false knight? Very well. You'll have that chance."

Gwenyth felt Robert's arm around her as he said, "In that case I choose to fight not for myself but in defense of Gwenyth, daughter of Glendower. I will sustain her innocence with lance and sword." The deep voice rang deep and clear as echoes of the formal challenge rolled across the dark valley. "I defy any challenger you name, my lord earl, and with my body against his I will prove my just quarrel by the grace of God."

In her horror she protested in Welsh. "You have been imprisoned for so many days—you will be weaker than the well-fed, well-rested knights of the earl's household."

"Tell the witch to stop spitting out her curses, they'll not help her now," the earl mocked.

Sturdily Robert replied, "I place my life and the life of this lady in God's hands and ask only that the combat is fair and honorable."

This time the mutter that swept the ring of lords and knights was approving, and an elderly, gray-haired lord spoke up. "That is well said. I for one would not judge the outcome of this trial before the combat itself." Then, turning to the earl, he added, "When will you hold this trial of arms? I will stay and watch."

Others agreed, and Gwenyth, glancing at the earl, saw that his face had grown angrier. Through clenched teeth he said, "It will be held on the morrow after our return to Stoake Castle."

The elderly lord spoke again. "Until then, Sir Robert must be treated according to the laws of chivalry. He must have proper food and clothing, rest in a decent bed. And he should have spiritual comfort, too. A priest must be sent to shrive him and give him the sacraments."

Gwenyth saw the old earl smile. Nothing that had happened so far had frightened her as much as that smile. "I agree, but on one condition. My lords, Sir Robert has said that he is this Welshwoman's champion. He fights to uphold her innocence—not his own. *Hé* is still charged with treason. Before you all I say that whether or not he wins or loses the combat, his life is forfeit."

"But, my lord!" Sir Andrew protested. The old earl swung around to face him, and the plump knight stammered, "That's most irregular."

"Silence." At the earl's roar the young knight flinched. "Is that agreeable to you, Sir Robert Marne? You may fight for this woman, but you will not fight for your own life."

"No!" Gwenyth cried, but no one heeded her.

Holding the earl's eyes with his own, Robert insisted, "If I win in combat, the lady goes free." The earl nodded. "Say it, my lord, so all can hear. Do you agree?"

"I do agree," snarled the earl. "But as to the rest—do you accept your own death, Robert Marne?"

"Yes, but first I ask a favor. I would like word taken to the crown prince about what has been decided here."

"Who would run errands for an accused traitor, a man who consorts with witches?" Ulrick sputtered.

"I would, if my lord earl permits." Sir Andrew had shed his diffident air and looked determined. "His Grace must be told of this night's battle in any case. If you agree, I will send my esquire along with your courier and instruct him to give the prince Sir Robert's message."

Before he could say more, Gwenyth cried, "There is no need to send a message! Sir Robert cannot, must not agree to such terrible conditions." She looked around despairingly at the ring of the earl's allies. "My lords, this is not chivalry. If he fights, let him fight for himself—"

Robert's hand lightly covered her mouth, stopping further speech. "You cannot stop me from doing what I do. This is England, and it is the English law I follow. Besides, I can't call the challenge back." Then he added, "It will be all right, my love. Sir Andrew will help me get a message to the prince, and he'll ride back in time to save us both."

How could it come all right? In true despair she cried, "I will not have you die for me!"

Ignoring her, he turned back to the earl. "Let it be as you say."

Again, Gwenyth saw the earl's gloating smile. "All of you, my lords and knights, are witness to the fact that Sir Robert Marne freely accepts my conditions of this trial by combat. If he wins, the woman will be set at liberty to resume her natural life. None will lawfully hinder her. If he loses, they will both die. But win or lose, Marne's life is mine. And, sir knight, even if you best the challenger I send against you, do not look for a pleasant death."

Robert stood by the window of the small, spartan room assigned to him by the earl and stared out over the torchlit castle yard. There was a banquet in progress in the hall where the earl was feasting his allies before they began their march back to their own holdings, and he could hear the laughter and music that accompanied the feasting. The earl's entire household seemed to be merry tonight.

Instinctively he leaned over the sill of his window and looked up into the darkness even though he could not see the turret room where Gwenyth had been imprisoned since their return to the castle yesterday. He had not seen her since, though Sir Andrew brought word that she was well treated and had offered to take messages to her. The chubby knight had proven a staunch friend in more ways than one, even though there was little hope that his esquire could locate the prince by tomorrow. Robert hoped only that his royal friend would come in time to make sure that Gwenyth was truly protected, for he did not trust the earl.

He wondered who Stoake would send against him. Not Ulrick, for he was a coward, and there was little chance that he would brave an armed and desperate man in mortal combat. Sir Andrew, he knew, would refuse such a command. But there were many strong and able knights in the earl's service. One of them would no doubt be glad to win his master's favor by killing the Welsh witch's champion.

Below him another song was beginning, a sentimental song of romance that had little to do with real love. He wondered, as he stood listening, if Gwenyth heard it, too. The thought that he held her fate in his hands was like a hard fist clenched in his belly. Though not afraid of death, he had never wanted so much to live. Gwenyth had made life sweet, and the thought that he would never see her again except for a brief glimpse on the field of battle, never touch or hold her again or draw in her scent of roses and sunlight, or kiss her sweet mouth—this thought brought unbearable pain.

Footsteps outside his chamber and the challenge of the guards brought him back to the reality of the present, and he listened as one of the guardsmen spoke doubtfully. "Wait, now. We heard nothing of a priest being sent to the prisoner. By whose orders have you come?"

"Is it not true that this man has trusted God to see that right is done on the field of combat? Naturally, I have come to offer him comfort and make sure he fights in a state of grace."

The voice was muffled but oddly familiar. Robert crossed the narrow length of his chamber and listened at the door as one of the guards protested, "We have no orders from the earl to admit a priest tonight."

"Does not the earl believe in the power of God and the church? If you send me away, you'll be responsible for his soul's damnation. When your own death hour comes, you'll have that sin on your conscience."

Robert could almost see both guardsmen crossing themselves. "Don't be so hasty, Father!" one of them exclaimed, and the other added, "You can go in. Heaven forbid we stand between a man and heaven."

A key grated in the lock, and then the door swung

inward. Robert saw a flare of torches in the hall and then the stoop-shouldered, brown-cowled figure that stepped into the room. "See that we are not disturbed," the priest mumbled. "This man has many sins on his soul, and these must be absolved."

As the guards murmured respectful agreement and left the room, Robert said, "It was good of you to come, Father, but I didn't ask for a priest. Who sent you—the earl?"

"No, not he." Robert exclaimed aloud at the altered voice, and a soft hand quickly rose to cover his lips. Incredibly, the bent figure straightened, and the hood fell back from a lovely, tense face framed by golden hair. In that pale face, emerald eyes seemed enormous. "I came because I had to see you."

He caught her in his arms. Rejoicing in her nearness, in the warm, familiar press of her breasts against him and the softness of her lips, he still felt anxious for her safety. "It's dangerous for you to be here, dear one. How—"

"Sir Andrew helped me. He paid a great deal of money to a real friar who lent me his habit. There is no danger to me, but even if there were, who are you to speak of peril? There has not been word from the prince . . ."

"Not yet, no, but there is still time."

She wasn't fooled by the false cheer in his voice. "There is no time left. The combat takes place tomorrow, and win or lose you will be—" She broke off, unable to say the word, then drew away and met his gray gaze steadfastly. From under her robe she drew a dagger. "They didn't search a holy man, as you see. When they open the door for me, you must overpower the guards and escape. Sir Andrew has arranged for a horse for you."

He was shaking his head. "You know that the earl has doubled his guards inside the castle, tripled the watch. There is no way that we could get away."

"Not we—you. No, hear me, I have reasoned everything out carefully. Now that he's had a chance to think things through, I believe the earl will not dare to harm me since I am the prince's prisoner, but he will kill you tomorrow whether you win or lose. You must leave at once in the friar's habit." He began to grin and she said angrily, "Don't laugh at me, Robert Marne."

"I was thinking what the guards would say if a small, hunched over churchman came out considerably taller than when he went in. Even they would suspect, dear love." He kissed her quiet, and even now when she wanted desperately to persuade him to escape, those kisses were too sweet to refuse. "No," he whispered against her lips, "there is no running away this time. Did you really think I would leave you? Surely you had greater belief in my honor."

"I care nothing for your honor. I want you to live." Tears welled into her eyes and slid down her cheeks as she whispered, "Do you think I could go on living without you? If you die, so will I."

Stepping away he looked sternly down at her. "What talk is this? I don't fight only for you, I fight for what England can be under Prince Hal when he comes to the throne." Gray eyes held hers as he added, "When you are released, you must persuade your father of Prince Hal's honor and goodness. You must convince him to make peace with England. It is for both our countries, Gwenyth."

Wales is everything, we are nothing. Memory of those words brushed her mind, and she bowed her head and let the despairing tears fall. Robert was right, and she knew it. The ache of sorrow within her was like a fire that burned everything within her until she felt gutted. "Do you hear me, Gwenyth?" he was asking, and she nodded. "Do you promise?"

Dully she said, "Yes, but this I promise, too. There will be no life without you. No happiness."

"But there must be," he interrupted her. Holding her very close, he kissed her bright hair and her wet eyelids. "I don't pretend to know what happens after this life, but I believe I'll always rejoice in your happiness and be tormented by your sorrow. So live and be glad for me."

She raised her face to his and they kissed in an endless moment that shimmered outside reality. Their lips tasted, their teeth nipped gently. Their breathing mingled, became one, and the touch and thrust of their tongues brought longing for another, deeper union. Hands moved over bodies, touching, seeking, reestablishing the beloved reality of each other.

"You said that you came to comfort my soul," he murmured after a moment. "What solace have you for me?"

"Let me show you what I have to offer." She

moved sinuously against him, and they kissed again as he held her carefully, holding back the intensity of his passion. He drank the wine of desire from her mouth and then slipped his hands inside the rough friar's robe to smooth the silk of her back and the curve of her breasts. Gently, lightly stroking her arms and breasts, he courted her as tenderly as if they had a lifetime in which to make love. He kissed her sweet mouth and then lifted the bulky friar's robe from her to bend his lips to the smoothness of her throat. He rubbed his mouth lightly along the still-clothed rounding of her breasts, over the sweet tautness of her hidden nipples, until she murmured protest and helped him pull away the barrier of clothes between them.

Then they stood together, flesh against flesh and heart to heart, hardness against softness. I will remember, he thought as his lips traced the inner curve of one sweet breast and heard her purr with pleasure. I will remember the sweet-saltiness of her skin, the pale roses of her breasts and how they tauten under my tongue.

"My love, my dear love . . ." she heard his deep voice grow husky with desire as he picked her up and carried her to his narrow bed. The cool of the coarse linen sheets at her back, the warmth of his arms— she felt both coolness and heat within the swirl of longing that poured through her like honeyed wine. She trembled as he came to lie beside her, and she curled the crisp chest-fur about her fingers, then followed the path of her fingers with her lips.

Once before she had bid good-bye to him in this

way, and now she had the uncanny sense that they were back on the hill under the bright life-giving warmth of the sun. But now together with the reality of sorrow was also a promise that in some way they would always be close, the knowledge that their souls would always touch no matter who lived and who died, and that this sweet but too-short physical joining was only one expression of their love. She knew beyond doubt that their love would go on and on, echoing into eternity and beyond.

"We will be together always," she told him. "Wherever I go, and whatever I do—always, my love."

Passion for her was like a driving force in his blood as she stroked his chest and lean belly with her hands and mouth, then bent to caress his strong manhood with her lips. Yet he sensed the deeper need, a want that was more basic even than love. Though his body clamored with desire, his heart wanted more of her, more of her sweetness and her tenderness. He touched her and kissed in turn, loving the clean, slender line of throat and shoulder, each slender finger, the curve of her palm and wrist. Then he followed the sweet flow of her body from curve to curve, over breast and gentle concavity of navel and beyond that to the honey of her womanhood. Again and again he gave her delight until her body was aching-ready for the gift of his love.

She was moaning with need when he entered her, and she took him deep within her. They knew that this moment could not last, and yet the thought brought no sadness. Instead, they forgot tomorrow and yesterday and held to the now, kissing, touching, whispering words of desire and tenderness and love.

Then, slowly, their loving became less gentle. It seemed they could not move fast or hard enough and they were consumed with need: he wanting to immerse himself completely in the wine-rich honey of her body, she drawing his hard gift deeper and deeper within her woman's softness. Wanting, yearning, striving together until joy and sorrow and heartrending beauty coalesced in one incandescent moment, and they fused into one.

Chapter Twenty

Drums beat solemnly as Robert, flanked by the knights of the earl's household, rode his horse through the castle gate and into the red eye of the rising sun. Around him the summer air still held some coolness, but the hazy morning foretold a hot day. He thought of the unbearable heat of being strapped into armor on such a day and then couldn't help a lift of heart as a lark winged overhead, singing its high, pure song.

The song reminded him of Gwenyth, and for an instant her lovely face and sweet smile filled his mind and all his heart. He thought of their brief time together last night, and thoughts of heat and discomfort disappeared in grim determination. He would fight to free her today.

Beside him, Sir Andrew coughed diffidently. "We're coming to the field."

Set some distance from the castle, the jousting field was a wide, rectangular area of level land covered with sun-browned grass. For a day and a night the earl's servants had worked to ready the area for today's combat, and now seats for the earl's guests had been set up along one length of the field while a raised dais under a banner bearing the earl's crest marked the spot where the lord of Stoake would sit and watch the proceedings.

On the other side of the field rough wooden benches had been set out for the common people who were already streaming in from surrounding towns. Robert could see whole families arriving, with the women carrying baskets of food and drink. There were also several monks in dark habits and a fair sprinkling of yeomen, some with their bows strapped to their backs. One stout fellow, shaggy-haired and bearded, was leaning on a quarterstaff and staring downfield toward the black chair where Gwenyth was to sit.

"Look at how many people have come to see the sorceress get what she deserves," Ulrick said. He looked at Robert out of the corners of his drooping eyelids. "All England will be glad of her death."

Knowing that the man was baiting him, Robert did not reply. It was Sir Andrew who snapped, "Nothing has yet been decided. That is why we are here, if you remember, so that God can give victory to the righteous." He turned to Robert and added in a low tone, "I had hoped that my squire would return by this morning, but he has not—and there has been no news from the prince. It does not look good for you, my friend."

Before Robert could reply, a bell began to toll in the castle chapel, and drums beat again as a solemn procession began to ride through the gates. First came the priests of Stoake Castle, bearing high a gold cross that glistened in the sun. Next came a score of men-at-arms and behind them, in pomp and glory, rode the earl himself, fairly glittering as sunlight caught the silver thread and jewels sewn onto his satin clothing. Behind him came his allies and knights, and following them on a gray horse came Gwenyth.

She was closely guarded, and she wore a simple white linen dress over which her hair fell in a golden waterfall. As she rode closer to the field, Robert saw that she was pale and calm and so beautiful that even the common folk who had come to clamor for her death held their peace.

Young Sir Andrew sighed with admiration. "I vow the lady needs no witchcraft!" he exclaimed. "Her beauty would make any man do her bidding."

Silently agreeing, Robert watched her cross the field and ride slowly toward him on her way to the prisoner's seat. As their eyes met, her lips moved soundlessly on his name. For all her outward calm her eyes were anguished, and he knew that she was once more begging him to spur his horse and ride away out of danger before it was too late. Aloud, he answered the unspoken plea. "It was too late at

Rowyn. I was your man from the moment you looked down from your horse at me and smiled."

The loud drumbeat had drowned out his words, but she knew what he was saying. She had never seen him look so lordly as now, encased in glittering plate armor. His gray eyes were hard with determination, and understanding seared her heart with both joy and sorrow. It was not only she who had chosen, like Merryn, to welcome great love at the price of great pain. "My love," she whispered. "My dear love."

"Look how the witch curses us." Piously, Sir Ulrick crossed himself. "She should be muzzled and chained," he added petulantly, "not allowed to sit comfortably in that chair."

Again, and with difficulty, Robert restrained himself, but his fingers itched to close around Ulrick's windpipe. Sir Andrew was remonstrating angrily, "The chair is scarcely comfortable, and the poor woman is well guarded. The earl has seen to that."

The earl—Robert's eyes narrowed as he watched the great man take his appointed seat. Stoake's cold, pale smile never left his lips. Was he so sure of today's outcome? "Do you know who I am to fight?" he asked his friend.

The chubby knight shook his head. "It's been a well-kept secret. Not that we didn't try to find out, mind you. At first, we thought that the earl would demand that one of us fight you, but he did not. Then we considered that perhaps one of his allies would volunteer, but I see that all of them are with him on the stands."

So his opponent was to be some unknown knight, no doubt a sturdy fellow recalled from border duty for the sole purpose of fighting today. Robert felt his muscles tense and forced himself to relax, for he knew that control and mental balance were crucial in a fight of this kind. His body would have to be a well-honed instrument, all muscles and reflexes and learned responses working in disciplined unison. He looked across the field at Gwenyth and nodded to her to show that it would come right.

As their eyes met, the drumbeats quickened and echoed like rolling thunder across the field. Lords and commoners leaned forward in excitement as an armored knight mounted on a powerful bay stallion came riding toward them. Even from this distance he cut a powerful figure, and behind him came two esquires, one holding his lance and shield, the second his sword. Since his visor was closed, no one could see his face, but as he rode nearer, Gwenyth frowned, for there was something about the way this knight sat his horse that stirred her memory.

The earl's herald now rode out into the field and asked the newcomer's business on the field of battle. Raising his visor, the knight responded in a loud, rough voice: "I am the earl of Stoake's champion, come to do battle against the traitor knight Robert Marne."

At the sound of that unmistakable voice, Gwenyth bit back a scream. Her heart began to beat wildly against her ribs. She told herself that such things could not be, and that she must be mistaken, but as the herald asked for the knight's name and lineage, the rasping, familiar voice spoke again. "I am a Welsh castle lord in the earl's service. Huw ap Reese is my name."

Robert was too far from Gwenyth to hear her cry of recognition, but as Reese named himself, he looked involuntarily toward her. She was sitting transfixed in her chair and had gone as white as chalk. Involuntarily he spurred his horse forward to go to her, but the knights around him blocked his way. "You must wait here until the challenger rides up to you, Sir Robert," one of them protested. "You must obey the rules."

So Reese was the "unnamed" traitor who was helping the English. Robert's eyes narrowed as he watched the burly Welshman bow to the earl and his allies before wheeling his horse toward Gwenyth. What he said to her Robert did not know, but he saw her face stiffen into a mask of horror and disgust. He spurred forward again, this time breaking through the restraining line of knights.

"Huw ap Reese," he called loudly. "If you have anything to say, say it to me."

With studied indifference the burly castle lord trotted his horse across the field. "We meet again, Master Minstrel. Again you play the traitor, it seems."

"Not as well as you do. How long have you been selling your country, Reese?"

The Welshman grinned. "You must admit that it was very neat. Glendower thought that marriage and a high position in the alliance would give me the power I sought and means to wealth. Later, when his daughter ran away from me, the fool trusted to my hatred of the English." His lip curled in smug contempt as he added, "Glendower thought the English feared me because I raided their castles. He didn't realize that under the guise of taking prisoners, I was bringing English soldiers into Wales. Sometimes I pretended to ransom them and sometimes to kill them, but what I was actually doing was hiding them in unlikely places while Stoake bided his time."

That explained the presence of the Englishmen that he and Gwenyth had met along the Monk's Trail. As an ally, Reese would have known about that trail, of course. "And naturally you were paid in English gold."

"You didn't think I did it for love? There's nothing but money and power. The rest is sentimental drivel. Country—honor—the love of princes—none of this lasts." He leaned forward to add in an almost confidential tone, "Naturally, when the English overrun Wales, I've been promised all the land that Glendower now owns. Only fitting as his son-in-law, eh?"

"The game's not over yet, and Glendower bested you in the Valley of the Wye." Robert's voice was grim. "It's a pity I didn't have time to slit your throat in the woods, but that can be mended today."

Trumpets were blowing a signal that it was time for the combatants to ready themselves for battle. "You'll sing another song in hell," Reese gritted. "When you're hacking your blood out in the dust, remember that Gwenyth is still my wife. The earl has promised to release her to me after I have beaten you."

"He dares not!" Robert glared toward the dais under the fluttering flag. "Stoake swore before many witnesses that he would let her free and that no one would interfere with her."

"He swore that he would not let anyone unlawfully interfere with her," Reese purred. "I am her *lawful* husband." His voice dropped to a low rasp as he added, "You have no idea how I'll make her suffer for what she's done."

The herald now cantered up to them. "Knights, have you made your resolution to join in combat?" he asked formally.

Reese raised his voice. "I will fight this knight and so prove that Gwenyth, daughter of Glendower, is a witch. I will slay Robert Marne and then take the Welsh witch back with me to suffer her just punishment at Castle Reese."

The herald turned to Robert. "And you, sir knight?"

In a deep and ringing voice he retorted, "I denounce the earl's champion as a traitor and villain and will prove his lies upon his body."

An expectant hush fell on the crowd as the herald now cautioned both knights that this fight was mortal combat, to be joined to the death. He turned to the onlookers and solemnly repeated this pronouncement, adding, "There will be no interference of any kind with this lawful combat. If any man does interfere, he will die."

Though she listened to the grim words, Gwenyth

could hardly take them in. All she could think of was that Huw ap Reese had always been the traitor. She could now see that he had used marriage to lull Glendower into complacency while he grew rich on English gold and secreted English soldiers into the heart of Wales.

No wonder Reese had taken English "prisoners" —and no wonder, too, that he'd been reluctant to attack that English convoy. She remembered the looks she'd seen pass between Reese and his lieutenants and guessed that though the rank and file hadn't known this, Reese and his officers had realized that the gold was coming to them. Reese hadn't wanted her near the convoy because he'd feared that her "powers" would see through the deception, and when she didn't denounce him, he'd realized she had no magic at all. No wonder he'd had the guts to try and rape her.

"To your stations, noble knights," the herald was calling, and Gwenyth wrung her hands in helpless misery. Now this traitor, this liar and murderer, would fight Robert, and if she knew anything about Reese, he'd use every unfair trick to kill his adversary. He was strong, well fed, well rested. Reese would kill her love, and then he would own her, too.

Anguished, she watched Robert trot his horse back to one side of the field where Sir Andrew handed him shield, sword, and lance. He did not look at her, and she knew that he was not even thinking of her now. Every instinct, every nerve and reflex was concentrated on what was to come. She could almost feel the controlled tension of the big body she knew as well as her own, and she clasped her hands tight in her lap and forced herself to be still so as not to distract him in any way.

"Salute the lord earl, noble knights," the herald prompted.

They rode from opposite sides of the field on their strong war horses, their lances lifted in salute to the grim old man on the dais. There they waited until the lord of Stoake raised a thin hand in recognition, and then they wheeled away back to their positions.

"Laissez allez—begin!"

The herald's cry was drowned out as the jolt of hoofbeats punished the field. Sun-browned clumps of sod flew wildly as the horses thundered toward each other. Burly Reese leaned farther in the saddle as if eager to take his opponent down at the first encounter, but it was Robert's lance that splintered against the Welshman's shield. The assembled onlookers gave a cry as the Welshman tottered in his saddle but stayed seated.

Back the knights thundered to their starting positions. They were given new lances, and the herald shouted again, *"Laissez allez!"*

Gwenyth held her breath as sun flashed on armor. Horses neighed, their nostrils foam-flecked by the fury of the charge. There was a swirl of choking dust and then the grunting, shattering impact of lances meeting shields. Both riders rocked in their saddles, and to Gwenyth's horror, she saw that Robert's entire saddle was sliding from the horse and carrying him to the ground.

She screamed and got to her feet but was immediately pushed back into her chair by her guards. Before her horrified eyes she saw Robert struggling to disentangle himself while Reese thundered back downfield for the kill. "Oh, sweet Jesus," she moaned. "He'll be trampled."

Wanting to close her eyes, she could not. They remained wide open as the Welshman reached his still-helpless opponent and jabbed down with his lance. Then she cried out again, but this time with surprise and joy as her champion grasped the plunging lance and pulled, hard. Next moment all the spectators were yelling as Reese was pulled from his saddle and onto the ground.

The combatants were on their feet almost at once. Drawing their swords, they fell on each other. Reese landed the first blow, and it clanged down on Robert's upraised shield, spinning it out of the Englishman's hands. Bellowing triumph, Reese now began to rain blows on Robert, and as the English knight parried each one, the spectators howled their appreciation of a good fight.

One of Reese's wild blows connected, piercing Robert's armor under the arm. As dark blood seeped between the metal plates to stain the ground, Gwenyth was sickened to hear commoners and nobles alike shout encouragement. How could people actually enjoy this? But they were giving every sign of enjoyment. On the other side of the field a big, bearded English yeoman was waving his quarterstaff and urging on the combatants while others were clapping their hands and stamping their feet in glee. Her eyes flicked half unseeing over them before returning to the now bloodied field, but then some buried memory nudged her mind. That archer on the edge of the throng—she knew him.

"Evan Williams!" she exclaimed. But why was Reese's lieutenant masquerading as an English archer? The thought had barely time to fill her mind before another shout brought her eyes flying back to the combat on the field. With joy she saw that Robert was now pressing the attack, his sword rising and falling with a precision that was far more effective than Reese's wild blows. Then the crowd roared as Robert's sword bit down on Reese's mailed sword arm. With a yell, the big Welshman dropped his weapon.

Now, foot by foot Reese was driven across the field as the spectators hooted or yelled encouragement. Then his mailed foot trod on Robert's blood, slipped . . . "He's down!" Gwenyth's cry was muffled in the crowd's roar, but even above it she heard Robert's steely voice.

"Prepare for death, Reese."

Almost as he spoke, the Welshman began to plead. "Hold, Robert Marne. I yield to you. If you let me live, I'll make it right for you, I swear it . . ."

For a split second Robert hesitated, and in that heartbeat's time, Gwenyth saw Evan Williams reach for his bow. She screamed a warning, but it was too late. The arrow was already hissing through the air. It imbedded itself between the plates of Robert's armor underneath the arm and pierced the left chest.

Blood spurted from the wound, but Robert did not fall at once. Instead he raised his sword and brought it down before falling across the lifeless body of his enemy.

No one hindered Gwenyth as she began to run across the field, for her guards were heeding a new cry. "Treachery!" the earl's herald proclaimed, and Sir Andrew began to spur his horse toward the commoners' side of the field. "Seize that cur who loosed the arrow!" he was yelling.

Gwenyth had a brief glimpse of Evan Williams trying to run, but before he could do so the big, bearded yeoman near him raised a fist and brought it down on Evan's neck. Then she forgot everything and everyone but Robert, who lay motionless across Reese's body.

At first she was sure he, too, was dead, but as knights carefully turned over the heavy-armored body and loosened his helm, she saw that he was still breathing. "He's alive!" one of the knights exclaimed.

She cried, "He must not be moved until I can see where the arrow lodged." If it had missed the heart, if by God's grace it had not pierced the lungs, perhaps he would live. "I pray you, help me with his armor. Every moment may mean his life."

"Why worry about the life of a condemned felon?" The new voice was harsh, and numbly she stared into the white face of the earl. "Remember what was agreed. The man fought for your innocence, not his. His life belongs to me."

"Not so fast, my lord of Stoake."

The new voice was young and stern, and Gwenyth gave a glad cry of recognition. A solitary rider was urging his mud-spattered gray horse across the field, and the company bowed low as they recognized the Prince of Wales. He was as muddy as his horse, and his red-rimmed eyes were very angry.

"Your Grace." Gwenyth saw consternation flicker in the old earl's face for a moment before he bowed almost to the ground. "We did not hear your approach."

Prince Hal ignored the earl. "Are they both dead?" he asked Gwenyth.

"Only Reese. But Robert might die without help. I pray of your mercy, bid them help me with him."

The earl cut in, "He is a traitor to Your Grace. Caught trying to smuggle the witch out of the castle—"

Imperiously the crown prince cut him off. "Who is this fellow they are bringing here?"

Castle men-at-arms led by Sir Andrew and followed by the bearded yeoman were pushing and prodding a struggling Evan Williams across the field. Sir Andrew said in his diffident way, "This is the man who shot the arrow that felled Sir Robert, Your Grace."

The prince considered the struggling, snarling assassin. Then he said, "Fellow, if you are lucky, you will only hang. There are other unpleasant ways to die, however, so you had better tell us why you shot Sir Robert Marne."

"Because he was ordered to by his master, Huw ap Reese!" Gwenyth cried. The urgent need to save Robert's life made her ignore all thought of protocol. "Your Grace, this man is Evan Williams, one of my late husband's henchmen. Reese always fought as foully as he could. I wouldn't be surprised if his lieutenant cut the cinches of Robert's saddle."

Williams's lips drew back over his teeth in a snarl. "My master served the earl of Stoake, didn't he? The earl turned a blind eye to what my master and I were going to do."

Coldly the prince faced the old earl. "How do you explain this disgusting perversion of the laws of chivalry?"

Careful hands were now removing Robert's armor, so Gwenyth paid little heed to the earl's stammered excuses. The arrow was too high for the lung, and it didn't look as if it had pierced the heart, but it was deep and Robert was losing blood. She did not dare remove the arrow till she had him in the castle where she could tend to him, and she turned to seek the prince's permission. As she did so Prince Hal spoke sternly.

"Because of the irregularities that have attended this combat, I decree Sir Robert free and restored to all honors. I further declare that since he was the victor in this irregular battle, this lady is at liberty."

The earl's eyes flashed but he spoke humbly. "It is your right to so decree, Your Grace, but this man did commit treason. Besides, he and this woman are paramours against the laws of Holy Church. She is a married woman."

To everyone's surprise Prince Hal suddenly grinned. The grin made him look much younger and happier. "No longer," he pointed out. "She's a free woman now. And so I say before all of you here that if Robert Marne and Gwenyth, daughter of Glendower, wish it, they may be united lawfully in marriage."

"Marriage—between England and Wales?" the earl croaked, astounded.

"The laws on intermarriage can be broken by royal decree." Prince Hal raised his voice so that it rang across the field. "I need men like Robert Marne, and strong sons from courageous women like this lady here to help make our country strong."

Gwenyth interrupted this fine speech. "Your Grace, he is unconscious and bleeding. I beg you to order men to bear him to the castle and let me attend him." Her voice shook. "If we don't hurry, there will be no marriage or anything else. Robert will die."

Chapter Twenty-one

FOR THREE DAYS SHE WAS NOT SURE WHETHER OR NOT he would live. The arrow had gone deep, and though by some miracle it had missed the heart, she was afraid of shock that must follow such drastic blood loss. She also feared infection, for she had no ointments and no healing herbs with her. But the prince took charge here, and by royal order parties of servants scoured the countryside and the hills beyond for the herbs and roots Gwenyth needed.

Sir Andrew and many knights of the household helped, also, for everyone except Sir Ulrick admired the wounded knight's fighting spirit. They were also secretly glad when Prince Hal spoke to the earl in terms of strictest censure. "For my eye is now on you, Stoake. Do not think you are powerful enough to defy the Prince of Wales," he told the cowed old man. "If one hair of my friends' heads is harmed, you'll answer to me personally."

All this Gwenyth knew only because Sir Andrew told her, or because castle servants whispered gossip to each other as they brought food for her or hot water and newly gathered herbs so that she could tend the wounded knight. She cared little what was happening in the castle or anywhere else, for her world had shrunk until it encompassed only Robert's sickroom and the fevered man on the narrow bed. She cared for no sound except his breathing, and as she tended his wound and cooled his fever-racked body, she prayed only that he would live. And on the nights when he tossed delirious, she sat beside his bed and sponged him and talked to him.

"You must live, you will live, you must not leave me now," she begged him, as if her voice could reach him somehow and bring him back. "You must come back to me. I cannot bear to lose you. You must live—you will live."

She was sleepless for over forty-eight hours, but on the third day the fever broke. Bathed in lifegiving sweat he slept peacefully at last, and the healing sleep lasted for a full day and night. Even so she would not leave him but dozed on a chair beside his bed, and she was awake when he at last stirred and sighed and opened his eyes. The look in those gray eyes told her how far away he had traveled and how very close to death he had been, and she caught her breath in an involuntary whisper of thanksgiving. "My love, my dear love."

Her words seemed to reach him through thick fog,

and he felt disoriented. She was bending over him and one long, golden curl fell against his cheek, but he tried to turn his head to kiss it, and pain lanced through him. "God's bones," he swore.

"You mustn't move. That arrow went deep." Her eyes were enormous with worry, and he frowned to see the purple shadows under them and the wetness of her cheeks.

"What arrow—and why are you crying?" he asked her, wondering why his voice sounded so weak. Then memory came back. "Reese?" he demanded.

"Don't try to talk," she begged. "I will tell you everything if you don't try to talk. Robert, I so feared I would lose you."

She told him, but the telling took a long time—the better part of four days during which his strong young body began to mend. By the end of that fourth day, he insisted on dressing to receive a visit from Prince Hal. The prince was leaving that day, and he frankly glowed with pleasure when he saw Robert on his feet.

"Don't bow, for God's sake," he ordered. "I would not have you back in bed again, nor would I see your lady going pale and sleepless over you as if you were really worth such effort." Suddenly he winked, more boy than prince. "She is a fine woman, and you are a lucky dog to have found her. See that you live happily and peacefully with her on your lands, Robin."

"My duty is to be with you, Your Grace," Robert protested.

"Your duty is to get well. You have been so close to death that the vultures were gathering on the donjon of the castle." Prince Hal then became grave as he added, "I will call on you to help me again, Robin, and soon. My father is ill, and there is fear that he may soon die. If by God's grace I come to the throne, I'll need you to support my policies of peace. Fierce border lords like Stoake will want war, but we'll win them over." He held out a hand. "Will you be my man?"

"I always have been." As their hands clasped, Robert added, "We plan to ride to my own lands as soon as I am fit for travel, and there we'll be married. Both my lady and I would be proud to have you there beside us."

Somberly the prince shook his head. "I won't have the time. I must ride back to London immediately and see how my father is. Still, I promise to come and visit you on your estate and stand godfather to your first child." Then his seriousness vanished, and he smiled like an enthusiastic young boy. "Your children will be a bridge, don't you see? A bond forged out of love between England and Wales."

When he had gone Robert said, "You did not say much while His Grace was here."

"You men talked so much you left little for me to say." But though she tried to make light of it, he caught the trouble in her voice and put his arm around her shoulders.

"What worries you, my heart? I saw your face when I spoke of our marriage."

"Wales is everything—I am nothing." In a low

305

voice she repeated Glendower's words. "I forgot that while you were in danger. I would forget it again a hundred times to save your life, but now . . ."

She fell silent again and he grieved, for he knew and felt her pain. "We have gone over this ground before," he finally said. "I do not know what else to say to you. We don't have to live in England. There are other countries that we could call home . . ."

She shook her head. "I wouldn't have you turn your back on your country for me. But—Robert, supposing that marriage to me brings you scorn and dishonor among the English? Not many people are like Prince Hal. Not many would understand."

"It hurts you to think of being scorned and dishonored in Wales for loving an enemy. Is that it?"

Swiftly she threw her arms around his neck. "You are wrong. I will go with you wherever you will and live with you and die with you. Didn't I promise that marriage or no marriage I was yours forever? I will gladly, proudly say the marriage vows. It's only that I cannot bear to hurt him once again."

He did not need to ask whom she meant. "Your father," he said, and when she nodded, he kissed the rich gold of her hair. "Perhaps he will understand."

"No. He'll never forgive me for what he will see as a second betrayal."

Her voice was so sad that it seemed to tear open the healing wound in his chest. He thought of her as he had first seen her, blessing the marriage at Rowyn, and later as she escaped Reese's men, and later still as she had been that day beside the enchanted lake. He could not bear to see the bright, brave light of her dimmed by the push and pull of love against loyalty.

She was saying, "In my heart I know that Prince Hal is right. We must be what he said—the bridge between Wales and England, the beginning of peace between our countries. And yet I am afraid, dear love."

He kissed her eyes and lips. "As long as I live, I will strive for your happiness. But for your sake I wish that it was possible to make Glendower understand."

"How do you know that he does not?"

The new voice behind them was so unexpected that they both started. Robert's hand leaped automatically to his side. There was no sword there, and as his eyes went instinctively to the wall against which it stood, he saw a tall, bearded yeoman standing just within the chamber.

"Who in hell are you?" he demanded angrily. "And what do you mean, walking into this chamber uninvited?" Without answering, the yeoman closed the door and locked it. Then, with a quick movement, he removed beard and shaggy wig. "Sweet blood of Christ," Robert swore. "Glendower!"

With a little cry, Gwenyth ran to the supposed yeoman and caught him by the arms. "If the earl finds you—"

"Hush, girl. No one will find me if you lower your voice. I go by the name of Peter Simkin, and as I have earned the approval of that good knight Sir Andrew by stopping Reese's henchman, I have lately been in his employ." He smiled at their surprise. "Not even my family or my trusted Dafyd knows where I am. I am thought to be in Wales raising a greater army against the English king."

Recovering a little of his presence of mind, Robert demanded, "Why are you here?"

"I had the message you sent by Thomas Carpenter, and it saved me from being trapped at the Wye. I was a fool to trust Reese, but because I needed him to guard the coast I closed my eyes to what I should have suspected from the first—that a greedy man follows the master who pays him best." Shaking his head at his own folly, he added, "Because of Reese's lies I even suspected that Merdyn Pryse and some of my other allies could be traitors. Only after the battle did I make inquiries—and I found several inconsistencies in Reese's accounts of his so-called 'prisoners.' That's when I realized what he had been up to."

"And when you learned about the trial by combat, you came to help us?" Glendower nodded, and Gwenyth bowed her head. "Even after what I did—"

Her father interrupted. "You only followed your heart, as your mother followed hers. You are so much like Merryn, Gwenyth. Long before I had your English knight's message through Carpenter, I believed that you never were a traitor to Wales and that Robert wasn't my enemy. So how could I let the earl kill the man you loved or send you back to Reese?"

There was a silence in the chamber. Then Robert said, "What could you have done alone?"

Dark eyes twinkled with sudden and rare merriment. "Don't forget that I'm a sorcerer." Then he turned serious. "On the field of battle, I heard Prince Henry bless your union with this English knight. Wales is in your blood, Gwenyth. Yet you'd marry Robert Marne?"

She did not hesitate. "Yes."

"Even if this means exile? You said it yourself, daughter. People will not understand."

Tears stood in her eyes but again she did not hesitate. "Yes."

Glendower turned to Robert. "You take on more than you realize. She's a fine girl, but she has a will of her own, just like her mother. She'll need a firm hand."

Unable to believe her ears, Gwenyth cried, "Then you consent to our marriage, my lord father?"

He looked at her kindly. "The world is changing. I didn't come into this enemy stronghold just to save you, Gwenyth, but to see and learn more about this young English prince. I was impressed. When he comes to the throne, there may be hope for peace between our countries."

Robert moved so swiftly that Gwenyth feared his wound might reopen. "My lord Glendower, let me arrange a meeting between you and my prince. Speak to him. I'll stand surety for your safety."

The Welshman hesitated a moment and then shook his head somewhat regretfully. "If I were only Owen Glendower, I might be tempted to do as you say. However, I represent my country. While I live, I must be the symbol under which the people fight."

He paused and then smiled. "No long faces, now. You have not asked for my blessing, but I give it to you both. Love I need not wish you, for you have won that for yourselves."

He held out his hand and Gwenyth kissed it. Robert took and held it for a moment as he asked, "Must you return at once?"

The master of Eyri nodded, and Gwenyth's quick eyes caught the sadness in that gesture, and she began to plead. "Dear father, don't go. Robert speaks of his beautiful, peaceful estate. There is a hill there, he says, and a lake and meadows. Come and see us married. Surely you have worked and fought and toiled for Wales and can be allowed to rest for a little while."

But he was already shaking his head. "I cannot. And, Gwenyth—when I return to Wales, I'll have to denounce your marriage to an Englishman. Not even Dafyd must know how I truly feel, though he and his family love you and miss you terribly. You understand this?" She nodded sadly, and he added, "You won't be able to come back to your country for a long time, perhaps never. You and your knight must make your own world."

Struggling with happiness and sorrow, Gwenyth wondered whether every joy had its balance of sadness. As Glendower readjusted his wig and smoothed his false beard into place, she could not stop from murmuring, "Then I may never see you again."

"Who knows? When I am an old man and the fight for freedom has been won, I may visit you." He smiled a little wistfully. "We may even walk in the hills together, and I may then rejoice in my grand-children."

Robert and Gwenyth exchanged a glance. In that instant of time there was a slight sound at the door—nothing more—and when they looked up, Glendower had gone. Robert swore softly. "Is the man really a sorcerer? He seems to be able to appear and disappear at will."

Gwenyth tried to smile through her tears. "Then you believe that there is such a thing as Welsh magic?"

"I don't know much about sorcery, but I think it little less than wonderful that in the space of half an hour two royal princes have sworn to visit our home and bless our babes." Robert drew her into the circle of his arms. "I know of only one magic, Gwenyth. To be with you, to grow old together, to love and be loved through life and beyond—now that's worth more than enchantment to me."

She brushed aside the last of her tears and smiled her radiant smile that was like sunrise over the mountains. "It's the only magic worth believing in, my lord knight," she agreed as she raised her mouth for his kiss.

Author's Note

OWEN GLENDOWER FOUGHT FOR WALES'S INDEPEN-
dence for many years. Henry IV continued to attack
Wales with increasing harshness, however, and finally brought the brilliant Welsh patriot to the edge of
defeat. Glendower then went into hiding with a
handful of his followers, emerging periodically to
harry the English.

When Henry V, according to many historians the
best king that England ever had, came to the throne,
he offered amnesty to all Welsh rebels. He also sent
special envoys to Glendower, offering him every
courtesy if he would lay down his arms. Glendower,
who saw in himself the spirit of the fighting Welsh,
refused.

Some historians say that the old warrior died in
1516 while hiding in damp Welsh caves. Others offer

a much more pleasant end to his story. According to them, Glendower crossed the Welsh mountains and, disguised as a poor old peasant, journeyed to the home of one of his married daughters, there to live out his life in peace and happiness.

Perhaps that daughter's name was Gwenyth.

Tapestry
HISTORICAL ROMANCES

POCKET BOOKS

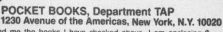